For Mum

You fostered my love of reading and inspired me to become a teacher. I wish you were here to read this book with me. Thank you xx

ELISA CALLAGHAN

First Class

A Reggie Quinn Mystery

ELISA CALLAGHAN

Acknowledgements.

Thank you to my amazing family and friends for all your inspiration and support. I would also like to thank all the phenomenal teachers I have worked with in both New Zealand and the UK. You go above and beyond every day for the children in your class. Finally I would like to thank Mike Palmer for answering my many questions about UK police procedure.

ELISA CALLAGHAN

CHAPTER 1

"Regina Anastasia Quinn! You've missed your bathroom slot and you are going to be late for school!"

The voice stabbed mercilessly into Reggie's foggy brain. It took a moment, but slowly and steadily the message filtered through to the rest of her reluctant body.

"Urgggh," she groaned. When would her mother stop treating her like a teenager? *Probably when I stop acting like one*, she reluctantly admitted.

Reggie had assumed that on graduating from university and taking on her first teaching position, she would naturally morph into a motivated early riser.

"REGINA!" her mum yelled.

"OK, OK, I'm up," she replied, pulling the duvet cover off her face and squinting as the light shot fire into her aching eyeballs. "Turns out I'm just not a morning person after all," she grumbled.

Reggie rose groggily from the bed, spared one last look of longing for her cosy duvet and stood in front of the mirror. She peered at her reflection, moving her head from side to side as she assessed her disastrous hair. Keeping her long unruly mane under control was an ongoing battle, one that despite the use of many products and electric hair straighteners, she feared she was losing. Today was no exception, especially without precious shower access.

"Ponytail it is then!" she grumbled, quickly dragging a hairbrush through the uncooperative brown tangle.

The room with its familiar built in wooden desk and wardrobe and comfy single bed of her childhood was another niggling reminder that life was not living up to recent expectations. She heard the magical sound of the bathroom lock jiggling. Spurred into action, Reggie moved quickly and dodged past her emerging sister. She speedily brushed her teeth and splashed water around. In approximately two minutes time her mum would begin banging on the door.

"Morning Reg, You know you need to leave for work in like one minute don't you?" Stella – Reggie's sister, stuck her head back around the door, smiling.

"It's all your fault," Reggie moaned, gently massaging her aching head. "Who has birthday drinks on a Sunday night? And how the hell do you manage to still look so good this morning?"

"I guess I got the good genes," Stella smirked.

At 5ft 9, with beautiful straight, blond hair and sparkling blue eyes, Stella was the epitome of loveliness. Reggie had the same lovely blue eyes but that was where the similarity between the sisters ended. After studying herself in the mirror, on numerous occasions, 'unremarkable' was the word Reggie had decided suited her best. Everything was in proportion and her complexion was clear - if a little freckly. On a bad week she was only ever a couple of pounds overweight. When she bothered to exercise, she could actually tone up quite nicely, but she had no exceptional features and certainly nothing to make her stand out in a crowd.

"Hey Reg, did you see the hot guy talking to me at the bar last night? We're meeting for drinks tonight after my shift."

"No time to talk, fill me in later." Reggie finished her thirty seconds of makeup application with a swipe of lipstick and frowned at the dark circles under her eyes. She would need more than concealer to hide them. Quickly, she headed back to her room. She emerged one minute later, wearing a black pencil skirt and a fitted blue shirt. Now she felt more like a successful professional ready to face the working day. She headed resolutely out to her car. As she started the engine a tapping on the window startled her. She wound the window down and her dad passed two packages in.

"Don't forget your lunch sweetheart. I figured you might be running late this morning. That was an impressive performance of 'It's Raining Men' you sang in the hallway at one a.m." He grinned at Reggie's pained expression. "I've also made you some toast to eat on the way."

"Oh God, sorry Dad," she groaned as the memory of arriving home flooded back.

"Have a great day. Expand the minds of the next generation," he laughed. With a wave he headed past his beloved flowering rose bushes and back inside the house.

Reggie gently butted her head against the steering wheel. "Shit, shit, shit!" Some professional I am, she thought. My mum gets me out of bed and my dad makes my lunch. "Oh my God I need to sort my life out!" Snorting in disgust, Reggie finally started the engine and pulled away from the kerb.

The drive would take fifteen minutes, not enough time to even begin to put her life into order. Shrugging, Reggie switched on the radio, turning the volume down to placate her throbbing head. She nibbled on the slice of toast, knowing that what she really needed was a Diet-Coke and packet of Doritos. The drive would take her past lush green farmland and over to the next town, much larger than the small pretty canal town of Cairn, where her family had always lived. She always enjoyed the calming colour pallet of the green fields, before the busy traffic fumes and grey buildings of Stapwell welcomed her to her new workplace.

Reggie had been the newest and most enthusiastic teacher at Amberidge Primary School for three weeks now. The excitement of finally being a professional in the workforce had managed to survive the lengthy beginning of the year INSET (in service training) days of information overload. She'd happily endured planning sessions, discussions about meetings and it seemed to Reggie, more meetings about the discussions about the original meetings! She'd spent all her spare time organising her classroom, creating displays and doing all the things she'd learnt at university that excellent teachers did. By the time school actually started she already felt like an experienced teacher and was feeling a little bit smug.

Three weeks on and the smugness had been crushed under a mounting pile of mistakes and near disasters. Her enthusiasm was becoming just a little bit tarnished around the edges as she realised that the reality of working life was far removed from the glossy image she had created in her mind.

The plan itself had seemed simple. She would dominate her new school with amazing skills and a bottomless well of enthusiasm. Her fellow colleagues would welcome her with open arms, while the students would recognise that she possessed wisdom beyond her years and hang rapturously on her every word. Finally, and most importantly, her new boss would immediately see the talent she possessed and come to rely on her as her indispensable right hand woman.

The plan had failed spectacularly. She definitely possessed the teaching skills, but what she had forgotten to factor into the plan was the reluctance of the people involved to value her at all. In fact, some of the teachers seemed to see it as a personal challenge to pop any and all bubbles of enthusiasm she dared to share with them. Reggie had been initially puzzled by the negative response of the teaching staff towards her. She was now beginning to suspect that it was the other Year Three teacher – Veronica Barkwich who was turning public opinion against her. The fact that Veronica had been personally chosen by the head teacher to be Reggie's mentor made the situation difficult. Reggie had no proof and no idea why, but it seemed that the one person who should be helping Reggie navigate the difficult waters of her first year of teaching was in fact trying to sink her career.

Even the children were somewhat of a disappointment. Not her class, they were lovely and enthusiastic – as the majority of seven year olds can be. It was the eleven year olds who seemed to have teamed up with the teachers to suck the joy out of every day. Straightening her shoulders Reggie mentally shook herself. You can do this, she thought. Professionals have to overcome many obstacles to achieve their goals.

Reggie swung the old blue Hyundai into the staff car park; it juddered a little as she dropped it down to second gear before parking. She stepped out, shutting the door carefully to avoid brushing dirt onto her outfit. Reggie's theory was that if she washed the dirt off the car, more of the rust would be visible. She carried her box of books around the building towards her classroom, wondering why none of the teachers were in their rooms.

"Shit! The Monday morning meeting!"

The teachers were all in the Staffroom receiving their weekly briefing from the head teacher - Ms Darwin. She was the scariest and most exacting woman Reggie had ever encountered. Dropping the box in the foyer, Reggie grimaced at the school secretary, who rolled her eyes at Reggie from behind her desk. Reggie tiptoed at top speed along the corridor to the Staffroom. Taking a deep steadying breath Reggie knocked quietly on the door and eased it open. "So sorry I am late, I-"

"Miss Quinn, delightful of you to join us!" Ms Darwin's clipped tones cut Reggie's apology off at the knees. Piercing eyes impaled Reggie and the slightly malicious smile curving at the edge of Ms Darwin's lips warned of the danger to come. The staff collectively held their breath, each relieved that it was not their turn to face Ms Darwin's wrath. They were, however, more than ready to enjoy the current victim's pain.

Ms Darwin gestured to an empty chair and then clasped her hands in front of her severe black skirt suit, under which as usual she was wearing a crisp white shirt. Reggie scurried to the chair, wondering briefly if Ms Darwin ironed her shirts or if perhaps the shirts were just too scared of her to dare to have creases.

"Miss Quinn," Ms Darwin continued, "you arrive at a fortuitous moment. I was just informing the staff that Mrs

Smith will be absent today and we therefore need a volunteer to take on an additional playground duty this morning." Reggie's heart sank. "I'm sure you would be most happy to volunteer your services?"

"O..of c..course," Reggie stammered. "No problem at all." Reggie breathed a slow sigh of relief as Ms Darwin moved onto a discussion of other school matters. She sat quietly listening, waiting for the burning of her cheeks to fade from fire engine red back to her usual freckled complexion. She promised herself that if she managed to stagger through to the end of the day she would reward herself with a coffee and some window-shopping in the town centre. Her first paycheque still seemed a lifetime away.

As Reggie was now painfully aware, drizzle was the enemy of any duty teacher. If it started to rain, the teacher on duty had the power to call 'wet playtime' and send all the children inside. This would force all the other teachers out of the cosy warmth of the staffroom and back to class to supervise their children. Duty teachers who called wet duty were never popular and Reggie needed all the help she could get in the popularity stakes. She had quickly worked out that although drizzle could cancel a sports day or stop a school trip in its tracks, it was a regular occurrence during playtime and neither staff nor children batted an eyelid. That was of course, unless, like Reggie you had hair with frizzy tendencies. Today Reggie's fuzzy ponytail was quickly growing sideways into wide, bushy proportions.

"Miss, your hair's massive," snickered a girl as she strutted past, her arms linked together with two friends. The other girls were also gigging and looking at Reggie out of the corner of their eyes.

Reggie resolved to find a way to make the Year Six children respect her, even if she had to get up thirty minutes early every day to straighten her hair. At the sound of the bell Reggie was relieved to begin shepherding damp children towards their classrooms.

The 3.30pm bell sounded and Reggie looked around at

the eager faces of her class. The room had been tidied, chairs stacked, recycling paper placed carefully in the container. All children wore their jackets and bags and were standing quietly by their desks waiting for dismissal. She smiled proudly. This was how she should feel all the time. She just needed to find a way to expand her success in the classroom to other areas of her career.

"Good afternoon 3Q" Reggie beamed.

"Good afternoon Miss Quinn," replied the class as one; in the sing song voice children adopt when speaking as a group. There was a good-natured shuffling and nudging as the children made their way out of the classroom door. Reggie boxed up the books she was going to mark at home and organised the sheets she wanted to photocopy in the office for tomorrow's maths lesson. She shrugged into her long black coat and headed out across the playground towards the office.

Reggie's progress came to an abrupt halt as the fierce and intimidating figure of Mrs Underhill appeared in the office doorway. Mrs Underhill was a large and very aggressive lady. Reggie's Gran would say she was built like a brick shithouse. Reggie had the unfortunate pleasure of teaching her daughter – Opal (who was as precious as her name). Mrs Underhill was the epitome of a pushy parent and was every bit as scary as Reggie's head teacher. The difference was, that while Ms Darwin would slay you with a pithy putdown; in Mrs Underhill's company you had the constant feeling that at any moment she would use her massive treelike arms to land a knock-out punch on your face.

Mrs Underhill set a course for Reggie, her oversized tent of a smock billowing in the breeze created by her purposeful strides. Her right hand was clamped tightly around Opal's wrist. The rest of Opal's body seemed to drag behind like a ragdoll in her mother's wake.

Reggie took the only course of action open to her. She put down her box of books and stood statue still, a fake welcoming smile plastered on her face.

"Mrs Underhill, what a pleasure to see you!" Reggie lied.

"It's not a bloody pleasure it's a bloody pain, that's what it is. I should be at the shops right now but Opal here, says how you kept her in at lunchtime. Isn't that right Opal?"

Mrs Underhill yanked the terrified girl from behind her. Opal nodded dutifully while staring at her shoes. "You see!" Mrs Underhill pointed an accusatory finger in Reggie's direction. "You got no right. My Opal is entitled to bloody fresh air to keep her healthy."

Reggie took a moment to try and quiet the heartbeat rampaging in her chest. She made sure the smile was still in place and bent slightly to address Opal.

"Did you happen to mention to your mother the reason why I kept you in at the beginning of lunch time?" Opal, who was now squirming in place, shook her head, clearly regretting setting her mother on this dramatic path.

Reggie looked at Mrs Underhill and spoke in what she hoped was a confident and unwavering voice.

"I'm afraid that Opal was caught swearing at some of the other children in our class this morning. Our school rules are very clear. Foul language is not tolerated. I kept Opal in class to talk to her about using different, more appropriate words to express her feelings to other children in the class."

There was a moment of silence while Mrs Underhill processed this new information. Her wrath then shifted visibly from Reggie (who had to physically prevent herself from sighing her relief out loud) to her daughter, who sensed what was coming and began to duck. Unfortunately for Opal her mother's size masked ninja like precision and accuracy. Opal was too slow to avoid the swing of the tree trunk arm, which whipped around to smack the stunned girl in the side of her head. Reggie winced as she saw the reddening mark on Opal's cheek. She made a mental note to ask a colleague about the correct procedure for dealing with violent parents.

"What have I bloody told you about swearing at bloody school?" Mrs Underhill ranted at Opal. "I'm sorry Miss Quinn, you did right keeping her in. You're doing a bloody good job, keep up the good work." She threw a smile in Reggie's direction. "I'm going to take this little bugger home. No device time for you tonight!" She glared at Opal.

Before Reggie could utter a word, Mrs Underhill grabbed poor Opal's hand and set sail across the playground towards the office. Reggie took a moment to make sure Mrs Underhill was truly gone and then dissolved into near hysterical laughter.

"No bloody swearing at school!" she forced out as a second wave of laughter swept over her.

The relief of weathering Storm Underhill was huge. The additional joy of finally ending this disastrous workday, gave Reggie a feeling close to euphoria. She cranked up the radio and hummed along as she turned the steering wheel and headed away from school towards the town centre and freedom.

CHAPTER 2

Finding a parking space was usually mission impossible in Stapwell town centre but this afternoon Reggie's luck was in. Stapwell had the honour of being the county town of the area and boasted some beautiful old buildings. It housed the council, library and indeed many of the larger banks and businesses within the town-square and high street. Other newer buildings had been slotted in between these and in the surrounding streets, creating a haphazard arrangement of old and new around the main centre.

Reggie was still humming as she swung into the first available slot on floor two of the shopping centre car park. She headed down to the ground floor in the lift.

"Clothes then coffee," she decided. Reggie revelled in the joy of trying on the outfits she was determined to own - as soon as payday came around. Though many more days like today might see her needing a drastic rethink in her career choice. She might then require a very different wardrobe. After a waitress uniform flashed into her mind she mentally shook herself. It was too soon to even begin to think of throwing in the towel. All she needed were some new strategies to help her prove to her colleagues and especially her boss, that she could be a reliable and useful member of the team.

"Perhaps a trip?" Her eyes lit up at the idea. Her year group were studying the Romans. The nearest Roman town was only an hour's drive away. It would need some quick organising but there was a definite possibility it could work. Thinking that coffee might really help her new idea along she headed out of the shopping centre and across the cobblestones towards Starbucks. It always made her smile to see such a beautiful old Georgian building with a bright green Starbucks sign hanging from it.

Reggie queued to place her order and idled the time away watching a group of students in the line ahead of her. One had obviously made a funny remark and the others laughed, excitedly contributing one-liners and comebacks to keep the joke running. It was difficult not to feel a stab of jealousy for the easy friendship and shared experiences being at university provided. Another town a few months ago and this had been her. Reggie couldn't decide if it was coming home or being part of the workforce that had robbed her life of some of its joy. Perhaps it was a depressing combination of both.

Reggie collected her order and stopped for a moment to take a sip.

"Reg!... Reg, Reggie."

A persistent voice cut through her thoughts and she turned to see a familiar smiling face - wearing rounded glasses and a spiky mop of hair, waving frantically from a table by the window. Reggie's polite smile widened with recognition. She dashed over to the window and was grabbed in a tight bear hug. She noticed he was still wearing his trademark open checked shirt over a T-shirt with jeans and Converse shoes. It was like time had stood still and they were back in high school.

"Reg, I can't believe it's you!" exclaimed her friend. It's amazing to see you"

"Stocky! What the hell are you doing here?" Reggie stepped back. "How long have you been here, why didn't you tell me?" She accused. "You're supposed to be in London in some high-flying tech job, becoming rich and famous."

Steven Stockwell, or 'Stocky' to his friends sank back into his chair, hands raking through his spiky mop. "That's the problem. It all turned to crap. I'm laying low."

Reggie slid into the chair opposite, reaching across the table to him. "Hey, this is me, tell me what's going on?" she cajoled.

Stocky raised his head. "My life is totally over," he announced. Reggie laughed and flicked his shoulder.

"At least you haven't lost your sense of the dramatic. Come on, last holidays you were on a high. You had all those interviews lined up for amazing tech jobs. What happened?"

Stocky sniffed and sat up in his seat.

"Remember how excited I was to be the next Bill Gates or Steve Jobs?" Reggie rolled her eyes as she remembered the bragging. Focused on his story, Stocky continued. "It turns out that so many of us were inspired that you can't move in the city without tripping over a wannabe tech genius. Every interview had thousands of people for each job. The job market is totally saturated with tech nerds like me. Look at that guy over there!" He gestured to the barista behind the counter. "That's Kelvin, we went to uni together, did the same classes. His mum made him get a job here and I'm next!"

Stocky slumped in his seat and Reggie glanced over to study the guy who had served her coffee. Kelvin had the typical messy nerd hair do and pale complexion gained from too many hours spent indoors on the computer.

"It can't be that bad," Reggie reasoned. "How long have you been back?"

"I ran out of money and had to move back in with Mum two weeks ago," Stocky said.

"You're not the only one with money problems," replied Reggie. I don't get my first pay check for another couple of weeks and I've been living with my parents for a few months now."

"At least you have a job you love!" Stocky accused.

Reggie inclined her head and let the comment wash over her. Right now, it would be pushing it to say she even liked her job. I want to love my job, she thought. That must count for something. Shaking her head, she tried to focus on what Stocky was saying.

"Mum got Uncle Steven to give me a job working for him, as a favour!" Stocky groaned. "How embarrassing is that?"

Reggie ignored his question, replying instead with one of her own.

"Isn't he a police officer?"

"He was. He's retired now and has opened a private investigation firm."

"What are you doing for him?" Reggie asked. "Organising his computer and tech equipment?"

"I wish!" Stocky sighed. "He's got all that sorted. He paid a firm when he opened the business. I'm doing fieldwork. I'm supposed to be doing surveillance right now."

Reggie's eyes widened. Like many highly intelligent people Stocky was not strong on common sense or coordination. Then another thought hit her.

"Uncle Steven?" she asked warily. Stocky nodded. "Not the one from your family Christmas party last year?" Stocky shuddered at the memory.

"Yep," he said, "Sleazy Stevie, who kept pinching your bum and trying to put his hand up your top!"

Reggie scowled, then a whisper of a smile crossed her face as she remembered the satisfaction she'd felt when her high-heeled boot had *accidentally* come down hard on Sleazy Stevie's shoeless foot.

"Oh!" Reggie's hands grasped tightly onto her coffee cup as silence extended between them. "Maybe it is that bad!"

"No, it's way worse than that," muttered Stocky. "Look at these!" He pushed a brown envelope towards Reggie.

She opened it and pulled out several grainy and badly focused photographs of a man and a woman standing in a car park.

"What are these for, who are these people?"

Stocky pointed to the man. "He is my client's husband and I'm supposed to be getting pictures to prove that he's having an affair."

Reggie grabbed one of the other photos.

"Why is the quality of these so bad? Your camera would be perfect for this." She took a closer look at the picture in his hand.

"Why the hell is he waving at you in this one? I don't know much about surveillance but I'm pretty sure that the people aren't supposed to know you are watching them!"

"I know!" Stocky groaned. "I had to sell my camera to cover rent a few weeks ago so I'm using the one on my phone. It's got terrible zoom and I have to get close up to take pictures."

"Well I'm no expert but I would say your cover is blown," said Reggie.

"It's well and truly blown," Stocky nodded. "He knows me and my car now. Yesterday I was watching him outside a café. He brought out a drink for me and told me where he was headed to next. He actually seemed like quite a nice guy!" Stocky stared miserably down at his hands.

"Can't you borrow your uncle's car and his surveillance equipment? He must have some good stuff?" Reggie asked.

"No, he says he doesn't trust me with his gear. Basically, he just wants to get rid of me and be able to tell Mum he gave me a chance." Reggie made sympathetic sounds.
"Do you know what the worst part is?" Stocky continued. "Mum said this morning that she knows McDonalds is hiring! McDonalds! She's already made it clear that I have to bring some money in. This time next week I could be selling you cheeseburgers." He dropped his head into his hands.

"You'll come up with something," encouraged Reggie.

"No, this was my last chance to find useful evidence for the client. I'll be fired tomorrow for sure. Unless…" Stocky raised his head and stared thoughtfully across the table at Reggie.

"What!" Confused, Reggie stared back.

"Unless you do it Reg! You could do surveillance with me. We could use your car. I'd duck down while you take pictures." Stocky's face was alight with excitement at the brilliance of his idea.

Reggie stared open mouthed for a moment before words flooded back to her.

"No way. I have a job, remember? It may not be all that I hoped for and I may not currently be the best teacher in the world. But I have plans, ideas – a trip." She spluttered out.

"Please Reg, I really need this. We can totally work around your workday. I promise! Just help me out," he pleaded. "I can't work at McDonalds, I can't!"

Reggie could already feel her resolve caving under the pressure of his stare and the sheer desperation in his voice. Stocky sensed her weakening and went in for the kill.

"If we get some proof I'll get paid. I'll cut you in. You said you need money." Stocky could see the battle of emotions on her face. She was tempted, he could tell. "Fifty, fifty split. You can't say fairer than that?" He smiled - hope gleaming in his eyes.

"Ok, I'll help you," she said with resignation.

"Yes!" Stocky fist pumped the air. "This will be totally awesome. Now you're onboard we will totally nail this guy!"

Reggie looked on in amazement as Stocky's mood shifted like lightning from depression to cloud nine, and couldn't help wondering if somehow she had just been played. That was one of the downfalls of old friends – they certainly knew what buttons to push to get the response they wanted.

"I can't do anything until after school tomorrow." Reggie's comment had the desired effect of bringing Stocky back down to earth.

"That's fine," he replied. "We'll meet tomorrow afternoon. The guy we are following owns the Star and Anchor pub further along the main street. We can meet in the car park outside." Reggie stood up.

"Look, I'm not sure how much help I'll be but I'll give it a go," she shrugged. "I need to go home now. I've got books to mark and a trip to organise."

"Okay," Stocky agreed. "I'll wait here and see if I can borrow a decent camera from Kelvin. His shift finishes soon."

Reggie waved and headed out into the autumn afternoon sunshine. As she walked towards her car, she didn't need the sinking feeling in her stomach to know she had probably taken on more than she could handle. She should be devoting more time and effort to her own work she thought, not running around spying on people. What did she know about being a private investigator? Absolutely nothing, that's what!

Reggie turned the car towards home and knew she had a busy night ahead of her. Job number one would be to make a few phone calls and see if this Roman trip could work. Then she would have to catch up on all the work she should be doing tomorrow after school. Instead she would be sitting in her car spying on some guy. She felt a flicker of excitement in her stomach. At least life was never boring when Stocky was around.

The next morning Reggie woke early. Time was on her side and she not only made her bathroom slot but also had time to style and straighten her hair, until it hung in a glossy, sleek mane past her shoulders. Today needed to go well, she mused. For extra help she decided to wear her lucky top. It had never failed her on nights out at university. The top was a beautiful deep burgundy colour and its soft material showed off her curves. It also showed off an ample amount of cleavage - this was possibly a contributing factor to the good luck she experienced when wearing it. She knew she looked good in it but it was far too revealing for a teacher to wear. So, she paired it with a soft fitted cardigan in a deeper shade of burgundy, fastened with a single button to cleverly hide the cleavage area from view. She felt sophisticated and powerful, both useful qualities to help her through her meeting with Ms Darwin later in the day.

Time seemed to be moving at half speed this morning and she was even able to sit down to breakfast and coffee with her mum in the kitchen.

"Good morning darling," said her mum as Reggie sat down opposite her.

Elizabeth Quinn was tall and statuesque with short blond curly hair, always styled to perfection. She was a shrewd and determined woman whose personality dominated the house. When set on a course of action, she was a force to be reckoned with. Both her daughters had benefitted from this as they had navigated their way through high school. Reggie hoped she had inherited her mum's strength and ability to persist, even when success seemed impossible.

Unfortunately, both daughters also had experience of being the object of their mother's determined interest and this was never a pleasant experience.

"You look lovely today dear," said her mum in an overly pleasant and cheery manner. Reggie eyed her suspiciously.

"Thanks," she replied, carefully avoiding eye contact.

"Of course I hope you aren't doing this to impress a young man. This really isn't a good time for you," Elizabeth announced. "You need to focus on getting your career started. With your student debts and still no pay check, you're not exactly a catch right now darling!"

Reggie sighed and looked at her mother. "Mum, I'm just trying to look professional for work." Reggie held back the pithy response she wanted to make in favour of keeping the status quo. Instead she opted to try for a subject change. "I hope you had this same chat with Stella. She went out with some random guy from the bar last night." Her mother beamed.

"Such a lovely man, Stella says. Apparently, he's a lawyer." Reggie groaned inwardly. "Anyway," her mum continued. "Your sister has a successful career and a second job. She's not far off saving a deposit for a house. She should be looking for a nice young man to settle down with and give me lots of grandchildren. It's the next step."

Elizabeth Quinn looked dreamily off into the distance, probably naming Stella's future brood. Reggie smiled and silently promised that later in the day she would enjoy the look of horror on her sister's face as she informed her of her impending motherhood. No doubt her fun-loving sister would kick Mr Lawyer to the kerb and keep her dating exploits to herself for a while. Reggie liked the idea of watching from the sidelines as her mother launched a matchmaking campaign for Stella. While her mother focused her considerable talents on organising Stella's life, she was far less likely to be analysing and interfering with Reggie.

Reggie used the drive to school to go over her plans for the

Roman trip. The Roman activity centre had an opening for next Wednesday, due to a cancelation. She had a quote from the bus company and knew how much they should charge the children. If she sent a letter home today that should leave enough time for parents to send the money in. Everything seemed to be falling into place. She just needed to stay focused and sell the idea to Ms Darwin. The thought of the upcoming meeting with the intimidating head teacher had Reggie wiping a slightly sweaty palm on her skirt as she drove.

Reggie emerged from the meeting triumphant with success. Ms Darwin had approved the idea and had even managed a smile, not the sneer Reggie usually received but something Reggie liked to think resembled pride in her newest teacher's achievement. Okay, so her words hadn't exactly praised her to the rooftops but it was a definitely a move in the right direction.

"So, what do you think?" Reggie had said nervously, to fill the silence following her description of the trip.

Ms Darwin leaned her elbows on her immaculate desk and tapped her fingers together, seeming to mull over the idea further. Reggie shifted uneasily in the chair opposite. Finally, Ms Darwin nodded to herself, as if satisfied with solving a tricky problem.

"Miss Quinn," she announced in careful and deliberate tones. "You have not made the most impressive start to your time at Amberidge Primary School. Indeed, I was unfortunately beginning to conclude that your talents perhaps lie elsewhere." Reggie shrank self-consciously into the chair.
"However, it pleases me that you have finally taken it upon yourself to show some initiative. As you are a newly qualified teacher you will obviously need to work closely with your mentor - Mrs Barkwich, and she will be the lead teacher for the excursion."

Reggie's joy diminished slightly at the thought of working with her malicious mentor, who continued to be resolute in her disapproval. Perhaps I should see this as an opportunity to mend fences, thought Reggie, trying to remain positive. She forced her attention back to Ms Darwin as she continued to speak.

"I look forward to hearing positive reports from your children and Mrs Barkwich about the wonderful learning opportunities your class will experience."

Then came the smile. Looking back, Reggie now wondered if the smile had been in any way related to her achievements or if it was more about the comment Ms Darwin was about to make.

"It is so fortuitous we have had this little chat today Miss Quinn." Ms Darwin was still smiling. "Mr Banks has to attend a medical appointment after school today and will unfortunately not be able to run the Science Club. What a fantastic opportunity this would be for you to take on responsibility and get to know some of the older children." Ms Darwin inclined her head, raised an eyebrow and waited for Reggie's response.

Reggie knew this wasn't a request and her agreement was already taken for granted, but she felt flattered all the same that Ms Darwin had chosen her for this responsibility. It would mean that she would be slightly late meeting Stocky but not by much. It was definitely do-able and Ms Darwin was right, it was a great opportunity to get the older kids to like her. Reggie beamed at Ms Darwin.

"I'd love to take the Science Club. Thank you for thinking of me."

"You are welcome." Ms Darwin nodded, gestured her dismissal and bent her head to read the documents sitting neatly in front of her.

CHAPTER 3

Science Club had been a disaster from start to finish. As Reggie drove towards the pub to meet Stocky, the wail of the fire bell still rang in her ears. She lifted a hand to press against her sore temple and willed the aching to stop. Thank goodness she had been wearing safety goggles. The explosion had only been small; nothing to really worry about. It wouldn't have been a big deal if the smoke hadn't set off the overly sensitive smoke detector. Water had cascaded down from the new sprinkler system, soaking the room and the excited Science Club members. The caretaker had been effusive in his pronouncement that the saturated classroom would take days, maybe even a week to dry out. Mr Banks would certainly be unpleasantly surprised when he returned from his medical appointment to find his entire room and contents looking like it had been through a car wash.

The worst moment had been when Ms Darwin had arrived on the scene. Instead of the verbal takedown Reggie had been expecting, the head teacher stood and slowly looked her up and down. She raised one eyebrow, held Reggie's gaze menacingly for a few moments as if trying to express a million thoughts in one look; then she swept off to talk to the fire crew, who were patiently waiting by their fire truck in the staff car park. What a mess!

Hopefully in another couple of minutes the painkillers the school secretary had given her would kick in. Her lucky top had mostly survived the encounter but she'd had to speedily remove the cardigan as the acid had eaten its way through it. It was beyond saving and currently lay in tatters at the bottom of the caretaker's bin.

"Bloody kids!" she ground out between gritted teeth. Now she had to do this ridiculous stakeout, sitting outside a pub when what she clearly needed was to be inside drinking a large amount of wine.

Stocky was waiting for her as she pulled into the pub car park. He was dressed in black from head to toe, including a black beanie. All he needed was a ski mask to look like every stereotypical TV burglar. She chose a space among a line of cars with a good view of the back entrance.

"What have you come as?" snapped Reggie as Stocky opened the door. "You're supposed to blend in, not look like you're about to rob the place."

Stocky crossly sat down in the passenger seat. He opened his mouth to fire out a comeback but froze in place as he took in Reggie's appearance.

"Holy crap Reg, what happened to you?" he exclaimed, leaning back against the door to get a better look. Reggie pulled down the visor to look in the mirror.

"It's not that bad, is it?" she asked uncertainly.

Reggie gently touched the burn mark, which extended from her forehead down to where a portion of one eyebrow seemed to be missing. The sleek mane from this morning was long gone. In its place were sections of frizz from contact with the sprinklers and some charred sections that seemed slightly shorter than the rest. She moved the mirror to see lower down. Her cleavage was perhaps a little too magnificently displayed in her lucky top. The top itself was looking a little ragged around the sleeves and there were a couple of holes where the acid had managed to find its way through her cardigan. At least her skirt had survived. It was a little damp but otherwise undamaged.

Reggie sat back in her seat self-consciously trying to smooth some order into her bedraggled hair.

"There was a small incident at Science Club," she

mumbled.

"Small incident?" Stocky questioned. "You look like you've been soaked by a hose and rescued from a burning building!"

"The kids said that Mr Banks always lets them mix those chemicals together. I thought we were bonding. I was making progress." The explanation sounded dubious even to her ringing ears.

"Reg, that's crap! When we were eleven, the only teachers we respected were the ones we had a healthy fear of. Stop being their friend and start making their lives totally miserable," Stocky retorted.

"Hmmmm," Reggie licked her finger and rubbed thoughtfully at a smudge on her chin. "Maybe it's something to think about." She shook her head and folded the visor up. "Anyway I'm here, I'm alive – just about, so what's the plan?"

"Well," Stocky opened the glove box and passed a camera to Reggie. "Just before you got here, Dave Thomas – he's our target, arrived and went in that door over there. I think it's the back entrance to his office. We just need to watch and wait and hope something happens."

"So we sit here and if anyone comes I point and press, right?" Reggie asked.

"Yep. This is Kelvin's camera and it's fantastic. Just try not to drip on it!"

Reggie sat back, relaxing for the first time all day. The throb in her head had receded slightly and she was beginning to feel hungry. "We should have brought some snacks," she mused. "This could take forever."

Twenty minutes later, Reggie's eyelids were feeling heavy and her head was leaning comfortably to one side on the headrest. She was rudely shaken awake by the rocking car as Stocky threw himself down into the footwell of his seat.

"Reg," he hissed urgently. "Look, she's getting out of her car. That's her!"

Reggie, now fully awake, grabbed the camera and focused the zoom. The lady looked to be in her late twenties, well dressed with beautiful shoulder length blonde hair. Reggie felt a twinge of jealousy and reached up to touch her soggy, ruined mop.

"What's she doing?" whispered Stocky. Reggie continued to take pictures as the lady made her way over to the door and knocked.

"She's at the door waiting," Reggie described. "Some guy's come out. Ooh they're hugging. He's gone in again and she's still waiting." Stocky chanced a glance over the dashboard, dropping back down as the man reappeared.

"That's him," Stocky whispered. "That's Dave!"

"He's given her a cardboard box!" Reggie exclaimed," and she's putting it in her car."

"Is that it?" Stocky's disappointment was clear. He peeked over the dashboard in time to see the woman and Dave enter the office and shut the door.

Reggie put down the camera.

"All we have is a hug. Not exactly evidence of a passionate affair."

"We need more!" Stocky leaned his chin in his hand thoughtfully. "Either we wait here to see what happens when they eventually come out, or we go in and hope they walk out into the bar area."

"Let's go!" Reggie was out of the car and striding towards the main entrance before Stocky had time to grab the camera off her empty seat.

"Wait!" Stocky yelled. Reggie paused and turned around. She was feeling a bit jittery, must be all the adrenaline of the stakeout. She flexed her fingers to stop them shaking, and waited for Stocky to catch up with her. "We need to think about this before we go in," said Stocky. "We need to blend in, and no offence Reg, but you look like a reject from the *Rocky Horror Picture Show*." He gestured to her hair and top.

"Back at you cat burglar!" Reggie smirked as Stocky took off his black beanie and ruffled his hair. "Tell you what," she continued. Leave your hat in the car and I'll wear your jacket. Then people will just think you're a goth and I'm having a very bad hair day."

Stocky nodded. They made the changes and headed towards the bar.

"What about the camera?" Reggie asked.

"Too conspicuous," Stocky replied. "Besides, the camera on your phone is better than mine. If we see anything you can pretend to be texting and take pictures."

They reached the main entrance and Reggie pushed the heavy door open. She led the way across the carpeted entrance hall towards the two bouncers, positioned on each side of the bar's double doors. As Reggie walked, the jacket swung open allowing both bouncers a jaw dropping view of her barely restrained cleavage. She saw the eyes of the tallest man widen in appreciation. His smile of enjoyment switched quickly to surprise as he took in the rest of her bedraggled appearance. Reggie smiled back, enjoying the way his white shirt hugged his muscular frame.

"He's hot!" Reggie all but shouted as they passed through the double doors into the bar. She could hear the amused laugh of the bouncer behind her.

"Shhhh!" warned Stocky, grabbing her hand. "We are supposed to be blending in. I don't know what's got in to you but now is not the time to lose your inhibitions."

"Come on!" urged Reggie. "I need a drink. We'll blend in better with a drink." She pulled free from Stocky's hold and charged towards the bar.

Stocky paused for a moment not knowing what to think of Reggie's bold new attitude. Having no answers, he shrugged and followed on behind.

The Star and Anchor had previously been a popular two-screen cinema in a prime central location in the town. As the popularity of massive out of town multiplexes had grown, its own attraction had dwindled. However, when transforming it into a bar the renovators had cleverly left some of the key features in place, retaining much of the cinema's original charm.

As Reggie waited to place her order she studied the

large screen still in its original location behind the bar. She remembered coming here with her parents and Stella when she was younger. They had sat in one of the back rows. She smiled and turned her head to look at the balcony seats and projector room, which were still in place over the entrance. Reggie and Stocky collected their drink orders and headed for a table off to one side, but with a good view of the bar area. The place was beginning to fill up with after work drinkers. Groups of office workers in suits were sipping from glasses of wine and bottles of imported beer.

"At least it will be easier for me to hide from Dave with all these people around," said Stocky. He pointed to the door to the left of the bar. "That leads to the office and the one at the other side of the bar leads down to the cellars. Those are the two places we might see them." Reggie sipped eagerly at her wine.

"I'm beginning to see a flaw in your plan. They could be up to who knows what in that office and we can't get anywhere near."

"I know," replied Stocky. "But I'm running out of options. I have to show something to my client tomorrow."

Movement from the cellar doorway caught Reggie's attention.

"Stocky it's them!" She grabbed her phone out of the jacket pocket. Stocky turned his body so that he was sitting shadowed in the corner while Reggie pretended to write a text. She photographed the blond lady and Dave (carrying a box of wine bottles) as they made their way through the bar area to the office door. Dave walked into the office and the blond woman closed the door behind them.

"Great, they're back in the office," Reggie moaned. "We'll never see anything now."

Stocky thought for a second. Behind them was a high window, which had been added during the renovation.

"Not necessarily! Grab your chair," he instructed, already pushing his over to the wall and stepping up onto it.

Reggie joined him. If they craned their necks, the external

office doorway was partially visible. As Reggie pulled out her phone the door opened. She stood on tiptoes to get a better view and altered the camera function to full zoom. The couple emerged from the office and walked over to the blond lady's car. Dave placed the box of wine into the passenger seat. She smiled, pecked him on the cheek and moved around to the driver's side.

"The kiss, did you get it?" Stocky grabbed the sleeve of her jacket, practically jumping up and down on the chair.

"Hey stop that!" Reggie hissed grabbing onto the windowsill for support. "Yes I got it."

They moved their chairs back to the table, ignoring the stares from the nearest group of office workers. Reggie downed her drink as Stocky looked through the pictures.

"Do you think it will be enough?" he asked worriedly.

"Well, all you've got is a hug and a peck on the cheek, so you're probably screwed." Reggie announced cheerfully. "Come on," she nudged Stocky in the direction of the bar. "Your round!"

Stocky looked at her in concern. "Are you sure you're alright Reg? You don't seem like yourself." Reggie beamed at him.

"To be honest I felt really rough after the explosion. I still felt a bit off when we met up. But, now my headache's gone and I feel on top of the world." She threw her arms in the air to emphasise her statement, her smile just a little too bright.

"Er, Reg…" Concerned, Stocky leaned towards her putting a hand on her arm. "Did you take anything for the headache?" he asked quietly.

"Yep. The school secretary gave me some of her pills. Said they do wonders for her back. She's right, I feel amazing!"

"Oh crap," muttered Stocky as he looked into her wide staring eyes. "Um, Reg you're totally not supposed to take other people's prescriptions, and back medication would be really strong. Mixing it with alcohol can cause all kinds of side effects"

"Rubbish, I feel fine," said Reggie. She grabbed his beer bottle from the table. "If you're not going to the bar I'm drinking this. I'm so thirsty right now."

Before Stocky could object, she downed the remaining beer and slammed the empty bottle back onto the table. "Hmmmm, much better," she sighed, wiping the back of her hand across her mouth.

Stocky glanced across at the drinking crowds.

"Shit!" he exclaimed, shifting quickly back into the shadows. Reggie looked all around them.

"What's up, are they back?" she asked loudly.

"Shhhhh," whispered Stocky. "Don't look now but BF is here."

"Who?" asked Reggie. Stocky continued to whisper

"Bitch Face… from high school. She's over there with the big group of office workers."

Stocky pointed to a group of well-dressed executive types, who were enjoying a post work drink and chat. Reggie peered across and eventually identified the tall thin frame of Bridgett Fossington, wearing a beautifully fitting suit, and heels Reggie would kill to own.

"Yay, there she is, let's call her over." Reggie started to raise her arm in a wave but in a rare move of strength Stocky pinned her arm to the table, leaning in to hiss in her ear.

"ARE YOU CRAZY?" He emphasised each word slowly. "She made your life hell at high school. We named her Bitch Face for a good reason." Reggie shrugged him off.

"That's all in the past she'll have grown up now. I bet she'd love to see us." Reggie stood up and waved. "Woohoo" she shouted. "Bridgett, Bridgett over here. It's Reggie."

Stocky watched in horror as one of the suits pointed Reggie out to Bridgett. He recognised the superficial smile on her face as she began her signature model strut towards them.

All Reggie could see through her happy haze was Bridgett's perfect, deep chocolate brown halo of hair. It floated hypnotically around Bridgett's head and shoulders as she sashayed towards her.

Bridgett stopped in front of them striking a perfect model pose and shaking her hair out behind her. Reggie, who was still grinning inanely, began to gesture to the spare seat next to her, but froze as Bridgett raised one eyebrow and inclined her head.

"I'm smiling at you," Bridgett began disdainfully, "because I told my friends that you were special needs students I sponsored back in high school." Her lips formed a sneer, as she looked Reggie up and down. "Transvestite hooker is not a good look on you Regina. You're clearly off your head on some dropout drug or other. What a shame that your pathetic life, as I predicted, has amounted to nothing." Reggie stared, open-mouthed, still frozen in place. Bridgett transferred her vicious gaze to Stocky. "If I didn't already know that you are her nerdy, useless friend I would assume by your costume that you are her care worker." Stocky opened his mouth to respond but Bridgett cut in, her hand raised, palm flat-out, in front of his face. "Don't bother," she spat. Nothing you say can possibly interest me. Don't make the mistake of speaking to me again." She started to walk away but turned back to point at Reggie. "Oh and perhaps you should take her somewhere more suitable to drink, like the car park or under a railway bridge. She sure as shit doesn't fit in here."

Bridgett turned on her stylish six-inch heels and sashayed back to her group of friends, effortlessly re-joining the conversation. Reggie closed her mouth and stared, unblinking, at Bridgett's back.

"Um Reg, are you okay?" Stocky enquired after a minute had passed and Reggie still hadn't moved.

"Wine!" Reggie uttered the word without taking her eyes off Bridgett.

"Do you think that's a good idea?" Stocky asked quietly.

"Get me wine!" Reggie spoke slowly.

As Stocky rushed off to the bar Reggie let the full impact of Bridgett's words sink in. Any other week and it probably wouldn't have mattered. She could have laughed it off as Bitch Face just living up to her name. But today, with her clothes in tatters, her hair in a state and her career God knows where, it mattered.

Stocky returned with the wine and she had already downed it by the time he sat back in his seat.

"Hey Reg, remember the medication!" Stocky warned.

"Bugger the medication!" Reggie ground out. She turned furiously to face Stocky. "If I do nothing then she wins and I am nothing."

"What are you going to do?" asked Stocky, dreading the answer.

"I'm going to squash her bitch face in to the carpet, that's what!" Reggie jumped up out of her chair, her wild eyes scanning the crowded room for Bridgett.

While they had been talking, Bridgett's group had finished their drinks and were making their way - still chatting and laughing, towards the exit. Reggie spotted Bridgett walking out through the door into the entrance hallway and launched unsteadily in that direction. Stocky grabbed for her a second too late and watched in dismay as she rocketed towards the door.

CHAPTER 4

Reggie's progress towards the door was hampered by the large crowd. After a few detours and a fair amount of pushing and shoving, she finally made it to the exit doors. Stocky was hot on her heels but making slower progress through the throng. Reggie flung herself through the heavy doors, her wild eyes searching for their target. Her body vibrated with the rage pulsing through her veins. Bridgett was at the tail end of her group and making her way through the outer doors at the far end of the entrance hall.

Reggie's eyes narrowed as they focused on her goal. She stood up tall with a hand on each hip.

"Hey you!" Reggie yelled, pointing in Bridgett's direction.

Everyone in the entrance hall turned towards Reggie; some irritated by the disturbance and others excited, to witness the unfolding drama. Bridgett, still holding the door, turned to smirk at Reggie.

"Bitch Face!" bellowed Reggie, all control now gone. "I'm coming for you!"

Reggie propelled herself forwards, eyes focused on Bridgett's face. She saw the smirk turn into a grin a fraction of a second before she felt her legs leave the ground. Stocky, finally arriving, took in the scene before him. The tall bouncer had Reggie in a vice like grip, with her arms pinned to her sides. Her legs dangled pathetically as she tried to free herself.

Bridgett, who was now laughing, spoke loudly so everyone in the entrance hall could hear her.

"You want to be careful with that one. I don't think it's had all its shots!"

"That's enough Bridgett," said Stocky coldly. "There's no need for that. Please just go," he pleaded.

Bridgett threw a final smirk in Reggie's direction and left. As the door closed behind her, people resumed their conversations as if nothing out of the ordinary had occurred. Stocky looked with concern at Reggie, who was now slumped, defeated in the bouncer's arms.

"You don't know what she's done to me!" Reggie mumbled, glancing up at the bouncer. He relaxed his grip slightly so that her feat touched the ground.

"I can guess," he said sympathetically. "We've all been to school and we've all met her type. But you taking a run at her... that was never going to end well!"

Reggie was still breathing raggedly but could feel her body calming down. The spaced-out feeling was returning and her hands felt shaky again.

"If I let you go, you're not going to go all Rambo again, are you?" the bouncer asked with a small smile.

Reggie shook her head. He released her arms and took a step back. Reggie's knees buckled and she sat down hard on the floor. Stocky rushed over and crouched down next to her. He looked up at the bouncer.

"It's not her fault," explained Stocky. "She had an accident at work. Then someone gave her pain killers and she's had a funny reaction."

The bouncer nodded sympathetically. "She can't stay here though."

"Her car is in the car park," Stocky replied. "I can drive her home."

The bouncer bent down to a now drowsy Reggie, zipped her jacket right up to the neck and scooped her up into his arms.

Reggie opened her eyes. "What'ya doin?" she slurred.

"Just avoiding a wardrobe malfunction," the bouncer smiled. "Don't want to show the whole world what you've got."

Reggie's eyes widened with recognition. "Oh you're the hot bouncer guy!" She smiled dreamily up at him and nestled comfortably against his chest. "Mmmm, you smell nice," she murmured against his arm.

He grinned, "And you smell like you've been in a chemical fire." He gestured to Stocky. "Lead the way."

Stocky cringed and held the door open. "Sorry, she's not usually like this. Honestly!"

Hearing Stocky's voice, Reggie peered over the bouncer's shoulder. "Is that Stocky?" she asked. "He's great. He's going to be a top 'Private I' and I'm his sexy sidekick! We're catching your boss in the act!"

Feeling that she had successfully summed up the situation she settled back into the reassuring comfort of the bouncer's arms, smiling dreamily as her eyes began to close. Stocky and the bouncer exchanged amused glances. She's going to regret this in the morning, thought Stocky.

They reached Reggie's car and Stocky retrieved the keys from her jacket pocket. The bouncer carefully shifted Reggie's weight in his arms before gently placing her on the back seat.

"Do you think she'll be ok?" Stocky asked.

They both studied Reggie's still form. Soft snores began to escape from her mouth. The bouncer raised an eyebrow.

"I think she'll be fine," he said. "She just needs to sleep it off."

"I do wonder though," Stocky pondered. "What she might've done if you hadn't stopped her?"

The bouncer laughed. "I think we're both lucky we didn't find out." He looked towards the bar. "I need to get back inside. Take care of her."

"I will, thanks!" replied Stocky.

With a wave the bouncer turned back towards the building. Stocky noticed with a little jealousy that he moved with easy strides, non-the worse for having carried an almost comatose Reggie half way around the building. Stocky started Reggie's battered blue car and saw the bouncer watching his progress as he drove around the corner onto the main street.

Stocky used the drive home to reflect on the train wreck that this evening had been. His cover was now well and truly blown at the bar, thanks to Reggie's outburst. It was unlikely that his client would think the photo evidence was enough to prove that Dave was having an affair. He would have to try anyway and just hope she recognised the blonde woman.

Stocky glanced back at Reggie's sleeping form and frowned. He felt partly responsible for how things had ended up. He felt a twinge of guilt as he remembered how terrible she had looked after the explosion. He had been so swept up in his need to get evidence that he hadn't taken any real notice of how unwell she was until it was too late. He shook his head in disgust. He was so used to Reggie always being there for him and never letting him down. She was such a good friend that it hadn't even occurred to her to cancel their meeting and head home for a rest. Maybe it should have occurred to him!

He turned off the main road onto Reggie's estate and swung the car around the winding road to her parents' house. He pulled up outside and looked at the familiar home, welcoming in the dark evening. Lights blazed out of the kitchen and dining room windows downstairs, and glowed behind the closed curtains of Reggie's sister's room upstairs. At least he knew there were people home.

The last time he had been here was the previous Christmas, for the famous Quinn holiday open home. Each year friends and family gathered at the Quinn house at some point between Christmas and New Year, for food, drinks and a festive catch up. He smiled as he remembered them drinking as much of Reggie's parents gin, and vodka as they could, trying to look and sound sober as they chatted to her parents' friends. They had failed miserably every time but each year they resolved to make a better job of it next time around.

Stocky opened the back door and leaned in to gently shake Reggie. "Reggie, wake up! We're at your house"

Reggie groaned and squinted up at Stocky. "I'm so tired,"

she grumbled. She managed to push herself up into a sitting position and shuffle to the edge of the seat. Stocky helped her out of the car and she leaned on him for support. They made their way slowly down the drive towards the front door. Stocky rang the bell and they waited.

"Mum's gonna love this," Reggie mumbled into Stocky's shoulder.

The hallway light came on and Reggie's mum opened the door. Light poured onto them and Stocky heard Mrs Quinn's sharp intake of breath as she saw Reggie's bedraggled appearance.

"Good grief, what happened to her?" Without waiting for an answer, she leaned back inside the doorway and shouted for her husband. "Michael! Come here quickly and help Reggie."

Michael Quinn emerged from the lounge and with his customary tact, showed no surprise at the state his eldest daughter appeared to be in.

"Right then Reggie, let's get you up to bed," he announced casually. He gently took hold of Reggie and led her slowly towards the stairs. Mrs Quinn continued to hold the door open, her head turning to follow Reggie's progress with concern.

Stocky stood awkwardly on the doorstep unsure of what to do next. He felt some explanation was probably required but wasn't really sure what to say or how well it would be received.

Elizabeth finally realised she had been lost in her own thoughts. She pasted a smile on her face embracing the comfort of everyday social conventions.

"Come on in Stocky," she said gesturing to the kitchen. "Help yourself to a juice. You know where everything is. I'll just help Michael with Reggie and I'll be back down in a moment." She turned and quickly headed for the stairs. Moments later Stocky could hear muffled voices coming from upstairs, where he imagined they were deciding how best to deal with Reggie.

He grabbed a glass from the cupboard, poured himself a juice from the fridge and sat down at the kitchen table. Probably best to stick to the truth but keep it short he mused. He looked around at the clean and well-organised kitchen. The dark wooden cupboard doors were set against light walls and benches and farmhouse style tiles. The wall to the left of him was filled with family pictures and certificates celebrating Reggie and Stella's various achievements. The kitchen wasn't in the newest style but the overall feeling was one of comfort and practicality. It was the centre of a busy family home.

The sound of creaking stairs alerted him to the return of Reggie's parents. Stocky straightened in his seat. Even after knowing her for all these years, Mrs Quinn's direct and sometimes-abrupt way of dealing with people could be unnerving to face.

"Hi Stocky." Mr Quinn greeted him with a smile. "Thanks for bringing Reggie home." He walked over to the fridge to pour two more drinks of juice. Elizabeth took a seat opposite Stocky. She raised a hand to touch her hair and, assured of its continued perfection she clasped her hands in front of her on the table. Michael placed a glass of orange juice beside his wife's hands and moved to lean against the kitchen counter.

"Now Steven dear!" Mrs Quinn began. She looked across the table at him, her smile no longer forced and her eyes inquisitive. "What on earth happened?" she asked, direct as ever. Her no-nonsense tone showing she had regained her famous composure. Stocky took a breath.

"Ummmm… Look it totally wasn't Reggie's fault," he explained nervously.

Elizabeth and Michael exchanged a quick and knowing look.

"No, it never is dear." Elizabeth smiled reassuringly at Stocky. "Do go on!"

Very conscious that he could be digging an even deeper hole for Reggie with her parents, Stocky kept it brief. He explained about the accident at school, Reggie taking the prescription medicine and the resulting negative effects.

"Oh well, it could have been worse," responded Michael, unflappably positive as usual.

Stocky smiled in agreement, remaining silent as images of Bridgett Fossington and the bouncer flashed through his mind.

"Right then!" Elizabeth spoke as she stood up from the table.

Seeing this as his cue to leave, Stocky stood too and Elizabeth led him to the door.

"Thank you so much Steven. Reggie is lucky to have a friend like you." She peered out into the darkness. "I see you are driving Reggie's car," she said. Stocky nodded. "Well dear, you should take it home and perhaps you could come back at around 7.30am in the morning?" she asked, more of a command than a question. "Then you and Reggie can drive back to wherever your car is before she has to be at work."

She nodded to herself, happy that she had successfully organised what needed to be done. She ushered Stocky out into the night with a reassuring pat on the shoulder.

"Goodnight dear, drive safely!" she called out after him.

"Bye Mrs Quinn," he dutifully replied. With a sigh of relief Stocky started Reggie's car and headed home.

Reggie woke the next morning feeling relaxed and refreshed. For a few precious moments she enjoyed a leisurely stretch. That was, until she noticed that she was still fully dressed. After a moment of confusion, image after disastrous image tumbled into her mind and she froze, her mind trying and failing miserably to process the horror of the previous day. A gentle tap on the door interrupted her nightmare recap. She turned her head to see her mother's concerned face peer into the room.

"Oh good, you're awake dear," her mother smiled. "Quickly hop into the bathroom. I'm making you some breakfast, then we can have a nice chat before you go to work. Stocky will be here to pick you up at 7.30am."

The head disappeared and Reggie was left to wonder what exactly her parents knew about yesterday's events. Resolved to face the music Reggie quickly showered and dressed. Luckily the hair straighteners managed to hide most of the damage done to her hair. She entered the kitchen and her mother's glance of approval confirmed her own assessment, that her appearance was presentable and a far cry from the disastrous mess of last night.

Reggie sat at the kitchen table. Her mum placed a plate of toast and mug of coffee in front of her. She sat opposite, hands clasped, as she had done the previous evening with Stocky. Reggie waited as she had many times throughout her childhood for the axe to fall and her actions to be judged and punished. Her mum remained silent until Reggie had nibbled her toast and sipped her coffee.

Unable to put it off any longer, Reggie raised her eyes from her plate to meet her mother's gaze. Rather than the rage and frustration she was expecting, Reggie was surprised to see concern and disappointment.

When she spoke, her mother's words echoed her own thoughts. "Reggie dear, I can see you are expecting me to shout and rant." Elizabeth shook her head sadly. "Sweetheart you are not a child any more. I can't fix your mistakes by shouting at you and sending you to your room. Your actions at school yesterday put yourself and the children in Science Club at risk. You could all have been seriously hurt."

"I know, Mum," Reggie admitted. The truth was undeniable. She miserably sipped her coffee while her mum rose and began stacking the dishwasher.

"What you need to do now is take responsibility for what you have done, move forward and for goodness sake…" she paused with a plate in her hand waiting for Reggie to look up. When Reggie finally returned her stare, she continued. "For goodness sake Regina, make better choices."

A lengthy silence followed during which Elizabeth finished loading the dishwasher and began wiping down the benches. Reggie ate her breakfast quietly, all the while internally berating herself for all of her recent poor decisions. She really needed to get her shit together and grow the hell up, she thought. Reggie's mum finally broke the silence.

"By the way dear, the Star and Anchor pub rang and left a message for you last night. You apparently left your purse there! You can pick it up from behind the bar anytime today."

She turned to face Reggie, who had groaned at the news. "I'm not sure what part the bar played in last night's little episode, but I'm fairly sure I don't want to know about it, do I?" she asked shrewdly.

Reggie sat with the coffee cup gripped tightly in her hands. "No Mum, you do not want to know," she agreed.

The bar was the last place Reggie wanted to visit. After last night's humiliation, she'd been hoping to give it a wide birth for several months at least, maybe even the rest of her life. There was no way around it. She wouldn't get very far without her bank cards. When would be the best time to go? Perhaps at playtime this morning. The bar would be opening up and there would be few customers and hopefully none of the staff from last night. She had some NQT (Newly Qualified Teacher) classroom release time after playtime, so it wouldn't matter if she got back a few minutes after the next lesson started.

"Come on Reggie!" Her mum's voice broke through her thoughts. She lifted the empty coffee cup from Reggie's hands and headed back over to the dishwasher. "Stocky will be here any minute. You need to be ready," she urged.

Reggie reluctantly rose from the table and headed out of the kitchen.

CHAPTER 5

Reggie was waiting nervously by the kerb as Stocky pulled up in her car. Her long coat was buttoned up against the blustering cool wind. It ruffled the heavy pink heads of her dad's prize rose bushes behind her. Across the road the overly tall fir trees in the Taylor's garden were swaying hypnotically from side to side. Reggie forced her reluctant legs to move, opened the rear door and placed her school box on the seat. She slid awkwardly into the passenger seat, her eyes remaining forwards. Without a word, Stocky pulled the car away from the kerb and headed towards the main road. For a few moments, they both sat silently, neither of them knowing how to fix the strained atmosphere. Eventually, Stocky turned his head to take in Reggie's improved appearance.

"So… you look much better Reg," he said quietly, his voice carefully neutral. Reggie made no response, so he tried again. "Errr… How are you feeling?" He grinned and snorted as the laughter he'd been trying to contain exploded out.
Reggie smiled reluctantly, colour tinging her face.

"Embarrassed, very embarrassed," she answered, unconsciously rubbing the small burn still visible above her eyebrow. "Can we just pretend it never happened and move on," she pleaded, her eyes finally turning to meet his.

"Totally," said Stocky. He immediately changed the subject. "So, here's your phone." He pointed to where it sat by the gear stick. "I printed off the pictures you took. It's not great evidence but maybe she'll think it's enough to keep me on a bit longer."

Reggie nodded and they settled into a comfortable silence, both mulling over their own problems. Neither one was happy with the direction in which their lives seemed to be heading. Things were certainly different than the glossy university prospectus had promised. They should be prosecuted for false advertising thought Stocky bitterly, turning Reggie's car into the parking space next to his black Volkswagen.

Reggie noticed her surroundings with surprise. Lost in thought she had stared unseeingly out of the window as the lush farmland morphed effortlessly into the busy grey of town. She now noticed the skies above - full of menacing, prison grey clouds, hovering morosely over the metropolis below. The absence of cheerfulness suited her sombre mood, mirroring her own feeling of foreboding.

Finally, alone in her car Reggie attempted to rally her flagging spirits. Time to make good decisions, she thought. If she kept her head down and worked hard, hopefully she could get through this. The staff would be difficult to get onside, but not impossible. The majority of them were a decent enough bunch. She would have to apologise at the staff meeting. It would be embarrassing but she was big enough and determined enough to take that on the chin.

Maybe she could offer to be Mr Banks' assistant in Science Club, she thought. Then she could learn from him and gain enough skills to not blow up the school next time around. She shuddered at the thought. That is if they ever trust you enough for there to be a next time, whispered the negative voice at the back of her mind.

Reggie parked in the school car park in a spot close to the exit. This would guarantee a quick escape before playtime. Everything looked just as it did every other morning, except for the large blue school bin to the side of the building. Its lid was propped open by the overflowing, soggy mess of textbooks and equipment that had not survived the sprinkler system deluge. Reggie pushed down the guilt welling up inside her and stood up straight and tall. She took a couple of long, steadying breaths, pushed back her shoulders and marched towards the main entrance. She was remorseful, apologetic and damn it she was going to make amends and put this whole crappy week behind her.

The shrill sound of the playtime bell dismissed the children and allowed Reggie her first free moments in which to think about how operation 'Rescue Reggie's Career' was progressing. She quickly shrugged into her coat, locked the classroom door and descended the steps towards the back entrance of the car park. The apology had gone about as well as she had expected. Most of the faces of the staff members had softened slightly. Some had smiled reassuringly. Some even managed to make eye contact. There had been a couple of eye rollers, Veronica Barkwich (Reggie's vindictive team mate) topping it off with a loud tut and sigh. Reggie had been expecting the verbal dressing down from the head teacher but even that had surprisingly ended on a forgiving note.

Reggie's suggestion, that she help Mr Banks with Science Club had at first met with a lot of resistance. Neville Banks, who had refused to even look at Reggie until this point, stood up - his eyes wild with fury, and listed at length: the books, equipment and children's work that had ended up in the school rubbish skip. His hands shook and spittle gathered at the corner of his mouth, as he emotionally mourned the loss of his prized teaching resources, lovingly gathered over numerous years.

"This girl has ruined me!" he announced, dramatically removing his glasses and wiping at his eyes.

"Hasn't Neville been through enough?" asked Veronica, moving quickly across the room to place a comforting arm around Neville's shoulders. This show of support seemed genuine and heart-felt to all except Reggie, who saw the triumphant smirk Veronica fired in her direction. When all this grovelling was over, Reggie thought, and she had finally established herself as a professional among equals, she would find a way to take Veronica Barkwich down once and for all.

Surprisingly, help and support came from the most unexpected person. Ms Darwin rose and cleared her throat. All chatter ceased. As one, the staff turned expectantly towards the head teacher - resplendent as usual in a perfectly tailored power suit.

"How wonderful that we are so supportive of one another," she began. She beamed benignly at Veronica, who was still comforting Neville.

"It is that same support we now need to offer to young Miss Quinn." Reggie's eyes widened in disbelief as Ms Darwin continued. "Yes, she has made many mistakes and she may even make a few more."

Ms Darwin pinned Reggie with a look, which told her in no uncertain terms that future mistakes were not an option. Reggie shook her head rapidly. It seemed to be the required response.

"In this spirit of support we will all help Miss Quinn to fulfil her potential and become the teacher most of us feel she can be."

Ms Darwin glanced meaningfully at Veronica, who nodded in agreement, enthusiastically playing the role of Reggie's biggest supporter. Ms Darwin turned her attention to Neville Banks, who now that he had vented all his anger had returned to his seat, looking much better for the therapeutic experience.

"Dear Neville, you have had a most unfortunate experience," Ms Darwin soothed. "Although Miss Quinn has much to learn from you, her dedication and enthusiasm will be a great asset to you in your Science Club endeavours." Seeing Neville's eyebrows rise she added a final thought. "I see you are not yet convinced, but think on this Mr Banks. For the duration of the time Miss Quinn helps you with Science club, it can take place in her classroom. This of course means that if there are any further scientific mishaps… it will be Miss Quinn's classroom that explodes."

For the first time that day Mr Banks smiled. Noting that the smile did not quite reach his eyes, Reggie hoped fervently that he was not the kind of person who believed in revenge.

She couldn't afford to make any more mistakes, thought Reggie as she started the engine and headed towards the town centre. Luck seemed to be on her side. Traffic flowed quickly and for once all the traffic lights were green. After driving for only a couple of minutes, Reggie pulled into the Star and Anchor car park.

Get in, get the purse and get out, she thought. It should be simple enough. Ignoring the pictures flashing into her mind of the previous day, she locked the car and headed towards the entrance. The bar was just opening so there would be few staff and hopefully fewer customers. The added bonus was that there wouldn't be any bouncers working at this time of day. Reggie pushed open the heavy doors and made her way across the entrance hall, past the spot where the two bouncers had stood yesterday. So far, so good! She carefully opened the bar doors and scanned the interior. There were no customers and just one member of staff behind the bar, filling the fridges with bottles. Reggie made her way across the cavernous space. Without customers, it seemed like an overly large empty shell. More like the old abandoned cinema and less like the popular bar.

Reggie stood patiently at the bar for a moment listening to the melodious clinking of the bottles as they were added to the fridge.

"Excuse me!" Reggie began. "I'm here to collect my…" Reggie lost the rest of her words. Hearing her voice, the barman had turned around. Shock and embarrassment rendered her motionless, a fiery heat engulfing her face. For a moment he studied her, his sharp blue eyes puzzling to try and place her. Reggie saw the moment when realisation hit. His eyes began to twinkle and his mouth widened into a dazzling smile, almost taking her breath away.

"Well, hello again," he continued to smile. "We haven't been properly introduced. I'm hot bouncer guy and you, I believe, are sexy sidekick." He held out his hand, laughter brimming in his eyes, his face animated with humour.

Reggie didn't take his outstretched hand. Instead she sat down heavily on the nearest barstool with a whoosh, feeling like a fast deflating balloon. Noticing her distress. he took pity and poured Reggie a glass of water.

"Here," he pushed the glass across the bar to where she sat. "Have some water it will help."

Reggie mechanically lifted the glass and took a sip. "This is not happening," she murmured.

He found the fact that she was so flustered and embarrassed unusually endearing.

"Let's try this again," he said patiently. "I'm Jake, it's really nice to meet you."

He stretched out his hand for a second time. This time Reggie took it, glancing up into his eyes looking for any trace of sarcasm. She found none.

"I'm Reggie," she said, "and I'm really embarrassed to meet you," she added with a grimace.

"Don't be," he shook his head, still smiling. "I've seen a lot worse!"

"Really? asked Reggie, her interest piqued. "What kinds of things?"

Jake noticed that as Reggie's attention was captured by a different topic, her face became more animated and her complexion, which had been an alarming shade of red, was calming down. She was attractive, he noticed with surprise. He'd found her interesting the previous evening but mostly because of the amusing situation and the unexpected things she had said. He leaned towards Reggie over the bar, his warm, open smile relaxing her like the sunshine on a spring afternoon.

"One day when you have a few hours to spare I'll share my many stories of other customers and their tragic drinking experiences." He smiled ruefully, managing to look sexy and endearing at the same time.

Is he flirting with me? Reggie wondered. He certainly was amazingly good looking and she found she was intensely attracted to him. She coloured again slightly, remembering that she had already announced her thoughts about him to everyone standing in the entrance hall last night. Seeing her discomfort return, Jake opted for a change of subject.

"So, are you the teacher who tried to blow up Amberidge Primary School yesterday?" he asked cheerfully.

"Holy crap, how the hell would you know that?" Reggie asked incredulously. "Does the whole town know?"

"Relax," he smiled that warm sexy smile that Reggie was beginning to really appreciate. "Some of my buddies from the station came in for a drink after their shift last night. They described a sexy, dripping wet and slightly singed teacher, with boobs trying to escape from her top." He shrugged, the smile now apologetic. "Your friend told me you'd had a work accident and I put two and two together."

Reggie returned his smile. Jake's gentle and friendly manner was helping her to relax and making it easier to laugh at yesterday's events.

"It could have been worse I suppose," she replied. Jake raised an eyebrow. "Well, my boobs could have escaped from my top altogether," Reggie laughed.

"They came pretty close," he teased, relieved that she was able to laugh about it.

"I remember now," Reggie said. "You zipped up my jacket."

Jake shrugged, colour touching the top of his cheekbones. "Just being a gentleman," he replied, his voice a little gruff.

"Thank you," Reggie said simply.

"You are most welcome," he replied. His eyes found and held her gaze. Reggie was unable to look away. Her breathing slowed and she could feel an almost magnetic pull towards him. Leaning further forward Jake gently traced the burn above Reggie's eyebrow. Her skin heated beneath his touch.

"Who knew teaching was such a dangerous profession," he joked. He moved away to retrieve Reggie's purse from the back of the bar, deliberately breaking their connection.

Realising she had been holding her breath Reggie exhaled slowly, the after effects of their exchanged look warming her skin.

To reclaim some stability, she took another sip of water and moved the conversation to a less risky topic.

"So you're a bouncer and a barman?" she asked. Jake placed the purse into her hand, closing her fingers around it.

"Actually I'm a fireman," he replied.

"Of course," Reggie made the connection. "That's how you knew about the call out to my school. So why work here?"

My cousin is married to Dave - the owner. I want to open my own business, so I pick up a few shifts a week as a bouncer to earn some extra cash."

"And you do bar work too?"

"No, I don't normally work the bar. Dave quite often has meetings at this time of day. Jane - the Assistant Manager usually covers for him but she's off sick today. I'm just helping out. He smiled again and Reggie felt her temperature rise a couple of degrees. Making a mental note to analyse the unbalancing effect he had on her at a later time, Reggie glanced down at her watch.

"Shit, I have to get back to work," she said, quickly jumping off the seat. "Thanks for my purse." She hurried away from the bar, her thoughts already moving towards the rest of the day at school.

"Hey Reggie, wait a minute." Jake called after her. She paused and half turned back to him.

"Are you really investigating Dave?" he asked. Reggie hesitated for a moment considering how much, if any information she should give him. Let's face it she thought, between them, her and Stocky had blown any chance of keeping their investigation quiet. She decided honesty was the best policy.

"Yes, your cousin thinks Dave is having an affair so she has hired my friend Stocky, who you met last night. He's been having a few problems so I've been helping him out," Reggie explained.

"Oh is that all," said Jake with relief. "If she thinks he's having an affair he will be. I've known him since school and he was a player back then too. I never thought he was the right person for Caroline."

"Thanks," said Reggie. "I'll tell Stocky." She began to turn again and then a thought struck her and she walked back towards the bar. "Jake what did you think we'd be investigating?"

"To be honest I thought it might be dodgy business dealings. He gets all these packages and I don't think they are for the bar," said Jake.

"It could just be stock," Reggie suggested.

"Yeah … maybe!" Jake looked unconvinced. "Anyway it's none of my business," he continued. "The only reason I'm interested is that Dave has offered to invest in my business when I've got my start-up money together. If he's into illegal stuff I don't want his money."

Reggie looked at her watch again. "Look I really have to go." She retraced her steps quickly towards the door. "But if we find anything out I'll let you know," she called back over her shoulder.

"I'll look forward to it," Jake replied. His tone sent tingles down Reggie's spine. What was it about that man, she thought, that he could undo all her composure with a few words?

Reversing out of the parking space, she imagined his dazzling, breathtaking smile and couldn't help her own dreamy smile in response.

"Get a grip girl," she muttered and forced her thoughts away from Jake, towards more professional teaching matters.

CHAPTER 6

The drive home from work was a very pleasant experience; the sky no longer threatened rain and Reggie sang along, semi tunefully to the bouncy pop songs on the radio. The clouds above raced each other, dancing along to the beat, while the warm afternoon sun smiled proudly down on their childish antics. The only blip on the day's happy horizon was the text she had received from Stocky.

Been fired - not over. Need to talk.

Reggie had no idea how being fired could not be the end, but assumed she would find out more when Stocky came around later on, after family dinner. Reggie smiled, not at the family part but at the thought of her mum's home cooked lasagne for dinner - the reward every hard-working professional deserved.

Reggie hadn't really seen Stella to talk to since the other evening's incident. By now some of Stella's co-workers at the bar were bound to have taken delight in describing to her all the embarrassing details of Reggie's shame. Reggie knew that the joy of eating lasagne would be lessened slightly by sisterly digs, and embarrassing questions. Stella, unfortunately, was highly skilled at delivering both.

Dinner in the week was usually at 6pm sharp, cooked by either Reggie's mum or dad, depending on who was going to be home first. Reggie and Stella were still the clean-up crew; a tradition established when they were young, and rigidly enforced by both parents. Her mum and dad were both good cooks, but from a washing up perspective, Reggie preferred it when her dad cooked. He was from the school of one pot wonder cookery and this reduced the washing up workload substantially.

The delicious smell of lasagne set Reggie's stomach rumbling as she walked along the driveway. She waved to her mum, who was sitting at the kitchen table with a glass of wine and a magazine. She walked on, past the kitchen door, heading upstairs to change.

"Dinner won't be long!" her mum called after her.

Reggie changed into jeans and a long-sleeved top and rummaged in her drawer for a rare pair of matching socks. She returned to the kitchen. Feeling unusually helpful she set the kitchen table for the four of them. The dining room was more often saved for Sunday roasts and when guests visited. It quite often also acted as a second lounge where Reggie and Stella could sit together and watch their choice of TV shows.

"Is Stella not coming home for dinner tonight?" Reggie queried, hopefully.

"She's running a bit late," replied Reggie's mum. "She should be home soon." Elizabeth rose from the table and checked on the green beans simmering on the stove.

"These are ready. Can you pass me a bowl please darling, and go and tell your dad I'm dishing up?"

Reggie placed a bowl next to the sink, where her mum was draining the beans, and wandered over to the kitchen door.

"Dad...dinner!" she yelled loudly into the hallway.

Turning back around she met her mum's pained look with an innocent smile. Wordlessly Elizabeth handed her a plate of steaming lasagne and Reggie took a seat at the table, adding a token spoonful of beans while she waited.

Sounds from the hallway announced the arrival of whirlwind Stella.

"Hi everyone, won't be a min!" she yelled as she pounded up the stairs. She reappeared a few moments later wearing jeans and a fitted t-shirt. Reggie marvelled that after only minutes in the house and a frantic wardrobe change, Stella still managed to look beautifully presented. Her blond hair fell perfectly over her shoulders and her makeup was pristine. Clearly Mum has passed all those genes on to Stella, bypassing me completely, thought Reggie wistfully. Stella grabbed the last plate of lasagne and took the vacant chair.

"Isn't this great!" smiled their dad as Stella added a healthy pile of beans to her plate. "All my girls together for dinner."

"It sure is," mumbled Stella through a mouthful of pasta. Swallowing, she turned to her mum. "Great lasagne Mum!"

"You're welcome darling," Elizabeth smiled.

"So…" Stella switched her attention to Reggie. Her mischievous smile alerted Reggie to the imminent attack.

"Had any interesting experiences at my bar recently? Stella asked innocently.

"Can't think of any," Reggie replied blandly. She hoped Stella might take the hint and back off. No such luck.

"Oh," Stella feigned surprise, but the mischievous twinkle remained in her eyes. She went in for the kill. "Not even a misunderstanding with one of the bouncers and your old school friend, Bridgette?"

Reggie could see that her parents, who usually ignored most of the girls' dinnertime banter, were now listening with interest.

"Oh that," Reggie dismissed her most embarrassing experience ever, as if it was nothing. "I saw Jake today. It's fine, all sorted." Reggie took a moment to enjoy her sister's open-mouthed shock but knew it would take more than that to shut her down.

"You're on first name terms with Jake. Oooh is this a love connection?" Stella smirked, knowing she had scored a hit and that her mother wouldn't be able to resist joining the conversation now.

"Is this true Reggie? Have you met someone?" Elizabeth eyed her daughter with interest.

"No Mum. He's just the guy at the bar. He gave me my

purse when I went in today. Besides, after our chat the other day I've decided to take your advice and focus on my career for a while."

Reggie's mum nodded, pleased that her wisdom was appreciated by at least one daughter. Reggie smiled, knowing she had cleverly dodged a bullet. Now for payback!

"It's a good thing my love-life is non-existent; now that Stella has met Mr Right you'll be busy planning her future. You did mention she'll be wanting children soon!" Reggie sat back to enjoy the show.

Stella choked on a bean. "What…?" she managed to spit out, very much the cornered prey in her mother's matchmaking hunt.

"I've been thinking," Elizabeth began, oblivious to Stella's extreme discomfort. "We should have your nice lawyer friend over for dinner."

"Mum, no!" Stella was practically squirming in her seat.

Unperturbed, Elizabeth continued thoughtfully. "If he is 'The One', we should really start getting to know him."

Reggie watched her dad roll his eyes at his wife's determined expression. He wisely remained silent. It really was amazing how focused she could become when the chance to marry off one of her offspring was even a distant possibility. Stella, having finally managed to swallow her food was quickly on the defensive.

"Mum he's not THE one, he's just a guy who I had a drink with. Besides I'm far too young to settle down." She glanced sideways at Reggie. "Reggie's older! You should worry about her not me"

Elizabeth sighed, shaking her head.

"I do worry about Reggie, but she's in no position to settle down."

"Mum. I'm right here!" Reggie raised her hands in exasperation.

"Yes darling, I know you are, but we have to face facts. You did just almost blow up your school. You have a lot work to do before you are ready for marriage and children." She placed her knife and fork together on the plate and rose from the table. "Now I'm going to sit in the lounge and rest my nerves. If one of you could make a pot of tea while you clear up that would be lovely."

Stella and Reggie exchanged looks as the door closed behind their mum.

"Rest her nerves?" muttered Reggie. "I don't think she has a nerve in her entire body."

Their Dad laughed. "I'm going to join your mother," he replied. "Reggie try not to blow up the kitchen while you do the dishes." Reggie scowled. "And Stella, it's such a shame we won't be meeting your young lawyer friend. I was really looking forward to eating in the dining room for a change!"

Stella aimed a tea towel at his head but he was already through the door and chuckling as he sauntered away. They began the dishes, Reggie washing and Stella drying; the familiar routine soothing Reggie's ruffled feathers. After a while she commented thoughtfully.

"I'm not sure which is worse, being hounded by Mum's matchmaking or having a life too disastrous to even be considered worth matching up!"

Stella chuckled, "I'll swap you anytime. Hey, maybe you can give me some pointers on how to mess my life up more!"

"Here this will help." Reggie squeezed the wet cloth over Stella's head. Stella squealed as water and bubbles ran down her hair."

"Business as usual in the Quinn household, I see!" said Stocky, sitting himself down at the table.

Reggie spun around, surprised not to have heard him come in. "Make yourself useful," she ordered, "We're nearly finished here. If you make a pot of tea for Mum, then we can sit and talk."

Stocky busied himself with the teapot while Reggie wiped down the kitchen benches and Stella put the last of the dry dishes away. Minutes later they sat comfortably around the kitchen table; Stella warmed her hands on her mug of steaming tea and looked at Stocky.

"So, I hear your life has turned to shit!" she announced bluntly.

Stocky nodded. "Totally shit, but I have a plan."

Reggie raised her eyebrows and took a sip of her Diet-Coke. "How can you have a plan if you were fired?" she asked.

Stocky blew cooling air over his tea considering his response. "Well…" he paused to sip the tea. "I did get fired and to be honest she was completely justified. Turns out the blonde lady in the photos was my client Caroline's sister."
The girls stared at Stocky in confusion.

"She fired you because Dave is having an affair with her sister?" asked Reggie.

"No!" Stocky waved away her question. "I showed her the pictures and she just laughed. Apparently, Dave and her sister organised a surprise birthday party for Caroline last night. The box she was carrying had a cake in it and the wine and beer were for the guests to drink." Reggie began to snigger.

"Y..you mean that we went through all that trouble and I nearly got beaten up by Bitch Face, just to get pictures of party planning!" Giggling uncontrollably, she wiped at the tears flowing from her eyes with her sleeve. Seeing the state she was in, Stocky also began laughing. Stella stared in disbelief at the two giggling idiots.

"You two are the incompetent twins!" she exclaimed.

"Hey!" Reggie forced out between giggles. "I'm just the sexy sidekick!"

"And you!" Stella poked Stocky in the arm. "You're a freaking computer genius. Do the words 'background check' mean anything to you?"

Stocky had the decency to look sheepish.

"This whole 'Private I.' thing is a very steep learning curve, he replied defensively."

"Only if you've never watched a TV show in your life!" Stella bit back.

"You're right," said Stocky, now serious. "I've been doing some internet research on surveillance skills, so next time I'll be ready for him."

"What next time?" asked Stella. "You were fired."

"Well, here's the thing, Uncle Steve has no idea she fired me. He was out of the office all day on a case. I am sure that Dave is having an affair. I just need to follow him around and catch him with the actual 'other woman'. If I show Caroline real evidence, she might rehire me and Uncle Steve will never know."

Reggie sat up, the urge to laugh suddenly gone. "Actually you might be right," she said. Reggie filled them in about her conversation with Jake that morning at the bar.

"I knew about Jake being Caroline's cousin, but I didn't know he went to school with Dave," Stella added.

"What's your take on Dave?" Stocky asked. "You've worked for him for a while."

Stella thought for a moment. "He's just your typical bar owner," she said. "Charismatic, likes a laugh, loves chatting up the ladies when they are buying drinks. That's what men buy bars for, isn't it? He's 'accidentally' patted my bum a couple of times when I've been working," she smiled cheekily. "But who can resist this?" Laughing she leaned in her chair and patted her rear. "Seriously though, I know he's had several affairs in the past. He's always meeting up with different blond bombshells at the bar. Although, now that I think about it, there hasn't been anyone new around for a while."

"Oh my God!" Reggie put her hand on her forehead as realisation struck. "I know when he does it!" she exclaimed.

"Go on," urged Stocky, now all business.

"Jake was covering for him this morning because he had a meeting. He said Dave has had a lot of morning meetings lately; Jane was sick today but he said she usually covers for him," said Reggie.

Stocky turned to Stella. "Do you know Jane? Can you find out if she's covering for Dave tomorrow?"

"Sure," she replied, "I'll text her now."

The urgency in Stocky's tone spurred Reggie into action.

"You'll need a plan. What about your friend, Kelvin?" she asked. "He could help you." Stella's phone pinged and they both paused expectantly while she checked her message.

"Ha," she said triumphantly. "She is working tomorrow morning. She's covering while Dave's at a meeting."

"Yes!" Stocky fist pumped the air. His excitement was contagious.

"Ring Kelvin now." Reggie urged. Kelvin was quick to answer and Stocky speedily briefed him.

"Yep… yep, we'll use your car and equipment… Thanks man… Yep I'll be at your house at 8am… See you." Stocky ended the call, a satisfied smile on his face. "We're in business," he said, still smiling. "This will totally work, I know it!"

"What will you do?" asked Reggie.

"We'll wait outside his house and follow him from there. That way we can't miss him," Stocky replied. "Kelvin is really pumped. Says he needs something more exciting than Starbucks to focus on." Stocky thought for a moment then looked at Reggie. "It's still early. Do you think we should do what Stella said?"

Before Reggie could answer, Stella jumped in. "My advice is always worth following, but I don't remember giving you any!"

"You know, watching TV shows for tips on what to do," said Stocky. Stella rolled her eyes, but Reggie's eyes lit up.

"Yeah, we could watch *C.S.I* or something!"

"No you idiots!" Stella stood up, frustrated. "*C.S.I* is about what happens after they find a dead body. They don't do surveillance. You need a show about detectives or Private Investigators."

"*Magnum P.I.*" Reggie announced triumphantly. Stella groaned. "What?" Reggie asked defensively. "Dad says he's the best. We've got the DVD box sets in the lounge."

"You do know there's a new version out now." said Stella.

"You can't beat the classics, they're totally brilliant," enthused Stocky. "We can watch a couple of episodes and analyse them for helpful hints. Are you in Stel?"

"As tempting as that sounds," Stella replied, "I have stuff to do." The sarcasm practically oozed out of every pore. "But I'll join you later for the analysis and debriefing." She smirked and left the room.

Ten minutes later Reggie and Stocky were comfortably slouched in the old oversized leather chairs at the far end of the dining room. The curtains were closed against the chill of the autumn evening and Reggie had switched on the lamp, giving the room a cosy warm glow. Reggie sat back comfortably, her feet up on the footstool, remote in hand. Stocky reached across, helping himself to popcorn from the bowl on her knee.

"Was the popcorn strictly necessary?" he asked.

"Of course – brain food," she replied. "Now shut up and watch."

Half an hour later when Stella entered the room she found the DVD paused and an animated debate in full flow.

"That's total crap!" Stocky announced passionately. "How can you follow someone around in a bright red Ferrari without being seen?"

"At least people know you mean business in a Ferrari!" Reggie countered. "They won't wave at you and buy you a 'pity coffee' if you are driving a Ferrari."

She hammered her point home, carried away by the spirit of the debate. Stocky's face fell and she was immediately contrite. "Sorry Stocky!"

"No you're right," he said mournfully. "What does he have that I don't?"

Stella sighed, exasperated.

"Apart from the fact that it's all fake and a TV show... he has swagger." She walked over to them, squeezed into the seat with Reggie and helped herself to popcorn. "He believes he can do it and his clients believe he can get the job done. Even when he doesn't believe it he fakes it until he makes it happen." She shoved a handful of popcorn in her mouth. "Oh... and he has dress sense, she mumbled between crunches, pausing to pick escaped bits of corn out of her cleavage.

"Classy Stel!" grumbled Reggie as she brushed Stella's popcorn debris off her lap. "*Magnum P.I* is set in the 80's. There's no fashion sense."

Stella swallowed and licked her lips before talking.

"What I mean is," she spoke slowly as if addressing idiots, "he has the sense not to dress like a student." She eyed Stocky's clothes with distaste; he blushed under her scrutiny and moved his hand to cover the rip in his jeans. He looked down, as if noticing for the first time the faded, worn out t-shirt he was wearing under his usual open shirt.

Stocky could see Reggie bristling at her sister's comments and so spoke before the sister bashing could begin.

"You're right!" he announced. Both sisters were caught off guard and shocked onto silence. "The clothes - I can't do anything about," he looked regretfully at his T-shirt. "At least not until I start getting paid. But the 'fake it till you make it' stuff – I can totally do that." He stood and headed for the door. "Thanks girls, you've given me a lot to think about." He waved, grinned and walked out, a noticeable spring in his step.

"Told you it was a good idea to watch *Magnum*," said Reggie.

"Who knew it could be so …," Stella searched for the right word, … "inspiring," she added in surprise. She hopped over into Stocky's empty seat, grabbing the bowl of popcorn off Reggie's lap.

"Go on, press play, let's see what else we can learn," she laughed.

CHAPTER 7

Finally, it was Friday. After the week from hell, Reggie only had to stagger through playground duty, administer the weekly tests and stay awake during assembly. She would then be able to enjoy a relaxing weekend of freedom. Not that she could afford to go anywhere or buy anything during her precious free time. Her first pay cheque was still a distant two weeks away. Sadly, by the time she had paid her parents the money she owed for her new work clothes, plus the rent check they were eagerly anticipating, not to forget the student loans people - who would grab their chunk of cash, she'd be lucky to have money left for a coffee.

Reggie thought wistfully about the money Stocky had promised her for helping him with his case. That would presumably go to Kelvin, now that he had taken over surveillance duties. Unfortunately, she had mentally spent the money so many times that it felt like it was hers by right and that Kelvin had stolen it away from her. She pushed down the feelings of resentment. Kelvin was just helping a friend – her friend. What kind of a person begrudged someone success like that? A desperate one, that's who. Reggie searched in her pocket for the key to her classroom door. Once inside she carefully placed the box of marking on her desk and slumped into her chair.

It was very depressing, she thought, that her greatest achievement in life was probably going to be appearing in the Guinness Book of Records as the oldest woman in the world still living with her parents. She smiled ruefully as the image of the three of them shuffling around the house with matching Zimmer frames and cardigans, popped into her mind. Reggie's thoughts turned back to Stocky. She hoped his surveillance was going well. He'd had a real run of bad luck lately; if anyone was due a change in fortune, it was Stocky.

The subject of her thoughts was currently parked down the road from Dave's impressive house, sitting unobtrusively (he hoped) between a blue Fiat Panda and a Volkswagen Polo. From his internet research, Stocky knew to position himself carefully so that his quarry wouldn't need to pass him in the street. Luckily the street was a dead end so he didn't have to consider which direction Dave would leave in.

Stocky's mood was still buoyant after the *Magnum P.I* revelations of the previous night. In a determined effort to 'fake it till he made it', Stocky had searched out a pair of un-ripped jeans from his closet. He had ditched his faded T-shirt and instead he had buttoned up the front of the shirt. He had even managed to find a fairly un-student-like dark blue shirt with small checks on it at the back of his closet. He had vague memories of unwrapping it on Christmas morning last year. His mum was always trying to update his wardrobe, but until today he'd never thought it necessary. A couple of extra minutes with the hair wax and his transformation was complete. Stocky had stood thoughtfully in front of the mirror, studying his improved image. Not quite the businessman yet, he thought, but definitely someone who meant business and who hopefully looked less like a student.

As agreed, Stocky had met Kelvin at his house at 8am. Kelvin had bounded out of the house with puppy like exuberance, wearing a black Nirvana T-shirt and matching black jeans. By the look of his clothes Stocky suspected that they had recently been retrieved from a pile on the floor.

"Dude, this is going to be amazing!" enthused Kelvin, vigorously patting Stocky on the back.

A minty fresh blast of breath met Stocky's nostrils, quickly overpowered by the strong smell of Lynx deodorant. For all his enthusiasm, until about five minutes ago Kelvin had still been in bed.

"Get in, get in," Kelvin urged. Once in the car he turned to the objects on the back seat. "I've got Dad's bird watching binoculars and my camera."

"What are these for?" Stocky pointed to a collection of wigs, hats and sunglasses.

Kelvin sat back and smiled smugly. "It's obvious dude – disguises. I have so got this Private Eye thing down." Stocky stared, open-mouthed as Kelvin continued. "My Auntie Agnes is in the local drama society, she said we could have make-up too… but I figure maybe next time…?" He pulled the visor down and looked in the mirror. "I think-" he ran his finger over his lips and bunched them up into a fish pout, "-that I would probably need to practise lipstick first."

Stocky fastened his seatbelt. "Words totally fail me!" he replied drily. "Come on, let's go!"

Kelvin revved the engine of the old Fiat into life. It quickly died. Kelvin saw Stocky's lips purse.

"Chill dude!" he reassured. "It always takes about three tries." True to his word the engine roared to life on the third attempt. "Tunes, we need tunes," announced Kelvin. He pressed play on the CD player and Nickelback began blasting through the old speakers. The bass vibrated painfully into Stocky's skull.

Kelvin crunched the gears and swerved backwards out of the driveway onto the road, then roared away down the street. Stocky clenched his fists, his nails digging into the palm of his hand. Kelvin took the corner at breakneck speed, slamming Stocky hard against the passenger door.

"There's no rush," said Stocky, forcing his voice to sound calm. "Dave never leaves home before 9am." Internally every fibre was fighting the survival instinct to yell "Stop!" so he could escape from the car and run… anywhere.

"Relax dude…" Kelvin paused. He casually gave the finger

to the man who tooted as he ran a red light. "I've done my advanced driving test so if there's a car chase I can go all 'Fast and Furious' on their ass!"

Stocky pulled his seatbelt tighter; he took hold of the door handle with a death grip, his knuckles turning white under the strain.

"There won't be a car chase," Stocky ground out through gritted teeth. "This is surveillance, remember… we're not supposed to be seen."

Kelvin braked hard, crunched the car into second gear and launched them onto the roundabout. Stocky felt sweat forming on his forehead. He hadn't thought it possible but he was beginning to realise that Kelvin was probably an even worse surveillance partner than Reggie. At least her meltdown at the bar had led to information from the bouncer guy. At this rate they would never reach Dave's house alive.

"It's the next street on the left," yelled Stocky, straining to be heard over the music. Kelvin was in the zone. His head bobbing to the beat and foot still flat on the accelerator. They were approaching the turning at ridiculous speed. Stocky jammed his feet into the foot-well. He closed his eyes. Silence. Nickelback had paused momentarily to start their next song.

"We should slow down…" the words tumbled unbidden out of Stocky's mouth… "so, no-one notices us," he added quickly to cover the embarrassment of his outburst. His body slammed back into the seat and then jerked painfully forwards, straining at the seatbelt as Kelvin screeched the car to a halt.

"Good thinking dude… stealth mode!" announced Kelvin. He carefully manoeuvred the car around the corner, moving at a snail's pace. Stocky sent up a silent prayer that no one had been driving behind them. He painfully uncurled his fingers from the handle and surreptitiously wiped his sweaty palms on his jeans. When he was sure his voice wouldn't shake, he switched off the music.

"Dave's house is there on the left," he said, pointing to an impressively grand mock Tudor structure with a large driveway and electric gates. "Go to the end of the street, turn around and we can park over there between those two cars." Stocky gestured to a spot a little way down the street, which would give them an unobstructed view of Dave as he drove out through his gates.

With the car safely parked and hopefully blending in, they both stared thoughtfully at Dave's house.

"That dude has money!" exclaimed Kelvin. "The bar business is where it's at. Maybe I should get into the bar business. Hmmm." He stared off into space. Stocky studied the goofy grin plastered across Kelvin's face. *He's probably picturing fast cars and hot blond models – so predictable.*

"You need money to own a bar and right now you've got none." Stocky's sharp words ripped through Kelvin's daydream. He jolted back to reality with a scowl. Seeing the look, Stocky backtracked slightly. There was no need to ruin his surveillance by antagonising his only help. "But… there's nothing to stop you getting experience," Stocky placated. "Have you considered getting a bar job?" he suggested, relieved to see the scowl replaced as Kelvin gave the idea some thought.

"To be honest," Kelvin said, shaking his head. "This whole coffee making gig is not turning out as I had hoped it would."

"What were you hoping for, I thought this was a temporary thing?" Stocky asked.

"You know, dark haired mysterious barista charms the ladies with his sexy coffee making skills." Kelvin reached into the back seat and placed a pair of sunglasses low on his nose. He struck what Stocky assumed was his sexy barista pose. In reality it looked a lot like the lipstick pout from earlier, with perhaps some Derek Zoolander, Blue Steel thrown in.

Stocky cleared his throat, feeling the urge to laugh build in his chest and asked the obvious question.

"Why would you think that making coffee would get you girls?"

"The movies dude. The hot ladies write their number on the cup and the guy gets a date. Happens all the time."

Stocky finally understood Kelvin's train of thought.

"But..." he said thoughtfully, "isn't it the person making the coffee who writes their number?"

"Whoa there," Kelvin took his glasses off and gesticulated wildly, narrowly missing Stocky's face in the confined space. "Apparently, that is frowned upon!"

"You tried it didn't you?" Stocky smirked. Kelvin grinned in return.

"Sure did man, she was super-hot."

"And did it work?" Stocky asked eagerly.

"Nah," Kelvin sighed wistfully. "I was called into the manager's office. He went on and on, blah blah...human resources...blah, blah...sackable offence blah, blah...sexual harassment."

Stocky grimaced sympathetically "Oh"

"Should've known it wouldn't work... it's the apron," announced Kelvin with resignation. "You can't make sexy coffee to charm the ladies in an apron!"

"Yeah, the apron... that'll be the reason," retorted Stocky, unable to restrain his sarcasm any longer. Remembering he was supposed to be keeping Kelvin on side he quickly continued. "Barmen don't wear aprons."

Stocky watched as Kelvin's face lit up with a new idea. "Barmen do get a lot of girls. Hey I could be one of those mixologist dudes who throw stuff around."

"Totally" said Stocky, seeing signs that Kelvin was about to drift off again, he continued. "Then all the hot women will stand at the end of the bar admiring your amazing skills."

"Dude you are so right," Kelvin agreed. He stared dreamily out of the window failing to notice the wrought iron gates at the end of Dave's driveway begin to smoothly and silently open.

"Quick, start the car," urged Stocky. "He's leaving!" Kelvin jumped, not yet quite ready to let go of his suave sophisticated barman persona.

"Come on!" Stocky shoved his arm. "You can daydream about hot girls later." Kelvin started the car, which true to form died. Stocky forced himself to wait for what seemed like several hours while Kelvin went through his three try start up routine. Stocky watched helplessly as Dave's sleek black Mercedes exited the driveway and began to disappear towards the end of the road.

"Oh thank God," muttered Stocky as the engine finally coughed and spluttered to life. "Remember, stealth mode," he reminded Kelvin.

Kelvin pulled carefully away from the kerb. After making the turn at the end of the road they found themselves two cars behind Dave.

"This is good." Stocky spoke more to reassure himself than for Kelvin's benefit. "Dave is less likely to notice us if we are a couple of cars behind him."

Stocky was all business. He really hated working for his uncle but failing at this would be an even worse outcome. The thought of proving his smarmy uncle wrong hardened his resolve and raised his anxiety levels substantially. Kelvin, in an uncharacteristically perceptive moment sensed the increased tension in Stocky.

"Don't worry dude, you've got this," he reassured, punching Stocky's arm for added emphasis. "You've got the equipment and your secret weapon."

Stocky dragged his eyes away from the Mercedes moving smoothly through traffic ahead and fixed his puzzled gaze on Kelvin.

"What secret weapon?" he asked. Kelvin laughed.

"Me of course, and my disguises." He turned to point at the back seat, shifting the wheel as he did, swerving dangerously close to the car parked on the side of the road.

"If you crash the car, we'll never find out where Dave is going," shouted Stocky.

"Chill dude, I'm a driving pro." With a wink and a smirk Kelvin pushed the stereo button. His head began to gently bob as Nickelback blasted their way through a new song.

An hour and a half later Kelvin's enthusiasm began to wane.

"You should have bought food!" he moaned, his voice distinctly huffy. "I brought the wigs and camera. You didn't even let me get snacks from the petrol station," he continued, his voice taking on a petulant tone.

"Dave might have seen you." Stocky kept his tone neutral but he was fast losing patience.

"That's what the wigs are for!" Kelvin snapped back.

"Surveillance can be tough," said Stocky, "but you're doing really well," he continued, in what he thought might be the tone you would use to placate a bored child. Out of the corner of his eye he noticed Kelvin's demeanour soften slightly. "We've followed him to the drycleaners, the wholesalers and the carwash without our cover being blown and that's more than I've managed before, said Stocky. "How about we give it another hour and then we'll give up and get some snacks?" he asked. Kelvin shrugged, unimpressed. "Okay, okay," Stocky caved. "You can wear a disguise, whatever you want."

"Really!" said Kelvin a smile lighting up his face as he reached enthusiastically for the items on the back seat. "You won't regret this," he gushed. "I've thought it all through. I'm going with the messy black wig and baseball cap. I won't add the shades yet, I can include them later if necessary to mix things up."

"But... you've already got messy black hair!" said Stocky.

"Exactly dude, they will never see it coming. Is it real, is it fake - who knows?"

Kelvin pulled the red baseball cap over his wig with a flourish while Stocky silently placed his fingertips on his temples trying to will away the nagging pain gathering behind his eyes.

They both watched in very different degrees of excitement as Dave's now sparkling Mercedes emerged from the carwash. Kelvin had thoughtfully left the motor running, so they were able to bypass the three try start up routine, smoothly following Dave back into the flow of traffic. They followed Dave's car into the centre of town, around several roundabouts, continuing to head south.

"He's heading to the motorway," said Stocky, anticipation stirring in his stomach.

Kelvin sat up straighter behind the wheel. "This could be something," he said, hopefully. "Alright dirt-bag, let's see who you are shagging!" In his excitement, his foot pushed on the accelerator.

"Careful," warned Stocky. "Don't blow our cover now!" Kelvin resumed his previous cruising speed and remained casually two cars behind Dave as they joined the motorway. Fifteen minutes later Dave led them off the motorway into the pretty market town of Waverly. They followed the winding road towards the town centre. Tidy streets, hanging baskets and other floral arrangements advertised small-town pride. After crossing the small river bridge, Dave turned right and drove into the main street. He slowed and pulled into the small car park of a well-maintained two-story brick building. Luckily today was not market day so there were a few parking spaces on the side of the road. Kelvin parked in one of them and they both stared in dismay as Dave got out of his car and walked towards the building.

"Great," spat out Kelvin. "I've wasted all my petrol to watch the dude visit his lawyer."

Stocky's heart sank as he looked over at the sign on the building. Spratt, Caulder & Associates – Solicitors, seemed to be a very sober and respectable legal business - if the sensible gold writing on both the sign and tinted windows of the door could be believed. The chances of having incriminating pictures to show to the client or his uncle seemed to be fading away before his eyes. The thought of failure and the total humiliation of having his uncle fire him settled heavily on Stocky's chest. He leaned forward, elbows on knees and hands cradling his head.

Resisting the temptation to rock, he muttered under his breath, "I am totally screwed!"

CHAPTER 8

"Stocky... dude, you've got to see this," Kelvin shouted. He shoved hard on Stocky's shoulder, dislodging his elbows from his knees, forcing his head to snap up.

"The camera, get the camera!" yelled Stocky. They both dove into the gap between the seats, each straining to reach the equipment in the back. After a brief tussle Kelvin emerged victorious, wig and cap only slightly out of place.

"Take the pictures," Stocky scowled.

"I'm doing it dude, chillax," reassured Kelvin, pointing the camera and clicking shot after shot.

Across the street Dave had emerged from the solicitor's office but he wasn't alone. A petite blonde goddess followed him across the car park. She wore a navy-blue sheath dress, which hugged her perfect curves - a small belt accentuating her tiny waist. The dress finished at the knee revealing a pair of beautifully toned legs, dressed in what Reggie would call killer heals. Her hair fell softly around her tanned shoulders, one of them supporting the strap of a very expensive looking document bag.

"She's way too hot to be Spratt or Caulder... right?" asked Stocky hopefully.

"Dude, whoever she is I want her to be my lawyer," Kelvin practically drooled, his eyes never leaving the camera lens.

They both stared as Dave opened the passenger door of the spotless Mercedes. He gently caressed her shoulder as he removed the document bag and the goddess slid gracefully into the seat. Dave walked around the car, deposited the bag carefully in the boot and got in.

"Yes, yes," hissed Stocky. "Did you see that? He is totally into her. He was beaming like a love-struck teenager after she got into the car."

"Let's do this," said Kelvin thrusting the camera at Stocky and beginning the start-up routine.

"Be careful," warned Stocky. "There aren't many cars around so stay back."

They watched Dave drive out of the car park, waited a few moments, then pulled out behind a red Toyota Corolla and continued along the road. They drove along the length of the main street, past several charity shops, a busy café and a newsagent. At the end of the street Dave turned into the cobbled driveway of the Wheat Sheaf Country Pub and Hotel.

"We've got them!" cheered Stocky. "I bet they come here all the time. Go slowly into the car park and head towards the other side."

Kelvin moved the car carefully over the bumpy cobbles. The car park was small and private, perfect for an intimate romantic getaway. Guests were shielded from the road by a neatly trimmed hedge and from the prying eyes of any neighbours by ornate brick walls. There was a scattering of cars already parked there and they watched the Mercedes move into a space close to the main entrance. Kelvin chose a space between two other cars. It was further away but with a perfect view of the hotel entrance.

Stocky raised the camera to his eyes. "Come on, come on!" he urged; tension in his body made it almost impossible to hold the camera steady. After what seemed like an eternity, he saw Dave emerge from the car. Stocky began clicking and captured the moment when, after taking the document bag out of the boot, Dave finally opened the passenger door and swept the goddess into an intense kiss. She laughed as she untangled herself and then the two of them walked hand in hand through the entrance.

As the door closed behind them Stocky let out a long slow breath of relief. He sagged shakily back in to his seat, the adrenaline all gone now. Finally, he had some solid evidence to take to the client. He'd even managed to capture part of the hotel sign behind the couple to confirm the location. Uncle Steve couldn't fire him now. He'd bought himself a little more time. Maybe he was good at this after all. He began to scan back through the images and smiled as next to him Kelvin moved on from whooping and yelling to drumming on the steering wheel.

"Dude let's see the evidence," said Kelvin, pausing in his celebrations to reach across and yank the camera out of Stocky's hands. The camera beeped and Stocky watched Kelvin's eyes widen as he began to frantically push buttons.

"Are they amazing pictures or what?" smiled Stocky, the triumph evident in his voice.

"Ummmm, Stocky... dude-" Kelvin's voice cut off as he stared miserably down at the camera.

Finally realising he was the only one of them celebrating, Stocky glanced across at his surveillance partner. Kelvin sat ramrod straight staring blankly at the empty screen of the camera. The wig and hat combo sat crookedly over one ear. His usually pasty face was tinged red and tiny beads of sweat were forming along the top of his lip.

"Where are the pictures?" Stocky's question hung unanswered between them for what seemed like hours. Eventually Kelvin shuddered and emerged from his trancelike state.

"I'm so sorry man," he shrugged apologetically. "My finger hit the button by mistake and-"

Kelvin broke off abruptly as Stocky, who was barely containing his urge to punch the idiotic wig off Kelvin's head, lasered him with a rage filled stare.

Instinctively leaning away from the threat, Kelvin went on the defensive.

"Mate it could have happened to anyone," he wheedled. He was beginning to panic at the uncharacteristic twitching and all over muscle clenching that appeared to have taken over his friend.

Stocky was no longer listening. He found himself immersed in a mist of uncontrollable rage. The urge to hit out and destroy anyone and anything was engulfing him, taking over the rational part of his brain. Swaying backwards and forwards he hissed breath in and out through his clenched teeth. Reaching boiling point, a guttural noise rose up from deep within his chest finally emerging as a roar. As if driven by the momentum of the noise his clenched fist swung, coming down hard on the dashboard in front of him.

"Aaaargh!" Stocky's scream of pain brought the world back into focus and he gently cradled his injured hand to his chest. Breathing more steadily he leaned back in his seat, eyes closed still hugging the injured hand.

"Dude, I thought you were going to Hulk out for a moment. I swear you were turning green." Kelvin gushed. Now that he sensed that the danger had (for the moment) passed, Kelvin had bounced back to his default setting of cheerful.

Stocky was not recovering so quickly. Anger turned to desperation. He leaned forward, chin resting on his clasped hands. Outwardly he was motionless but his mind raced to find some way back from disaster.

Kelvin watched cautiously - from his position of relative safety against the door, for any sign of returning anger. As seconds stretched out to minutes he began to wonder if perhaps he should go and get medical help, or maybe Stocky's mind had snapped and he should drive him to the mental hospital in Stapwell.

Unsure of his next step, Kelvin decided that maybe it would help the decision-making process if he put some distance between himself and the crazy guy. He slid back fully into his seat and reached towards the door handle.

"Stop!"

Kelvin flinched as the unexpected sound exploded through the silence like a gunshot. Stocky was still sitting forward but he was now nodding as if part of a busy internal conversation. Still unsure what to do, Kelvin waited. No move was better than the wrong move he figured. Finally Stocky stopped nodding, sat back in his seat and spoke.

"It's going to be alright. We can still do this…"

Kelvin waited. No move seemed to be the right move so he was sticking with it. Stocky turned, and Kelvin was relieved to see that his eyes were now calm and focused.

"It's a total balls-up, that's obvious… but they've got to leave at some point, right?" Stocky looked hopefully at Kelvin who nodded frantically.

Stocky was quickly rationalising himself into a better mood. "We've still got your camera and it has great zoom so we just sit and wait, right?"

It was crunch time. Kelvin knew he had to say something and the news wouldn't be good. He unconsciously wiped his damp upper lip and clasped his fingers to his neck. Unwilling to reawaken the beast but with no better option he went for brutal honesty.

"Sorry dude, batteries have run out… erm… sorry." Kelvin tentatively reached over and patted Stocky on the arm. He'd seen his mum do this to Great Uncle Fred when his wife died. He'd seemed to find it comforting.

Stocky's heart was pumping. Was it wrong that his future happiness relied heavily on proving another guy was a no-good cheat? He made a mental note to spend some time later analysing the terrible life choices that must have led him to this. He rolled his eyes up to the tattered upholstery of the roof. Kelvin had certainly been a disappointment. He usually enjoyed his friend's quirky and unpredictable personality. But if Stocky had learnt anything from today's debacle it was that Kelvin (although well-meaning) was a liability. Shit, if they were in the army together, Kelvin would probably have accidentally shot Stocky in the head by now.

Kelvin's behaviour had seemed more and more wacky lately. Take right now, for instance. Kelvin was busily patting him like he was a Labrador. Either Kelvin was losing his marbles or this was just another disappointing example of post university life. At university Kelvin was a quirky individual, an eccentric guy dancing through life to the beat of his own drum. Out in the real-world Kelvin was just odd.

"Right!" announced Stocky decisively. He mentally gathered his wandering thoughts and focused on the task at hand. Luckily, Kelvin stopped his patting and turned expectantly. "Your camera is out of action but we still have my phone. The zoom is crap though so we'll need to get closer. Over there between those two cars, that would work. Kelvin followed the direction of Stocky's gaze and saw that at the front of the car park on the other side of the entrance two cars were parked next to each other. "We can sit between those cars and peer around the front of the nearest one to get a great view of the entrance," continued Stocky.

"Yes!" agreed Kelvin, enthusiastically. "We've done the stake-out now it's time for the takedown. They won't know what's hit them!"

"That's kind of the opposite of the point," Stocky explained. "They aren't supposed to see us at all."

"Dude, you are right." Kelvin nodded thoughtfully. "We shouldn't be seen together. You go out first and I'll casually make my way over there when I've adjusted my disguise."

"Suits me!" Stocky's hand was already on the door handle and he quickly exited before Kelvin could say any more. At this stage in the day his ragged patience was barely hanging on by a thread. Any excuse to put distance between the two of them was a great idea.

Stocky walked briskly across the car park. He quickly checked the ground for glass or any other debris that could ruin his newish jeans and sat down between the two cars. The only flaw he could see in his plan would occur if either car owner chose to return to their cars. That would indeed be unlucky he mused, but he was due a lucky break... right?

Where the hell was Kelvin? Carefully he crawled to the

back of the cars and peered over the boot. Stocky gaped as he saw Kelvin in a long curly dark wig, top hat and oversized sunglasses, move across the car park, darting from car to car. It looked like Slash from Guns N' Roses was playing hide and seek and couldn't find a decent place to hide.

Kelvin finally arrived and triumphantly threw himself down onto the ground. "Ta da!" he grinned.

"Take the ridiculous hat off," barked Stocky. "It sticks up above the bonnet."

Kelvin removed the hat with a flourish. "Haters gonna' hate," he shrugged.

"What does that even mean?" Stocky hissed, his eyes firmly on the entrance doors.

"It means..." Kelvin paused for dramatic effect, "that some of us are gifted with flair and creativity and others -like you- who aren't, try to crush our soaring spirits."

Fortunately for Stocky's sanity, the heavy wooden doors of the entrance way began to open. Stocky leaned around the front of the car, one hand on the bumper for balance and the other holding his phone. He clicked disappointing picture after picture, watching as Dave - smiling smugly, strutted out of the hotel alone. He straightened his collar, raised a hand to straighten his dishevelled hair, hopped in his car and was gone.

"Dude, that guy has had good time. Did you see the state of his hair?" The sound of car wheels bumping along the cobbled entrance way cut off Stocky's reply. An expensive looking black Jaguar pulled up outside the entrance. A tall man wearing a long black coat over a business suit and tie emerged from the driver's side. His face was clean-shaven. His broad powerful shoulders, square set jaw and bald head wouldn't have looked out of place in a movie about east-end gangsters. Stocky snapped a couple more pictures. After a brief conversation on his phone the man got back into the car. Moments later the goddess swept gracefully out of the hotel, her hair and clothing both still immaculate. She took the document bag off her shoulder and entered the passenger side door. The car reversed out and drove away.

"Noooooo!" Stocky's cry was almost a whimper. "I've got nothing."

Kelvin shook his head sympathetically.

"Bad luck mate." The gesture was ruined somewhat by the top hat wobbling precariously on top of the curly wig.

"This day has been a disaster from start to finish," Stocky muttered through gritted teeth.

"Yeah but dude," Kelvin slapped him on the back. "At least you had me to help you through it."

"You! You were the cause of it." Stocky's temper boiled unleashing his pent-up rage. "You… drove like a maniac, you… whined, you… brought stupid dress up clothes."
Each 'you' was accompanied by a sharp finger poke to Kelvin's chest. "Oh and saving the best for last, you were the freaking idiot who deleted my photos. You're supposed to be a tech guy for Christ's sake." Stocky threw his hands in the air and moved away from Kelvin to rest his aching head on the roof of the nearest car.

Kelvin stood up tall and pushed back his shoulders. He spoke slowly and calmly.

"The way I see it, you asked for my help. I gave up my day off to drive you around because you'd rather follow dumb strangers around for your uncle than get off your arse and try to find a decent tech job. Who's the real freaking idiot?"
Kelvin spun around, flicked the long curly wig locks over his shoulder and flounced in the direction of his car. Four strides in he paused and turned back to face Stocky. "And for your information dude," he yelled. "I get low blood sugar. I haven't eaten all day. You try operating a camera with low blood sugar. All you had to do was bring snacks. This whole day would have turned out different if you'd just bought snacks. Dumb ass!" Rant over he strode over to his car to begin the start-up routine. When the car eventually roared into life the engine revved, wheels spun and it screeched painfully across the car park and out into the street.

As the smoke cleared Stocky stood dumbfounded, staring

after the disappearing car. Could this day really get any worse? Oh crap, he hoped not. He looked at his watch. It was just after twelve o'clock. It would be hours before Reggie would be free to come and pick him up. With resignation he brushed the dust and dirt off his jeans and walked towards the hotel doors. He had a few coins in his pocket, enough maybe for a couple of Cokes. Ignoring his rumbling stomach Stocky headed for the hotel bar. He took out his phone to begin carefully crafting his text to Reggie.

CHAPTER 9

Reggie could honestly say that this had been the worst week of her entire four-week career. She leaned back in her chair and surveyed the four walls of her small mobile classroom. Everything had the look of an organised and professional learning environment. Reggie allowed herself a tiny smile of pride. In this room she was queen. Beautiful wall displays showcased work completed by her class with both enthusiasm and pride. Shelves and cupboards were tidy, trays were labelled and assessment data was filed away neatly in appropriate folders.

It was frustrating that while everything inside her lovely classroom was under her control, everything else about her job was chaos. Reggie leaned back in her chair keeping her eyes focused on the head teacher's office, all the way across the other side of the playground. One of the best features of her room was its hilltop location, well away from the main school building. Reggie imagined it as her hilltop fortress. It took Ms Darwin a full two minutes of striding to cross the playground and climb the steps to Reggie's classroom. All she needed to arm her fortress was a machine gun nest; she would have plenty of time to aim, fire and even miss a few times before obliterating the starched white shirt and power suit from the face of the earth. Reggie smirked at the image then sat up feeling a little guilty. Perhaps it was just gallows humour she mused. Each day it was looking more and more likely that her career was approaching sudden death.

Looking on the bright side it was now after 3.30pm and she could escape for her much anticipated weekend of bliss. Eat, drink, sleep and repeat – at least until Sunday when she'd need to spend the whole day focused on schoolwork.

Her phone was flashing in her bag. She'd had it on silent all day. No need to give Ms Darwin more reasons to hate her. Seeing there were two messages from Stocky she hesitated before reading. There was a slim possibility that he was suggesting they go out for celebratory weekend drinks. She read the first line.

I need help! It's an emergency!

Sighing loudly as the possibility of drinks vanished, she read on - cursing when she saw how far she would have to drive to pick him up. In the second message he seemed less sure of himself.

Are you there? Can you come?

After sending the shortest possible reply Reggie gathered everything she would need for the weekend and headed towards the staff car park. She noted with a smile that she wasn't first to leave. It wouldn't do for the newest and most notorious member of staff to look like she was slacking off.

Half an hour later she was sitting grumpily on a bar stool next to Stocky in the Wheat Sheaf Hotel bar. Reggie had never been there before but from its plush seats, thick carpets and shiny wooden bar she assumed it must have recently undergone a refurbishment. Stocky was staring morosely into his glass of water - having run out of money a couple of hours ago. Reggie was sipping her glass of Diet-Coke (which she'd had to pay for herself) while she scrolled through the photos Stocky had taken earlier.

"It might be time to give up," Reggie said in what she hoped was a concerned tone.

"I can't Reg, I really need this!" Stocky sounded so forlorn. This time Reggie's concern was genuine.

"But all you've got here are pictures of two random people, three if you include bald mobster guy. There's nothing to connect them."

"What if," said Stocky, "I show her the pictures and tell her what I saw. Once she sees what the bombshell looks like she might pay for me to find more proof."

"It's a possibility," admitted Reggie grudgingly. "But I still don't see why you need me?" The angry edge was back in her tone. She glanced at her reflection in the mirror behind the bar and reached up to massage the pronounced frown line in the centre of her forehead. Damn it she was aging by the day.

"Like I said -" Stocky's tone was a carefully calculated blend of calm and reasonable, "-she already associates me with the surprise party balls up. If she sees I'm part of a professional team, and you back me up about my previous associate's technical error-"

"You mean clumsy Kelvin being a calamity Kate," Reggie interjected, unable to hide her delight. Stocky rolled his eyes and continued.

"So it would really help me if you could be there." The wheedling tone was back. "I can pick you up. It will be totally stress free for you."

"No!" Reggie was staying strong. 'I've got my weekend planned out. Sleeping in, followed by sitting on the couch eating junk food." Stocky saw his window of opportunity and took it.

"Fat chance of that. What about your Mum and her no rent extra chore policy?" Reggie's mum was very clear about the importance of all housemates contributing and doing their bit domestically at home. As Reggie was yet to pay any rent her mum gave her a weekly list of jobs to do around the house. It wasn't a case of here are your jobs, complete these when you have time. Reggie's Mum knew exactly when she expected the jobs to be done and it was usually 'right now!'

Reggie groaned; she had a feeling she would be on toilet cleaning duty, amongst other things.

"Fine!" she muttered. Going on this fools mission with Stocky might –if she was lucky, force her mum to reduce the length of her to-do list. "What time will you pick me up?"

Stocky had the grace to look sheepish.

"Umm, I was hoping you could find out from Stella what time Dave gets to work on Saturdays so we don't bump into him." Stocky's face reddened further under Reggie's arctic gaze. Without a word she fired off a text and returned to noisily moving the ice around her glass and sucking the dregs of Diet-Coke up the straw.

Stocky watched Reggie's scowling reflection in the bar mirror. He didn't have that many close friends and he seemed to be alienating the ones he had left. At this rate he could end up jobless and friendless. Maybe it was time to re-evaluate. After the meeting tomorrow he would leave Reggie out of it. Perhaps he could think of a way to help improve her situation at school. Maybe he could do some background checks and recon' on some of the other teachers and see if he could dig up some dirt. The ping of Reggie's phone stopped his train of thought.

"He'll be at work before lunchtime," announced Reggie.

"Great, I'll pick you up at 11am."

Reggie slid slowly off the barstool. "I don't suppose you have any petrol money to give to me, do you?" Stocky grimaced, placed his arm around her shoulder and started leading her towards the doors.

"Look Reg, I know I've messed up. I'm really sorry. I promise I'll make it up to you when I can... ok?" Hearing the apologetic tone Reggie softened.

"Yeah, I know you will." She finally smiled. "At least I get to sleep in tomorrow morning."

The high-pitched wailing woke Reggie. For a moment she was back in the classroom, fire alarm siren screaming and water gushing down from the sprinklers above. Then her bedroom door opened and her mum entered, dragging the noisy old vacuum cleaner behind her.

"Oh good you're awake," her mum yelled over the noise. Reggie pulled the covers over her head in a futile attempt to block out some of the noise. Taking the hint, her mum switched off the vacuum but remained standing ominously over the bed. Reggie gave up and uncovered her face.

"What time is it?" she muttered trying to keep her tone civil.

"It's 8am darling," her Mum smiled brightly. I've got the vacuum out for you. I like to get it done when Stella isn't home so she isn't disturbed if she is sleeping." Reggie rolled her eyes. "Well she does pay rent and she works really hard at her two jobs," her mum continued.

Reggie remembered that Stella had stayed over at a friend's house last night. She was probably watching TV and eating a cooked breakfast... lucky her. Her mum pulled a folded list out of her pocket.

"These are the jobs I need you to get done this morning please." Reggie wasn't fooled by the please or the pleasant tone. She could tell that her mum was still upset over the state she had been in when Stocky had brought her home the other night.

"I have to go out at 11am to help Stocky with something," she ventured.

"Well that gives you three hours darling, you'd better get busy." Her mum glanced around the room. "You should probably add this to the list too." Tutting she headed for the door.

Reggie toyed with the idea of mentioning that she was an adult, but ruefully acknowledged that she would be setting herself up for another lecture. Instead she cast her eyes over the bedroom, assessing it for cleanliness. It actually wasn't that bad. Last night's clothes were dumped on the floor and the shelves could do with a bit of a dust but apart from that it was okay.

Reggie knew her mum was just being picky to make her point. They both remembered a time when Reggie's bedroom had regularly resembled a warzone. Clothes, both clean and worn would be strewn over the floor among books, magazines and all the other junk teenagers manage to accumulate. The situation had become so bad that Reggie had developed the habit of clearing a path to the door each evening to prevent tripping over if she had to get up in the night. Reggie glanced down at the extensive cleaning list. Wow her mum really was mad.

Three hours later the house had been vacuumed and dusted. The bathroom and toilets sparkled. The dishwasher had been emptied and restacked and there was a strong smell of bleach wafting off the recently mopped kitchen floor. Reggie had even managed to squeeze in a quick shower. She glanced at her reflection in the bathroom mirror and added a final sweep of lipstick. Not bad. The blue fitted t-shirt she wore with her jeans, accentuated the bright blue of her eyes. At the sound of the doorbell she ran downstairs to let Stocky in. She sat down on the hallway floor to fasten her Converse shoes.

"The house looks clean," Stocky smiled.

"Modern day slave labour, that's what it is," retorted Reggie. She finished fastening her last shoe and jumped up. "Quick let's go before Mum comes back and finds me something else to do." She grabbed her bag and headed out of the front door.

As the car headed down the road, Reggie felt safe enough to relax. She laid her head back against the headrest and took a moment to enjoy the warmth of the sun heating her arm through the window.

"So what's the plan?" she asked. Stocky glanced across at her then returned his eyes to the traffic ahead.

"I've spent a lot of time thinking about this," he said. "Hopefully once Caroline sees the picture of the woman, we will have her full attention. Then I can explain that I actually saw them kissing in the hotel car park. You can back me up if needed about Kelvin deleting the pictures." Reggie nodded. It sounded like it might work. "I'm really hoping that actually seeing the woman Dave is cheating with will spur her on to want more evidence." Stocky's hands tightened on the wheel.

"What if she's not home?" Reggie asked the obvious question.

"Then we wait and hope she comes home before Dave does." Reggie groaned. "I've got snacks," said Stocky quickly, pointing to a bag on the back seat. Reggie reached back and pulled the backpack onto her knee. Stocky had obviously raided his mother's pantry. There were packets of crisps, chocolate biscuits, apples and two bottles of water. Stocky sensed Reggie relax again and thanked his lucky stars that he had learnt from the disastrous stakeout with Kelvin. No more whinging sidekicks and low blood sugar mistakes.

The journey through busy Saturday morning traffic took forty minutes, during which time Reggie happily demolished half of the pack of biscuits and an apple. Stocky remembered his death-defying journey with Kelvin along the same route yesterday. He'd have liked to see Reggie trying to stuff that many biscuits in her mouth then. It would be like trying to eat on a rollercoaster.

There were a lot more parked cars as they turned into Dave's road this time. Not needing to worry about where he parked today, Stocky pulled into the first available space on the same side of the road as Dave's house.

"That's it over there," he pointed.

Reggie took in the large modern home with spacious driveway and manicured lawn. It was impressive. I'm not greedy, she thought wistfully. I don't need anything huge like that, just a tiny place of my own where I make the rules. Unaware of her daydreaming Stocky focused on the task ahead.

"We just need to confirm with Stella that Dave is at work and we can go in," he said. Reggie reluctantly moved her thoughts away from her tiny dream home and sent a text to Stella. In the time it took for the reply to arrive she ate a couple more biscuits.

"He's there," she mumbled through a mouthful of crumbs.

Stocky jumped out of the car and headed down the street. Reggie reluctantly trailed behind, brushing biscuit crumbs off her top and jeans. Stocky paused outside Dave's driveway and waited for Reggie to catch up. The electric gate was open, a good start. Stocky had been worried that they would have to talk through the intercom and it was likely that once she knew it was him, Caroline might cut him off. At least now he could see her face to face at the front door.

They wandered up the wide cobbled driveway and paused outside the oversized front door. Stocky froze, overwhelmed by the intricately decorated stained glass window panels which sat within the giant doorframe. Reggie nudged him.

"It's just a door," she reassured. "And it's pretty ugly too."

Calmed by Reggie's words Stocky leaned forwards and pushed the doorbell. He held the photos out in front of him as if they could offer some kind of protection and they both waited.

Reggie heard the sound of heels tapping on a tiled floor and then the door swung majestically open. Facing them with a quizzical expression on her face was a stylish blond woman in her late twenties, wearing an expensive looking trouser suit. Her hair was beautifully styled in a trendy bob and her makeup was perfection. Wow thought Reggie, if someone like this can be cheated on then the rest of us don't stand a chance.

CHAPTER 10

Stocky was rooted to the spot. Reggie nudged him sharply in the ribs with her elbow. The painful stab catapulted him back to the here and now.

"I know you probably don't want to talk to me," he gushed, "but I have evidence you are going to want to see." The words tumbled out of Stocky's mouth and he waved the photos in front of his face. Caroline looked thoughtful for a moment.

"Actually, this is perfect timing. Why don't you and your associate come in and we can talk?" She gestured them inside and then led the way down the tiled hallway into a spacious and luxurious kitchen. "Have a seat." She pointed towards a huge rectangular table, which dominated the centre of the room. Not that it was a tight squeeze Reggie noted. She was amazed that anyone could need so many sleek cupboards and marble kitchen benches. A kitchen island bench sat gracefully to one side of the table, holding a beautiful flower arrangement. The sun streamed in through the open French doors, illuminating the crystal vase and creating dancing, shimmering diamond lights on the shiny bench surface.

The three of them sat comfortably around one corner of the table. Stocky had used the walking time to gain control over his emotions. He had his game face on. He knew this was his final shot.

"Thank you for seeing us Caroline," he spoke calmly, all trace of previous nerves gone. "This is my colleague Reggie Quinn, who is helping me with my investigations."

"Pleased to meet you," Caroline held out her hand. Reggie shook it with a smile. Stocky pushed the photos across the table towards his client.

"Now before you say anything," he cautioned, "I know they aren't together in these pictures but I did see them kissing and-" Caroline cut him off.

"Things have moved on since we last spoke Mr Stockwell." She reached across and took the picture of the bombshell and studied it in silence. Stocky and Reggie exchanged anxious looks. It felt rude to interrupt but she had been staring silently at the picture for a while. It was a huge relief when she finally spoke. "So... that's the bitch who's sleeping with my useless husband."

Stocky felt he should regain control of the meeting.

"Can I ask how things have moved on? Last time we spoke you weren't even sure if your husband was having an affair!"

Caroline smiled bitterly.

"I have my own evidence now," she said.

Stocky nodded encouragement but internally alarm bells were ringing. People who could find their own evidence didn't need the services of investigators.

"What happened?" he prompted. Caroline took a deep breath and brushed a strand of hair behind her ear. She sat forward and clasped her hands together on the table in front of her.

"The problem I had," she began, "was that Dave is very careful and devious. He rarely leaves his phone lying around and he always deletes all his messages."

"That would make anyone suspicious," Reggie added, unable to remain silent any longer.

"Exactly," agreed Caroline... Anyway, yesterday I was supposed to be out meeting a client all afternoon - I'm an interior designer," she explained.

Reggie took another quick glance around the splendour of the kitchen and wondered how amazing the other rooms in the house must look.

"Halfway through the consultation my client was called

away to an emergency so I came home early. Dave was here in the shower. He must have come home to change before the evening rush at the pub. I saw that he had left his phone on the bed and it was flashing with a new text message."

"Did you read it, what did it say?" Reggie was leaning across the table with excitement. Caroline blushed.

"I did think about not reading it and respecting his privacy but in my gut, I've known something was happening for a while. The text was from a woman called Sabrina Warrington." She picked up the photo. "I assume this is her." Caroline placed the picture face-down on the table.

"The text said, **You were amazing today. Can't wait to have you in my bed again**. *Saturday usual place.* Caroline paused and let out a shaky breath. "I mean it's one thing to suspect but when you know…"

"Did you confront him?" Stocky asked quietly.

"No I couldn't, I was so angry but I just needed to get away. I took her number from the phone and then deleted the message. I left the house and went for a drive. He doesn't know I saw it… I mean he suspects that I know what he's up to, because he knows I hired you." Stocky flushed slightly at the memory of his first failed surveillance attempts on Dave.

"He's been making more of an effort lately," Caroline snorted. "Only because he knows he's onto a good thing and doesn't want to mess it up. A loving wife at home," she grimaced – "and a sexy mistress… what more could any red-blooded man want?"

"In what ways has he been making an effort?" asked Reggie.

"You know," she gestured towards Stocky. "Helping my sister with my surprise party." Reggie smirked as Stocky shuffled uncomfortably in his seat. "He keeps leaving little gifts outside the front door, like we are teenage valentines again," she sneered. "Yesterday flowers, the day before it was chocolates. He thinks he can buy his way out of a messy divorce with pathetic gifts."

She stood up and began to pace the length of the kitchen.

At the far bench she turned to face them and despite outwardly appearing calm her eyes overflowed with pain.

"I just want to make him pay," she sobbed – struggling to regain her composure. She took a few breaths and walked back to her seat at the table.

"How can we help?" asked Stocky.

"I need more evidence... I want to divorce him and hit him where it hurts, in his pocket."

"We can get that for you," said Stocky, feeling confident now they were back on familiar ground.

"It may not be as easy as you think," Caroline sighed. "I was so angry and I just wanted to tell her how I felt. So last night when Dave was at work, I rang her... It was stupid, I know. Now they will be even more careful." Reggie was impressed.

"What happened, what did she say?"

"She didn't answer, it went straight to voicemail. I was so angry that I left her a message... a bit of a rant really, empty threats." Caroline cringed at the memory before finally smiling sheepishly. "I felt a lot better afterwards though, it was quite cathartic."

"Can you remember exactly what you said?" asked Stocky.

"Yes, I said – I know what you've been up to. I know everything and I'm going to make you pay, bitch. You need to look over your shoulder 'coz I'm coming for you!"

"You certainly told her," laughed Reggie.

"I think I've watched too many gangster movies," smiled Caroline sheepishly.

"So what you want from us," said Stocky, trying to bring the conversation back to business matters, -"is to get more evidence of them together for you to take to a divorce lawyer."

"Exactly," said Caroline. "I spoke to my cousin Jake – who works with Dave at the pub, and he seems to think you are reliable people."

Reggie's stomach lurched at the mention of Jake. The memory of his smouldering eyes looking deeply into hers, sent her temperature skyrocketing and tingles rushing up her spine.

"I've got £50 in my purse," continued Caroline, "Will that do as a retainer and you can bill me the rest?" Stocky was overjoyed.

"Yes, thank you, thank you. We won't let you down." He took Caroline's hand and pumped it vigorously. Caroline smiled at his enthusiasm. Gently detaching her hand, she opened a drawer and pulled out a corkscrew.

"We should celebrate… wine anyone?" She collected a bottle of red wine off the pristine marble bench and placed it in front of her on the table. After politely declining a drink Reggie noticed the decorative bow on the neck of the bottle.

"Is that a gift for a special occasion?"

"No," Caroline laughed bitterly. "It's another one of Dave's guilt gifts. He left it on the steps this morning." She finished twisting the corkscrew and began carefully easing the cork out of the bottle. "Although how he can think that bringing a bottle of wine home from work is a grand romantic gesture, I have no idea."

"We should probably get going and start gathering your evidence," said Stocky, rising from the table.

In the hallway Caroline stopped and reached into a small and expensive looking bag. She handed £50 to Stocky with a smile.

"Consider yourself officially rehired Mr Stockwell."

Stocky waited until they were two houses down the road before he began his fist pump celebration.

"Yes, we totally rocked that. It could not have gone better."

As the car moved off into traffic Reggie had to admit that she felt relieved. Part of her had been expecting them to be on the receiving end of an enraged rant. Caroline had surprised her, both in her response and her demeanour. She was a poised and elegant woman. Dave was more of a rough diamond, one of the lads. She had pictured him with a different type of woman entirely. Then again, Reggie mused, opposites definitely attract. She allowed her thoughts to drift momentarily back to Jake. One thing was for sure; there were some good-looking genes in that family.

"We should celebrate," announced Stocky. Reggie smiled, unable to resist his infectious enthusiasm.

"Great idea, champagne and caviar for everyone," she laughed.

"Or... McDonalds," said Stocky.

"Even better."

The lunchtime rush was in full swing at McDonalds. Reggie clutched their drinks and manoeuvred through the queuing throng, while Stocky manfully followed behind with his overflowing tray of food. Reggie squeezed past a harassed mother who was squashed around a table with four boisterous children. She collapsed with relief onto a stool at a tiny table for two in the far corner. While she waited for Stocky to negotiate the crowds she used her napkin to carefully flick onto the floor the lettuce, sauce and chip remnants left by the table's previous occupants. Finally Stocky flopped down on the stool opposite, dumping the tray of goodies on the table between them.

"Did we really need this much food?" asked Reggie. She watched in amazement as Stocky stuffed fries in his mouth with one hand whilst deftly unwrapping a cheeseburger with the other.

"I need to think," he mumbled, his mouth now full of burger... "and eating helps." Reggie took a sip of her Diet-Coke, enjoying the familiar fizz of the bubbles over her tongue.

"I've been thinking too," she said. "If you are going to be doing more surveillance on Dave, you are going to need help. Dave knows who you are but he hasn't noticed Kelvin yet. It might be time to apologise."

Stocky grimaced. Taking a break from shovelling food, he thoughtfully sipped his drink.

"It's going to take a big gesture," he said. "Kelvin knows how skint I am so if I give him what's left of Caroline's £50 for petrol money he might come around."

They ate in comfortable silence for a few moments, Reggie

enjoying the free food and Stocky considering his options.

"The main problem is the car," said Stocky. "There's no way I'm letting Kelvin drive, he nearly killed me last time." Reggie smirked at the traumatised look on his face. "But Dave knows my car."

"I don't mind swapping with you." She said.

"Really!" Stocky beamed.

Reggie sat up tall, willing the food to move lower in her stomach so she could cram in a little more. "Your car is way nicer than mine so it's win, win for me," she explained.

"That could totally work." Stocky was re-energised and ready to plan out his next move. "I'll take you home then go and see Kelvin. Once he's on board we can find out from Stella if Dave is working tomorrow and plan from there…"

He paused remembering guiltily that Reggie was dealing with her own work problems, and helping him had only made things worse for her.

"Um Reg, I'm really sorry for dragging you into all this. I know you've got your own stuff to deal with so I'm going to leave you out of this from now on."

"Thanks," she said, relief evident in her face. "I'm really looking forward to us both getting paid. Then we can forget about all our work problems and go out and get some drinks like we used to."

"Count me in," said Stocky, stuffing yet another cheeseburger into his mouth.

CHAPTER 11

Sunday morning was heavenly. Reggie woke late, having enjoyed an undisturbed and much-needed sleep-in. 10am found her sipping coffee on the couch, still wearing her pyjamas and a comfy fleecy robe. The TV was blaring out one of her favourite reality shows. Reggie felt smug and superior as she watched the fame-hungry participants make one disastrous life choice after another.

Ha, she thought. I may do some stupid things but at least I don't do them in front of a TV audience. She allowed herself one more self-satisfied smile as she watched the weeping blotchy faced girl on screen ask her TV show bestie,

"How did he find out I slept with his brother?"

"Don't worry Bex," her heavily made up friend comforted. "I slept with him too."

The delicious smell drifting in from the kitchen set Reggie's stomach rumbling. Stella had generously (so she told Reggie) offered to make them both bacon sandwiches. Reggie knew it was probably Stella's hangover, rather than sisterly kindness, which had prompted this generous act. She smiled; never look a gift-horse in the mouth.

As usual Stella had finished her Saturday night shift at the pub, then headed out dancing and drinking until the early hours. Reggie pushed aside the twinge of jealousy. She chose instead to focus on the fact that in a very short time regular pay cheques would begin to arrive. Then she could join Stella on her weekly party pilgrimage. The only blip on the horizon was the large pile of schoolwork waiting for her attention. One more hour she thought, cuddling deeper into the couch cushions, maybe two.

"Here you go," said Stella handing Reggie a plate.

She took a bite, the butter on the fresh white bread melting with the heat of the crispy bacon. She savoured the taste – perfection.

"Thanks Stel," she mumbled.

They sat together on the couch eating in comfortable silence. Reggie glanced around at the familiar decor of the cosy lounge. From the textured white paper on the walls to the brick surrounds of the imitation fireplace, this was where she felt most relaxed. How many Sunday mornings had they spent like this over the years, watching Sunday cartoons together in their PJs? Their choice of TV show might have changed, but sitting in her favourite spot on the oversized couch, legs tucked up under her, it was easy to forget that the world and all of its problems were still out there waiting.

At the sound of a text message she reluctantly reached for her phone. Reggie frowned as she read, not sure what to make of it. She turned to Stella, who was busily mopping bacon grease off her chin with a paper towel.

"Stel!"

"Hmmmm," Stella answered, attention focused on the trail of grease and melted butter that was now making its way down her pyjama top.

"Stocky says he just drove past Dave's house. He says there are police everywhere and the house is cordoned off with tape." Stella met Reggie's puzzled gaze.

"That's odd." She said

"I know," Reggie continued to frown. "We were there yesterday. Caroline rehired Stocky to find more dirt on Dave."

Stella's eyes began to twinkle mischievously. "You didn't rob her on the way out, did you?" She smirked. I've heard they're loaded."

Reggie resisted the temptation to lob a conveniently

placed cushion at her sister's head and recalled the luxury of the rooms she'd seen yesterday.

"Their house is pretty amazing, she agreed. I bet there would be heaps of stuff worth stealing." She took another bite of her sandwich before remembering the rest of Stocky's text. "Stocky's heading over here now," she mumbled, quickly swallowing the delicious mouthful, "and he wants you to find out if anything dodgy is going on."

Stella tutted and reluctantly dragged herself off the couch.

"Anyone would think I work for bloody Stocky," she muttered heading off to the kitchen in search of her phone."
A short while later Reggie heard Stella's footsteps heading back into the lounge.

"So what's the goss?" she began, breaking off suddenly as she saw the pallor of Stella's face. "Shit Stel, what's wrong? Are you ok?"

Stella sank heavily into the chair nearest the door still grasping her phone.

"It's Dave… he's been arrested,"

"Arrested?" Reggie repeated. "Arrested for what?" She remembered her conversation with Jake and his concern about the mysterious packages Dave had been receiving. "Has he been doing illegal business dealings?" she asked.

"No!" Stella shook her head slowly. "He killed his wife."

"What?" Reggie shouted in disbelief. "Dead… Caroline's dead?"

Stella nodded slowly, still frozen in place in the chair. They sat for a moment in silence, the brash voices of the TV unable to penetrate their thoughts. Reggie recovered first.

"How did it happen?" she asked.

Stella regained enough control to stand and move back to her comfy seat on the other side of the couch. When she spoke she sounded less shaky.

"I don't know," she placed her plate on the floor, appetite gone. "I spoke to Jane and she doesn't know much. Dave apparently rang her and asked her to take over while he's at the police station. They're short staffed; they're going to have to put one of the barmen out front as a bouncer. She wants me to go in and help with the lunchtime rush." Reggie was confused.

"Why do they need a barman to be bouncer?" she asked.

"Think about it!" Stella demanded, incredulous at Reggie's stupidity. "Jake's cousin was just killed by his boss. There's no way he'll be fronting up to work for him today."

Reggie let the enormity of the situation sink in.

"Shit!" was all she could manage. Then another thought occurred to her. "Yesterday, when we saw Caroline, she said that she had found out who Dave was having an affair with." Stella's eyes widened with surprise. "She also said," Reggie continued, "that she'd left a threatening message on the woman's phone. Do you think maybe they fought over that and that's why he killed her?" Stella checked the time on her phone and stood up.

"It's possible," she replied. "Look, I need to go and have a shower. I'll see if I can find out more when I get to work and I'll let you know."

Left alone, Reggie sank back - deflated, into the couch cushions. She didn't know what to think. Maybe when Stocky arrived he'd be able to put all of this into perspective. Thinking of Stocky, she grabbed her empty cup and plate off the coffee table and headed into the kitchen. The bright yellow of the kitchen lights cast a comforting glow over Reggie as she busied herself filling the kettle. Stocky would want a cup of tea and she could certainly do with another cup of coffee.

Reggie was thoughtfully sipping her coffee when Stocky rang the doorbell.

"Well, what do we know?" he asked, impatiently dropping his denim jacket on the floor in the hallway and heading for the kitchen table. Reggie poured him a freshly brewed cup of tea while recounting everything Stella had found out. Reggie returned to her seat and watched as Stocky thoughtfully stirred sugar into his drink.

"Of course I'm totally buggered," he eventually announced.

"Shut up!" Reggie bit back, unable to keep anger from her tone. "This is way bigger than you. Someone is dead... someone we talked to yesterday." Stocky had the grace to look ashamed.

"Sorry Reg. It's just so unexpected. It's hard to accept that one minute she's fine and talking about divorce and then the next she's dead." His eyes met Reggie's worried gaze.

"I've been thinking," she said. "What if it was our fault? What if something we said set this whole thing off. What if we're to blame?"

Stocky slowly raised his cup and took a sip of his tea. He cast his mind over their conversation with Caroline the previous day.

"No, I don't think so," he said. "Maybe if we had told her who Dave was having an affair with... maybe then, but she already knew. Let's face it," he grimaced, placing his cup on the table, "even the pictures were useless. Nobody is going to fly into a murderous rage over pictures of individuals in a car park.

"So we're off the hook then?" she asked, hopefully.

"We were never on it," said Stocky. "Although, I would like to know what drove Dave to it?" he wondered. "I mean divorce is one thing but murder... that's next level stuff."

Reggie's phone began to ring. She glanced at the display and seeing Stella's name grabbed it.

"It's Stel, maybe she knows something more."

"Put on the TV," yelled Stella down the line. "Channel 1, it's on the news. Dave's on the news."

Reggie flinched as her eardrum pulsed with pain. Stocky was already on his feet having heard the shouted message from across the table. He switched on the small TV on the kitchen counter and turned it so they could see it from where they sat.

On screen was an image of Caroline and Dave's house, no longer the peaceful image of relaxed wealth but a hive of police activity. Yellow incident tape was strung across the gap left by the open gate. Several police cars and a police truck were parked along the road. Officers in uniform and people in the white overalls you'd expect to see on a *CSI* show were milling around busily in the driveway.

Reggie stared, open-mouthed unable to process the image. Stocky was back on his feet. He rushed at the TV.

"I can't find the remote. Where's the bloody volume button?" he hissed. His finger stabbed madly around the edges of the TV set and it rocked dangerously.

"On top," Reggie managed to blurt.

Stocky frantically pressed the button until the sound boomed out around them, rattling the glass in the serving hatch to the dining room. They both listened intently.

"... *The cause of death has not yet been confirmed. A person of interest is currently cooperating with police inquiries. Witnesses saw a man and woman fleeing the scene at approximately midday yesterday and urge anyone with any information about the identity or whereabouts of these persons to contact the police information line.*"

A phone number flashed up on screen for a moment, then the image moved on to a story about teenagers stealing coins from a Laundromat. Stocky moved to switch off the TV and stood leaning against the kitchen bench. The absence of sound was a welcome relief as they both struggled to gather their scrambled thoughts.

"Do you think he had help?" Stocky eventually asked. At Reggie's blank expression he continued. "You know... the people fleeing the scene. He could have hired them to do the deed while he sat somewhere with an alibi."

"No, it can't have happened then," Reggie said, puzzled. "We were at the house until midday and we didn't see anyone... Oh my God... it's us!"

Stocky turned and gripped the bench for support as he realised what she meant.

"B.b.but," he stammered. "We didn't flee... I may have hopped a bit but I was happy, I'd just been rehired." He moved back to the table and sat heavily opposite Reggie. She noticed his hands shaking slightly. He moved them self-consciously off the table and gripped them together in his lap, as if he could will the shaking to stop. Reggie was feeling more pragmatic about their situation.

"People see what they think they should see," she suggested. Once people know murder is involved their view changes. Instead of two people walking, or in your case prancing down the street-" she grinned at Stocky's instant scowl and was relieved to notice his hands had stopped shaking; "-suddenly people see criminals fleeing the scene of the crime."

"That's great in theory but right now we are prime suspects in a murder," scoffed Stocky. "I've seen all those true crime documentaries. They put the wrong people in prison all the time." He slammed his now steady hands on the table for dramatic emphasis.

"I don't think we are on death row yet," Reggie reassured him. "We just need to go and talk to the police and clear it up. We are witnesses, not suspects. Maybe we saw something that will help."

Stocky was unconvinced. Alarm bells were sounding in the back of his mind and he couldn't ignore them.

"If only we knew someone in the police, then we could talk to them and they'd be on our side."

"Your uncle," she suggested, raising an eyebrow.

"Yeah, right!" Stocky scoffed. "He'd lock me up the first chance he got. It would be problem solved for him. He'd get me out of his business and be able to blame my mum for raising a rotten apple - a blight on society."

Reggie inclined her head. Although it sounded dramatic, Stocky was probably not far off the mark. Uncle Sleazy Steve had never struck her as someone who was big on family loyalty, or in fact in possession of any admirable qualities. She had a sudden idea.

"What about Teresa from school?"

"Teresa Fairweather?" Stocky asked. "Has she finished training?"

"She qualified a year ago and the best news is that she's posted here at the local station. I saw her last Christmas. She says working here is more like running a lost and found than being a police officer but she figures she'll get a more exciting position eventually." The wrinkles on Stocky's forehead relaxed slightly.

"I like her, I could totally talk to her."

"Great!" Reggie jumped up. "Let's go now before you change your mind, or worse, Mum and Dad get back and start asking questions."

CHAPTER 12

Stocky parked in the small car park attached to the aging parish church. The church services had finished for the day but a few cars remained. The one nearest to them proudly displayed a bumper sticker proclaiming-

"Try Jesus. If you don't like him Satan will always take you back!"

Reggie could see a small group of people through the church hall window. They were gathered around a hot water urn, sipping cups of tea and probably putting the world to rights. The ancient clock in the church tower chimed midday. After stepping through the rusty gate they wound their way through the overgrown churchyard. Reggie drew her cardigan around her, as a breeze seemed to emerge from nowhere. Why were graveyards always so cold she wondered?

They trudged on in silence picking their way carefully over the uneven ground between gravestones. They wandered past a statue of a praying angel and a marble carving of Jesus on the cross. Both were worn and leaning slightly to the side. After years of struggle they were finally admitting defeat to the elements and the uneven ground. Reggie liked them. They were giant billboards advertising how families of the past had felt for their precious lost loved ones. It was a far cry from the modern, regimented rows of identical stones, sitting soullessly in the current town cemetery.

They found the path and wound their way to the matching exit at the other end of the graveyard. Relieved, they stepped through the creaking gate and out of the shadow of the towering church building. The chill instantly dissipated and they felt the warmth of early autumn sun on their faces. Reggie looked back through the higgledy-piggledy collection of gravestones and statues. The few golden leaves, freshly deposited under the trees were the only clue that winter would soon be on its way.

On the other side of the road sat the police station, a no-nonsense practical building built to last. It was a triumph of symmetrical Georgian architecture and looked like the house every child draws but never actually lives in. Four stone-surrounded sash windows were arranged around a central stone doorframe. The door itself was painted a practical police blue and a large stone sat over the doorway with the word police boldly carved into it.

"It looks empty, said Stocky. Maybe they don't use it anymore."

"No," said Reggie confidently. "Dad told me they wanted to close it and move into the council offices but there was a big town meeting and a petition to keep it open."

They crossed the road and Reggie took a closer look at the fabric of the building. The wooden window frames were split and looked like their many layers of paint were all that held them together. The bricks were cracked and crumbling in places and in some areas, the cement between them was missing.

"I can see why they wanted to move though," she added. "It must be very damp and draughty." She reached out to open the oversized door.

"Wait!" Stocky urged, grabbing her wrist. "We need a plan." Reggie lowered her arm.

"It's simple, she soothed. We go and ask for Teresa and if she's not there we find out when she's working next and we'll go home to make a new plan."

"OK." Stocky agreed. He took a deep breath and followed Reggie through the heavy door, shuddering slightly when it swung back with force. It closed firmly behind him with an ominous click.

The interior was even more dilapidated. Clearly some effort had been made to fight the ravages of time, but a new coat of paint couldn't hide the damp spots on the wall. The polished wooden floor was creaky and uneven and the musty damp smell was a clear indication that all was not well. In medical terms - this building was terminal.

A petite but athletically built girl in a pristine police uniform stood behind a counter on the other side of the room. Her blond hair was neatly tied up in a bun. She looked up as they entered, her face registering surprise and then pleasure as she recognised them.

"Wow, long time no see," she beamed. "Should have known you two would still be hanging out together. What brings you here then?" A thought occurred to her and she frowned. "Not a lost dog, please tell me it's not that... or dentures... no of course not dentures." Teresa pounded her fist onto her forehead and shook her head, her smile returning somewhat ruefully.

"Are you ok?" Reggie asked. "You seem a little stressed."

"Sorry, it's just my new assignment it's driving me insane," Teresa replied.

"We can see that," Stocky smirked. "Job not what you thought it would be?"

"No, no, I knew I would have to pay my dues. Eventually I'll get posted to a bigger town and will be able to work towards being a detective. The problem is that my sergeant was sick of dealing with what he calls the 'Grey Brigade'. He said the grumbling grannies were doing his head in, so he's making me deal with them. He even gave me a fancy title to make it official. I am the Community Constable Liaison Officer in charge of elderly relations!" She sighed, placed her elbow on the desk and rested her head on her hand. "He even gave out my email address. I never knew the older generation were so tech savvy. I get emails day and night. If that weren't enough I have to run a clinic three days a week at the retirement complex. By the time I get there at

9am there's already a queue of Zimmer frames and wheelchairs stretching right down the corridor. I'm lucky to get out of there by lunch time". Her face brightened slightly... "Although they do serve an amazing sticky toffee pudding and custard." She rolled her eyes. "At this rate I'll need a bigger uniform."

Reggie took in her trim sporty figure and shook her head.

"No," she smiled a little enviously, "you look great. Are you still playing hockey?"

"Hell yeah," Teresa laughed. "Hitting that ball around is the only thing keeping me sane. Since I became the Grey Brigade Cop my game has really improved... although a couple of the team have mentioned that I'm a bit scarier out there on the pitch than I used to be." She shrugged. "Got to get the aggression out somehow."

Seeing the expression on her face Stocky took a half step backwards.

"You're kind of scaring me right now," he mumbled.

"Sorry!" Teresa visibly relaxed and the smile returned. "I think it was seeing your familiar faces that set me off... Now how can I help you guys?"

Reggie glanced at Stocky who was nervously playing with his fingers and refusing to make eye contact. He wasn't going to be any help.

"OK," she said, pausing to figure out the best way to start. "We have a bit of a problem and were hoping you could help."

"Of course," said Teresa, intrigued. "As long as your problem isn't over the age of seventy, I'm happy to help."

Relieved, Reggie launched into a full explanation of the previous day's events, finishing with the news report asking for the identity of the fleeing couple."

"So you're the fleeing couple?" Teresa asked. Seeing Reggie's nod, she fist-pumped the air "Yes... yes, finally something interesting to do." Her joy became excitement as a thought occurred to her. "You're not here to confess, are you?" she asked hopefully... "because that would make my career." She took in Reggie's raised eyebrows and Stocky's deathly pallor and dampened down her enthusiasm. "No of course you aren't here to confess." She ignored Stocky's involuntary twitch at the word confess and opted for a soothing (and hopefully professional) smile. "So here's what we need to do. You'll each need to be interviewed by a detective from the main branch at Stapwell. You can either go there or we can get someone to come over here." Stocky looked pained.

"Can't you do it? He pleaded.

"I wish," Teresa grimaced. "My rank is way too low... but if you get the interviews done here I could sit in with you," she added hopefully.

"Here sounds good," agreed Reggie. Stocky nodded his silent agreement.

"Great," said Teresa, barely containing her excitement. "I'll go out back and run this by my Sergeant while you two make yourselves comfy over there." She gestured to a row of three utilitarian plastic grey chairs balancing precariously on the dangerously uneven floor by the wall. "When I come back," she continued, "I'll bring you both a cuppa. You look like you need one." She looked at the still silent Stocky. "I'll put extra sugar in yours." Confident in her handling of the situation, Teresa breezed through the door behind the desk to share the exciting news with her beleaguered sergeant.

Reggie trod carefully over to the row of chairs and lowered herself gingerly into the nearest one. She found that if she leant backwards with just enough pressure, the chair would balance fairly safely on three of its four legs. After watching her progress with interest, Stocky followed suit. Unable to remain still he began rocking the chair, using the two stable legs as a pivot to rock backwards and forwards between the other two. The continuous tap, tap tapping was like a hammer in Reggie's brain.

"For God's sake stop, and snap out of it," she hissed. "You've been less than useless since we came in here." She eyed him accusingly and he blushed. He steadied the chair on three legs by leaning forward slightly and resting his palms on his knees.

"Sorry Reg," he mumbled. It's just that this whole situation freaks me out," he admitted. Reggie softened slightly.

"Me too," she said, "But panic and drama won't help us-" Before she could continue Teresa reappeared carrying two steaming mugs of tea. She held one out to Stocky.

"Get this down you and you'll feel much better," she reassured him."

Reggie took hers with a 'thanks' and began to politely sip the foul brown liquid. She wondered for the millionth time why the tea-loving gene that seemed to be a prerequisite for being British had apparently deserted her at birth.

"So here's where we're at," said Teresa. "Sarge spoke to the Stapwell branch and they are sending two detectives over. They should be here in the next half an hour. Apparently," she confided in a hushed tone, "they are pretty excited to have new suspects-" she broke off seeing Stocky's twitch return "-I mean witnesses," she corrected… "to interview. They are having a hard time with the husband." She leaned in further. "He's lawyered up and they are getting nowhere."

Lawyers were the enemy, she screwed up her nose, tutting in disgust. They were always getting in the way of locking up the bad guys.

"I'll grab you a couple of magazines to read while you wait."

Teresa bustled away, returning momentarily with a copy of *Knitter's Monthly* and *Narrowboat Companion*. She shrugged at their lack of enthusiasm.

"It's what the Grey brigade like. We used to have them on a coffee table next to a couch over there." She gestured to the empty area by the opposite wall. "But Sarge said it encouraged the old dears to settle in and get comfy, so they had to go."

Stocky downed his sugary tea, then thumbed distractedly through the much-read pages of *Narrowboat Companion*. He left his elbows leaning on his knees to maintain the chair's balance. Reggie gingerly placed her full cup on the floor and flicked through Knitters Monthly, hoping to find a puzzle page. She had a feeling they might be waiting a while for the detectives to materialise. She paused for a moment on a knitting pattern for a toilet roll cover, smirked and continued her search.

Loud yapping from outside announced a new arrival. Almost a minute later the huge door heaved open and a small elderly lady thrust herself through the gap. She was wearing her Sunday best. Once inside, she paused to rearrange the paisley silk scarf, which had fallen off the shoulder of her tweed suit jacket during her tussle with the door. She smoothed down her matching tweed skirt, satisfied that she had regained her respectability. She effortlessly untangled the yapping Yorkshire terrier's lead from around her legs, while managing not to dislodge the black patent handbag situated firmly in the crook of her elbow. Looking down she checked her matching patent shoes for imperfections. Seeing none she raised her hand to check that the rigid curls of her steel-grey perm were still in place.

The terrier had mercifully ceased it's yapping but was now glancing between Stocky and Reggie, a menacing growl emanating from the back of its throat. Stocky nervously lifted his magazine to block the dog's view.

"Phew!" the lady exclaimed, finally noticing their presence. "That door gets me every time. Anyone would think they were trying to keep people out. "Charlie..." she looked down at the snarling dog. "Where are your manners? Say hello to these two lovely young people."

Charlie let out a final snarl, then with a 'humph', threw his body to the floor and began to lick his testicles. The lady smiled proudly at Reggie - Stocky was still hiding behind his magazine.

At that moment Teresa breezed out from the back office having heard the silent door alarm. Seeing the lady and dog she froze, fighting the urge to run back to the safety of the office.

"Ahh there you are," the lady beamed maternally at Teresa. "Young Constable Teresa you are just the person I wanted to see." She strode across the wooden floor towards the desk, heels clacking. The dog lead pulled tight, dragging Charlie across the floor behind her until he managed to untangle himself and scramble to his feet.

"Mrs Babbage, how lovely to see you," Teresa lied. She plastered what she hoped was a professional expression on her face and gripped the counter for support.

"Now Constable Teresa dear, I wanted to let you know that I have organised the sign-up sheet for your police clinic tomorrow."

"But…" confused, Teresa began to reply, "we don't have a sign-up sheet-"

"We do now!" Mrs Babbage cut in, clearly pleased with her innovation. "Much more efficient this way. Obviously, I have put myself down first for a double slot." Teresa nodded weakly knowing it would be impossible to stop Mrs Babbage once she had her course set. "I don't want to reveal too much and ruin the surprise," she confided, but I think I have a lead on the case of the missing dentures."

Reggie and Stocky both stared, amazed at how effectively Mrs Babbage had steamrollered Teresa. As if sensing their stares the lady turned and beamed, offering them a glance at her perfect set of white teeth.

"Not that I need worry about dentures," she shared proudly. "The dentist says I am a modern marvel of dental hygiene. But…" she said thoughtfully, "One must help out those less fortunate. It is my Christian duty."

She smiled again, confident that her generous nature was evident to all. She turned back to Teresa who, caught in the act of sagging onto the desk straightened quickly, feigning interest.

"Now before I forget," Mrs Babbage switched topics at lightning speed, seeming not to need air, "I have pencilled your Nana in for the slot after me. She hasn't caught up with you this week so it will be nice for you both to have a lovely chat and a cup of tea after our serious business is concluded. That way," she added conspiratorially, "you'll be able to cope better with the whinging old codgers who come to see you afterwards." Teresa sagged, defeated. Mrs Babbage began to turn away but whipped back around. "One more thing," she remembered, opening the clasp on her bag and feeling inside. She thrust a packet of glucose tablets into Teresa's limp hand, closing her fingers over the packet. "Your Nana sent these for you. She wants you to keep your energy up tomorrow because you'll have a busy day. She says she wants you to do your best because you're representing the family."

She smiled, patted Teresa's hand and re-fastened her bag. "Right then, I'll be off. Lovely to meet you young folks," she nodded at Reggie and Stocky. She marched across the room - Charlie trailing behind, paused momentarily to fight with the door, tutted, and then was gone. Finally, silence.

All that remained was her flowery perfume. Teresa stood motionless still grasping the packet of glucose tablets.

"Wow does she ever take a breath?" asked Stocky admiringly. "She really did a number on you."

Teresa raised both eyebrows, finally placing the packet onto the desk.

"It's the same every time," she admitted weakly. "I can't even get a word in. She used to be the Headmistress of St Andrews's Girls School."

"Of course!" exclaimed Reggie as realisation struck. "That's why they were always the top scoring school in the area. She's a battle-axe. No one would want to mess with her."

"If only it were that simple," Teresa mumbled. "The retirement complex is full of ballsy women just like her, with a lifetime of skills, experience and grudges and nothing but time on their hands. Prison gangs have nothing on these women." She shuddered. "Tomorrow, when they find out about the sign-up sheet it will be all out war... and who will be stuck in the middle of it all? Me!"

Teresa swallowed. She reached out with a shaky hand for the glucose tablets and headed unsteadily towards the door to the back office. Teresa grasped the door handle for support. She took a breath, pulled the door open and walked through.

"Hey, where are you going?" shouted Reggie. Teresa kept

walking; her shaky voice echoing bitterly through the closing door.

"I'm going to lie down. Sarge'll make me a cuppa. He owes me."

CHAPTER 13

Reggie closed the magazine. She leaned her head back against the wall and allowed her thoughts to wander through the previous day's events. It was still hard to believe that Caroline – the vibrant and beautiful woman from yesterday was now dead. It was looking increasingly likely that Reggie had been one of the last people to see her alive. She just hoped that the police wouldn't think that she was the first person to see her dead!

How exactly had Dave killed her? Reggie pictured Caroline's beautiful home and wondered if it now resembled the gory crime scenes so graphically displayed on TV police dramas. She shivered and forced her thoughts in a different direction. Jake! How could she have forgotten his connection to both Caroline and Dave? Reggie wondered how he was coping. How on earth were you supposed to feel when your employer murdered your cousin? Her wandering thoughts led her back to the last time she had seen Jake and her promise to find out what Dave was up to. This had not been what either of them had in mind.

The memory of his slow sexy smile brought a flush to her cheeks. She moved uncomfortably in her chair, prompting a questioning look from Stocky. She shrugged dismissively, settling her head back against the wall. Frowning she focussed her gaze on a damp patch on the ceiling. Timing was everything, she thought, trying to banish Jake's image from her mind. Definitely wrong time and place she decided firmly. But... a small voice whispered in a secluded corner of her mind… but what if he was the right guy?

The heavy door began to open, its now familiar groan echoing through the room. With relief, Reggie brought her thoughts back to the present. Stocky leaned across.

"Don't worry about me," he whispered. "I've been thinking, and I can do this. I won't let you down."

Reggie couldn't speak. Nerves seemed to be turning her stomach to mush. Please don't vomit she thought, taking steady breaths in and out. Belatedly Reggie realised that she had never actually dealt with the police before. She was pretty sure that sitting in a police car and sounding the siren at a school fair did not qualify. Reggie had always had, in her opinion, a healthy fear of the unknown. It stopped her going on the biggest, scariest rides at theme parks, stopped her going white-water rafting and it was kicking in big time right now. Glancing across at Stocky she saw that he finally looked calm and composed. His gaze was resting on the opening door, waiting for his first glimpse of the new arrivals. Damn it! She thought. Maybe I was only being strong because Stocky needed me to be. Trust him to choose this moment to finally man up!

Two figures eventually emerged from behind the reluctant door. The younger man in front grimaced with the effort of holding the door open for the older, taller gentleman to walk though. They both wore suits, although the older man's dark blue suit was of a far superior cut to that of his young companion.

"Thank you Thomas," the older gentleman smiled at the younger, politely extending the smile to include both Reggie and Stocky as he ambled past them to the desk. Reggie relaxed slightly. It was hard to fear the unknown when it looked like an affable businessman and you were his next meeting. Reggie was surprised to see a much older man in uniform waiting behind the desk. That must be Teresa's long suffering Sergeant, she mused. He was a lot older than she had pictured. His grey balding hair was cut short and a pair of round glasses sat on a red bulbous nose - mirroring the redness of his cheeks. He had the face of a drinker and a potbelly to match, Reggie noticed. Her eyes were drawn to where the sergeant's shirt buttons battled to contain the flesh beneath.

After a short exchange with the sergeant the tall man nodded and turned back towards Reggie and Stocky, his arm outstretched.

"Good morning," he spoke warmly, shaking both their hands. "I'm Detective Inspector Andrews, and this…" he gestured towards his smiling companion … "is Detective Sergeant North. Reggie judged Detective Sergeant North to be only a few years older than she was. His grey suit looked every inch as pristine and well cared for as Teresa's uniform. As Reggie shook the Inspector's hand the last of her nerves evaporated. "I want to thank you both for taking the time to come forward and give a statement," he continued. His relaxed smile was both soothing and encouraging. "Unfortunately this facility only has one interview room, so we'll leave one of you to wait here and take the other through and get started."

"I'll go first," Reggie spoke quickly, while her nerve still held.

Teresa had reappeared behind the counter having seemingly made a miraculous recovery. She held open the bench-top as they all walked through, and gave an encouraging thumbs up, and a grin to Reggie as she passed by. The interview room offered no surprises. It looked to be in the same condition as the rest of the building. It was a small dingy room with a tiny window of frosted glass set high up in one wall. A wooden table dominated the room, surrounded by more of the same plastic chairs used in the waiting room. As she sank carefully into the offered chair Reggie noted with relief that all four of her chair legs rested sturdily on the floor.

The detectives took seats opposite and Detective Sergeant North held his police notebook and pencil and placed a recording device on the table. As there were no more seats, or room to add them, Teresa positioned herself in the corner behind the

Detective Inspector, still grinning.

"Right then," smiled Detective Inspector Andrews. "Let's get started. Reggie in your own words can you please talk me through your last contact with Caroline Thomas."

Half an hour later after much questioning and repeated explanations, Reggie was free. Another forty minutes saw Reggie and Stocky wandering around the corner towards the nearest pub. This one had been the town Post Office in a previous life. It boasted cheap food and drink and no music, so was the perfect place for them to debrief and compare notes. They made their way through the busy Sunday lunch crowd. Reggie navigated towards a small corner table while Stocky joined the queue at the bar.

Reggie sat comfortably. She allowed the babble of conversations to wash over her like lapping waves - releasing a tidal wave of relief. It was finally over she realised. There was nothing more she could do for Caroline, and Stocky would no longer need her help. It was for the best, she thought. She desperately needed money but not at the expense of her actual job. She'd just have to suck it up and be really poor for the next couple of months. Maybe next term when she'd put the science club debacle behind her and wowed her boss with her school trip she could get a weekend bar job to bring in some extra cash.

"Ta da," announced Stocky proudly. He deposited a Diet-Coke on the table in front of Reggie and whipped a packet of crisps out of his jacket pocket with magician like flair. "I used my last money to get these, I figure we've earned them."

"Thanks," Reggie smiled, stirring the drink with her straw and enjoying the clink of the ice cubes against the glass.

"So what did you think?" Stocky asked eagerly. He opened the packet and took a handful of crisps.

"About what?" Reggie queried.

"All their questions," he replied. "They're not even sure Dave did it!"

"How do you figure that?"

"They were fixated on her state of mind. Over and over

again they asked... was she depressed? Did she seem upset? Was she irrational?... mentally unstable? Did they ask you about that?" he demanded.

"Well yes but-"

"Exactly," he cut her off, eyes bright with excitement as he warmed to his theory. "Then there's the wine. They were really interested when I told them she was opening a bottle of wine. They kept going back to it. Reg it's totally obvious." He paused for dramatic effect... "She offed herself!" She drank the bottle of wine with a load of pills. End of story." Satisfied with his analysis Stocky sat back in his chair and began to shovel crisps into his mouth. Reggie reached across and lifted a crisp thoughtfully from the bag.

"Except..." she mused, "she didn't seem depressed or irrational or unstable. She seemed pissed off and revengeful." She took a moment to eat the crisp and take a sip of her drink. "In fact" she continued, "she wanted to take action, that's why she rehired you. Those aren't the actions of a defeated woman. She was gearing up for a battle. Anyway," she shrugged, "they'll find out one way or another when they do the autopsy."

"And so will we." Stocky grinned triumphantly. "I gave Teresa my number when we left. She's going to text me when she has more info."

"What will that accomplish?" asked Reggie. "Between the two of us we have more than enough to worry about. Finding out how Caroline died will not bring her back as a client. In fact," she paused, puzzled. "Why aren't you more upset about this? Shouldn't you be banging your head on the table right now bemoaning your fate and your future at McDonalds?" Stocky smiled sheepishly.

"That was the old me," he announced. "The new me has decided to learn from my experiences this week. You just never know what's around the corner. Uncle Steve will definitely fire me at some point, could be tomorrow could be next week. No point worrying about it. Something will come up." Reggie raised her glass.

"To the new, improved Stocky." Stocky clinked their glasses together and took a sip of lemonade.

"One thing is certain," he said sombrely. This time last week Caroline had no idea that she was living her last few days. No job, however crappy could be as bad as that."

Silently they finished their drinks. Each taking comfort from the lively every day sounds of the busy pub surrounding them. He's right, thought Reggie. Her mind turned to the mountain of schoolwork waiting for her at home. If Stocky could be positive about the future, then so could she. A new week, a new start and a renewed focus on lifting her fledgling career out of the dust.

CHAPTER 14

Taking no chances, Reggie was the first to arrive in the Staffroom for the Monday morning meeting. She carefully selected a corner chair, far away from the head teacher's seat of power. Arriving this early had taken a great amount of effort and mental fortitude. She had set her alarm for some ungodly predawn hour to ensure she didn't encroach on either of her parents' bathroom slots. With Ninja stealth she had tiptoed through the darkness putting together an outfit, which she hoped, declared serious, sensible teacher. She looked down at her neat black trousers and sensible black ballet flat shoes. Her crisply ironed white shirt was somewhat of a risk but as long as she didn't eat or drink anything, the chance of spillage was low. Reggie's hair was securely fixed in a knot at the nape of her neck so as to deter even the slightest hint of frizz.

Her hands gripped the notebook and pen in her lap so tightly that her fingers began to ache. I'm like a drowning woman clinging to the wreckage of my ship she thought. Ignoring the obvious metaphorical link with her sinking career she forced herself to release her grip and breathe slowly. She nodded and smiled to the other arriving staff members. It was probably a coincidence, she thought, that the seats furthest away from her filled up first.

At 8.15am precisely, Ms Darwin stepped ceremonially into the room. She paused until a hush descended over the gathering, then processed regally over to her waiting seat. She descended gracefully onto the upholstery, and with hands clasped in her lap and back ramrod straight she surveyed the room.

"How wonderful that we are all here so punctually this morning," she praised. Eyes lowered, Reggie felt the moment when the sweeping gaze focussed on her and was pleased that it quickly moved on. "As you are all aware," Ms Darwin continued, "there will be a school disco this Wednesday evening." She paused for a moment to allow the inevitable mumbling and groaning. "In light of last week's science incident…" Reggie felt the room glance in her direction and fought to control the redness creeping up her neck… "we will be changing the theme of the disco to 'Local Heroes'. Children can dress up as fire fighters, police officers and nurses, etcetera. Half the money we raise will go to the local fire station - as a thank you for all their help, and the other half will help the P.T.A replace important resources damaged by the sprinkler system."

Heads nodded and murmurs of agreement rose from around the room. "The only problem we now have is that we have a great deal to organise in a very short time frame." As Ms Darwin continued, Reggie felt her heart begin to sink. "What I think we need is a volunteer to take charge of organisation and make sure that the event is a success."

Silence followed the announcement. Reggie, her eyes glued to the notebook in her lap listened desperately, hoping to hear the voice of a volunteer. The silence extended. Hearing nothing Reggie chanced a glance upwards. Her eyes met twenty stares fixed meaningfully in her direction. Seeing the patiently expectant look on Ms Darwin's face, Reggie admitted defeat. Hesitantly she raised her hand and in a voice that was more of a question than statement she mumbled,

"I can do it?"

"Of course you can," Ms Darwin beamed. "Come to my office when the meeting ends and we can discuss your duties."

With that, the room collectively relaxed and the meeting trundled on along its usual course of housekeeping matters. Reggie tried to focus on the PE shed cleaning rota and the hall timetable but her mind kept coming back to the inescapable fact that she now had a ton of extra work to do this week. To top it all off Reggie's confidence had taken a severe hit in the last couple of weeks. She was having difficulty picturing any outcome other than complete and utter failure for the disco and then inevitably her career.

It was in that morose frame of mind that she knocked tentatively on Ms Darwin's door.

"I'm so pleased that you volunteered for this task Miss Quinn." The smiling Headmistress gestured to the empty seat across from the desk. She then launched into a detailed and lengthy explanation of her expectations. Reggie was swept along, nodding and smiling as required. The information washed over her, drowning her thoughts and threatening to force her under. Thankfully Ms Darwin finally offered a lifeline. She pushed a document across the desk towards Reggie, who grabbed it, fighting the urge to sigh with relief.

"This contains all the information you will need. I have also included the phone number of the PTA chairwoman in case you have any questions about the shopping list. Don't forget that the fire station is sending a couple of officers to do a quick fire safety game so you'll need to buy another couple of prizes."

Reggie nodded numbly, the pressure of the information overload becoming a very real throbbing pain at the base of her neck.

"Veronica Barkwich has kindly agreed to cancel her badminton club, so you will be able to decorate the hall after school on Wednesday afternoon... oh and I will rustle up a couple of keen colleagues to help you decorate."

Reggie drifted in the direction of her classroom, her feet moving on autopilot, brain temporarily numb. The morning routines of her classroom and the cheerful enthusiasm of her class relaxed her brain somewhat and helped her feel more in control. Once the children were all busily playing spelling games she took a moment to sit at her desk and study the document from the head teacher. The document really was a lifesaver. Ms Darwin had included detailed bullet points, outlining exactly what needed to be done. She had even made a shopping list including suitable prize ideas. Wow, thought Reggie, she is one crazy micro manager. Or… maybe she really wants me to succeed?

Perhaps there was hope for her career yet. Cheered by these thoughts Reggie re-read the to-do list with a little more confidence. Supervising the decorating committee would be fine, as they were all school councillors and really lovely children.

The only downside was that she'd have no breaks at lunch or playtime, but she could cope with that for a couple of days. Time to be organised, she thought. I'll do the shopping after work today. Then if anything else is needed I can easily pick it up tomorrow. Satisfied that everything was under control and with a new sense of purpose, she stood, placed the paper on the desk and felt ready to move forward with her day.

"Fantastic job, everyone," she praised. "Now I need you to collect your reading books and move into your reading groups."

Armed with the school credit card Reggie spent an enjoyable afternoon shopping for drinks, snacks, glow sticks and prizes. Her mood was buoyant as she made the drive home. She loved shopping, and spending other people's money was an added bonus. She hummed along with the radio as she drove and for the first time in a while felt hopeful about her immediate future. The to-do list was carefully folded in her bag and the back seat of the car was filled with the fireman's helmet templates she needed to cut out for the decorating committee. She was still smiling as she pulled up outside her house. "You've got this," she reassured herself under her breath.

As Reggie manhandled the card and templates out of the back seat she noticed the expensive looking car parked on the other side of the driveway. Her eyes lit up. Could this be Stella's lawyer friend? Had mum worked her match making magic and worn down Stella's resistance? Her eyes twinkled at the thought of the family dinner ahead. Revenge is sweet.

Reggie struggled down the driveway with the oversized

cardboard and pushed in through the front door. She carefully placed the precious cargo on the floor before turning expectantly towards the voices coming from the kitchen. She froze. Blood drained from her face as she realised the identity of the man sitting comfortably at the kitchen table enjoying a coffee with her mother. Dave! He was wearing a designer shirt and jeans and his hair was perfectly styled as usual. Only the dark circles under his eyes and stubble on his usually clean-shaven face gave a hint that all was not well. Panic churned her fragmented thoughts. Did he think she knew something?... was he here to kill her? ... her mum?... why was he sitting casually drinking coffee? Unwilling to move closer she called out the next thought that entered her mind.

"Mum, why are you having coffee with a murderer?"

The conversation stopped and two faces turned towards her. Dave, she noticed was attempting a nervous smile. Better nervous than murderous, thought Reggie. Her mother's face was more difficult to understand. The look was one she had seen many times lately – disappointment tinged with resignation. Before she had time to begin to figure it out her mum beckoned her into the kitchen.

"Oh good you are finally home," she stated in the clipped tones that warned Reggie of trouble ahead. "Young David here - who is Stella's boss by the way and speaks very highly of her," she glanced meaningfully at Reggie, who groaned inwardly... "has just been explaining his terrible situation to me."

Reggie opened her mouth to respond but thought twice about it as her mum continued.

"I made you a cup of coffee but you will probably need to heat it in the microwave."

Reluctant to enter but pleased to have something to do Reggie moved past the kitchen table taking the lukewarm cup of coffee with her. Her mum's next words cut across the sound of the whirring microwave.

"David thinks that you might be able to help him because you already have an investigation into him underway." Her mum paused for a moment and Reggie deliberately kept her eyes focused on the microwave door. "I have assured David that this cannot possibly be the case as you are not a private investigator but in fact a newly qualified teacher, who is pouring all of her available time and energy into successfully starting her career."

Her mother's words burned with anger. Reggie turned slowly from the microwave clutching the steaming coffee cup for support. How was it possible that a probable murderer was sitting in their kitchen and yet she was the one on trial? She had no idea how to respond.

Luckily at this point Dave chose to enter the discussion and saved her from further incriminating herself.

"I'm really sorry," he smiled apologetically, his famous charm wafting soothingly over them. "This is clearly not the best time for you." He glanced at Reggie as she rolled her eyes. "But," he continued urgently… "I'm in really big trouble and I need your help."

"Right," Reggie's mum rose decisively. I'll leave you two to talk." She locked eyes with Reggie. "And if it turns out that you actually can help, then you should. I don't need that on my conscience." She swung open the door and walked through. Her parting shot echoing back down the hallway. "I hope you have a job left at the end of all this."

Reggie cringed and leant back against the kitchen bench, reluctant to sit at the table with Dave.

"I always need bar staff," he offered with a lopsided grin. Reggie ignored him, cutting instead straight to the heart of the problem at hand.

"Look, my mum's right," she admitted reluctantly. "I'm a teacher not a private investigator. I don't know why you would think that I could help you. And to be honest… I think you might be guilty?"

Dave pushed his empty coffee cup away from him and turned to face Reggie.

"Jake spoke to me. He was concerned that your investigation of me would unearth evidence of illegal activities.

I have no idea what he thought I was into but he seemed to have faith in your abilities." He shrugged. "At the time I just laughed. I had nothing to hide." Seeing Reggie's sceptical expression, he continued, "not in business anyway. I may not have been the most faithful husband in the world but my business is all legal and on the up and up."

"So you've spoken to Jake, recently?" Reggie questioned. Dave's face fell. The sadness etched in his features making him look younger, like a vulnerable child.

"No," he spoke quietly, the jovial mask gone. "He won't take my calls. No one will take my calls since Caro…" He stopped for a moment staring past Reggie, lost in thought. His eyes finally found Reggie's and he straightened his shoulders, sitting taller in his chair. "Please," he pleaded. "Just hear me out, then if you still think I'm guilty I'll go and leave you alone." Reggie took a moment to think.

"Ok, here's what we can do," she replied. Stocky is the actual investigator and I'm not doing anything without him. We'll get him over here and you can talk to both of us. I'm not promising anything but we will at least listen to you."
Dave nodded his relief.

"That's all I can ask."

Reggie fired off a text to Stocky and was relieved when he quickly replied.

An hour later Stocky made his way along the carpeted hallway to the open dining room door. He paused in the doorway trying to make sense of the scene before him. Both Reggie and Dave were sat in amicable silence at the circular dining table. A protective pink tablecloth covered the dark wood and was littered with large pieces of card. Reggie seemed to be drawing what looked like large fireman's helmets while Dave was busily cutting one out. A pile of finished examples sat next to Dave's elbow.

"So this is cosy!" remarked Stocky. Reggie paused over her template and looked up.

"Hi, I didn't hear you arrive; Dave's helping me with

school stuff."

"Yeah I see that. Definitely not what I was expecting to walk into! While I remember... your Mum says that your Dad is bringing pizza home and there will be enough for Dave. She would also like a pot of tea for her nerves."

Stocky grinned at Reggie's eye roll. Reggie sat back admiring the pile of finished helmets.

"I guess I must be almost forgiven," she said. "Mum getting Dad to bring pizza has to be a good sign... right?"

Stocky shrugged and reached across to shake Dave's outstretched hand.

"Thanks for coming mate," said Dave. "I could really use your help. I'm in a tight spot."

Stocky heard the desperation in Dave's tone. He sat in a spare seat at the table and studied Dave's face.

"I totally agree 100 percent that you're in a tight spot," he replied. "But I'm not sure how you think we can help."

"Before we get into this," Reggie stood, "I have to make the tea for Mum. Why don't you two finish cutting these helmets out for me and we can talk in a minute."

She bustled out of the room leaving an awkward silence in her wake. Dave smiled, offering the spare pair of scissors to Stocky.

"It's actually quite relaxing," he said. Saying nothing, Stocky took the scissors and began cutting.

Reggie returned from tea making and stood in the doorway enjoying the site of the two men industriously cutting out her disco decorations.

"I've been thinking," mused Stocky, "that if your theme is fire fighters you should have flames and water on the walls in the school hall."

"Great idea," added Dave. "Paint the flames on black paper in fluorescent glow in the dark paint – we use that sometimes for special events at the pub."

"Nice one," Stocky agreed. "Then if the water droplets are made of foil they will reflect the disco lights." The pair exchanged high fives in celebration.

"Ok, calm down geniuses, don't give up your day jobs," said Reggie. The idea was actually quite good but she wasn't about to admit that. She sat back at the table with the others. "So what is it that you think we can do that the police can't?" she asked. Dave leaned forward, all traces of humour gone.

"The police are only looking at two options. Option one is that she killed herself."

"I knew it," said Stocky. "Didn't I tell you that's what they were thinking?" he looked across at Reggie.

"So, you have been discussing what happened" said Dave.

"We were the last people to see her alive, of course we have," Reggie replied.

"There's no way she would kill herself. She'd get mad at me sometimes, when I let her down." Reggie could hear the regret in his voice. "In fact, she'd been angry all week and I was trying to bring her around."

"Look, for what it's worth, I agree with you," Reggie stated. "Angry people don't kill themselves. When we saw Caroline, she rehired us to find more dirt on you so she could divorce you."

"We would have made up, we always did," Dave grimaced. "But that leads me to option two. The police are waiting for the autopsy results. If it rules out suicide then they are looking at me for poisoning. They think that poison was in something she ate or drank."

"Well the last thing she drank was the wine you gave her," Said Reggie. "She took the bow off and opened it while we were there. She even told us about you leaving presents on the doorstep."

"Flowers and chocolates, sure, replied Dave, looking confused. "But how dumb would I have to be to leave her a bottle of wine from work? It's a really cheap move. It would just piss her off."

"You're right," Stocky confirmed. "It made her really mad."

"If you think about it," Dave continued, "I would have to be the worst murderer in the world to give her poisoned wine that was clearly from me then lock myself in my office at work for the afternoon with nobody to confirm my alibi."

"Is that where you were?" Reggie asked.

"Yep. I had extra bar staff on so I thought I'd use the time to catch up on all my paper work. Of course, the police say that I could have left out of the side door at any point and dropped off the wine. As soon as the toxicology results come back they will get warrants to search the pub, my house and my mum's house, where I'm staying right now."

"The problem with what you're telling us is that it doesn't prove you are innocent," Reggie pointed out. "It just proves that if you are the murderer then you were really badly planned and are basically not very good at it."

"Ok, what could possibly be my motive?" said Dave impatiently.

"Off the top of my head, money," suggested Stocky. "Caroline wanted to divorce you. She told us she wanted to hit you where it hurts."

"No, she was just pissed off," said Dave. "We signed a prenup when we married because we both have our own successful businesses. The only asset we'd have to sell and split would be the house and she'd be more upset about that than me. She loved that place. She designed and redecorated every room. It's one of the reasons I can't go back."

He glanced at Reggie and could see she was still undecided.

"Look, I admit it." He raised his hands in defeat. "I was a shit husband. I see a pretty blond girl and I can't help myself. I'm a player from way back. But in my defence, I've always been that way. Caro knew that. We've been together since school. She was my best friend. It's a poor defence but she always knew the man she was marrying. Sometimes it really pissed her off but then I'd make it up to her, we'd go away for a few days or a week and be better than ever. I need you to find out who did this to her… who did this to me!"

Dave's emotions overwhelmed him. Oblivious to their presence he groaned, head falling forwards. He cradled his aching head in his hands on the table.

"She's gone," he sobbed. The police will take everything else... there'll be nothing left." The crying subsided "What's the point," he mumbled quietly under his breath.

CHAPTER 15

Reggie and Stocky exchanged troubled glances across the table. Silently Stocky mouthed, "What now?" Reggie shrugged, at a loss. She wasn't the best judge of character but it did feel like Dave was telling the truth. It seemed like this had emotionally hit him really hard. Reggie doubted Dave was the kind of guy who voluntarily shared his emotions with others. He seemed more likely to hide behind a mask of jokes and good humour.

Salvation came in the form of pizza. Reggie glanced through the serving hatch and realised with relief, that her dad had arrived home while they had been listening to Dave's explanation. A pizza box and three plates sat like a gift from the gods on the kitchen bench. She opened the glass hatch and deposited the pizza box and plates in the middle of the table. She placed a couple of slices on a plate in front of Dave.

"Eat this," she urged. "You'll feel better."

Reggie took a slice and pushed the box towards Stocky. The cheesy deliciousness revived her flagging spirits.

"What we need to think about," she mumbled, her mouth still half full, "is option three! If Caroline didn't do it and you didn't do it, then who did and why?"

"Before we can even get into that we need a reality check," said Stocky. He leaned forwards on the table, his pizza sitting untouched in front of him. "Reg and I are in a difficult situation. She's having a bad time at work and was only helping me because she's up to her ears in debt and needs the cash… and she's a good friend," he conceded. "Working for Caroline was pretty much my last chance to bring some money in and stop my uncle firing me. I'm happy to help you but it will need to be in an official capacity. You should probably count Reg out though; she's got enough on her plate right now." Reggie rolled her eyes but said nothing. Stocky was right.

Dave sat up, wiped his eyes and sniffed. He took a bite of his pizza and chewed thoughtfully. His eyes brightened a little. This was business; they were back in his comfort zone. He smiled as he replied.

"So, to sum up the situation, you?" he pointed at Stocky, "need job security by bringing in money to your firm, and you," he pointed at Reggie, "need to spend time at your school but are desperate for money."

"Nailed it!" replied Reggie dryly. Dave sat back, relaxing for the first time.

"Then, problem solved," he smiled. "Stocky, I will pay your company for the work you already did for Caroline. I'll sign with you and pay you a daily fee while you are investigating for me, plus, a bonus if you manage to get to the bottom of this and keep me out of prison." Stocky beamed, almost speechless.

"M..mate..thanks," he managed to splutter.

Dave looked at Reggie, all humour gone. "I really need your help on this Reggie," he pleaded. I know you have your school thing and I get that, but evenings and at the weekend you could help." Seeing Reggie open her mouth to decline, Dave quickly continued. "I know you need money and I hate to do this to you but this is my life we are talking about here. I'll pay you cash for every hour you spend helping and I'll pay you the same bonus as Stocky if we succeed." Reggie groaned, placing her head in her hands.

"Your Mum did say you should help me," Dave wheedled.

"Fine," Reggie raised her head. She wasn't sure if she was angrier with Dave for putting her in this position or herself for caving. "But I can't help till after Wednesday. I've got the disco to organise," she added firmly."

"Great, we're back in business," smiled Stocky with

renewed energy and enthusiasm. "Let's consider option three!"

"Before we do that," said Reggie. "I think we should try to find out if the police are considering any other leads or suspects."

"That's easy enough," Stocky replied. "I have to take all my surveillance pictures of Dave to the police station." He cast an apologetic grimace in Dave's direction. "While I'm there I can pump Teresa for information."

"Ok," Reggie agreed. "Then our other obvious lead has to be the wine bottle. If Dave didn't leave it then where did it come from?" She looked at Dave. "Was it one of yours?"

"The police showed me a picture of the bottle. It's red wine - Merlot with a magenta bow. I bought a few cases like that. It was a celebration gift offer, hence the bows."

"I could find out if anyone else in the area bought the same brand," Stocky offered.

"Good idea," Reggie replied. She turned to Dave. "What happened to the rest of the bottles, do you still have them?"

"Only a couple, I bought them as gifts. I gave a lot out to friends and people I do business with. We also had them at Caroline's surprise party. I told people to take any leftovers they wanted at the end of the night."

"So our suspect pool is everyone at the party, plus pretty much anyone you know or do business with. That's huge!" exclaimed Reggie. Refusing to be daunted, Stocky stepped in.

"We just need to trace all those bottles. It's totally doable. Dave and I have to meet in the morning to sign our agreement and then we can start making lists and making phone calls."

Reggie glanced up at the clock on the wall, realising with a jolt that it was after 10pm.

"Where's Stella?" she wondered. "She never came home for dinner."

Dave cleared his throat. "That's actually my fault. She was here when I arrived. I convinced her to go and cover for me at the pub tonight so that I could wait here for you."

"She's going to make me pay for that," Reggie grimaced.

"No, you're safe. I'm going to be the one she makes pay," he smiled ruefully.

"What did you promise her?" Reggie asked curiously.

"First I had to promise never to accidentally pat her on the butt again." Reggie snorted. "What?" He continued defensively. "Your sister's a hot blond. It's my kryptonite, what am I supposed to do?"

"Resist!... Man, you've got a problem," she muttered." Intrigued, Stocky joined in.

"Is that all?"

"No." Dave took a deep breath. "I had to promise her free drinks all night on two Saturdays of her choice."

Dave smiled amiably as Reggie and Stocky both collapsed with gales of laughter. Wiping his eyes Stocky gasped.

"You know she drinks like a fish, right?"

"Yeah. If the police don't finish me off Stella will probably drink me out of business."

"You're right," agreed Reggie, feeling much better about the Stella situation. "She'll definitely make you pay."

Cheerfully they munched on the remaining slices of pizza, refining their plans for the next few days. Stocky would deliver the surveillance pictures to Teresa first thing in the morning and see what he could find out from her about the investigation. Then he would drive to the pub to meet with Dave. Hopefully by then Dave would have created a list of most of the people who could have the wine bottles. Stocky could then start ringing people.

"Please be careful," Dave urged. "Enough people hate me already. I don't need my family and friends to think I'm accusing them of murder."

"Stocky just needs to act like he's from the wine company," suggested Reggie. "He needs to say there was a faulty batch and they are trying to recall the bottles. That way people will be happy to tell you if they've re-gifted the wine or if they have already drunk it." She looked at Stocky. "You can say that it could cause a mild allergic reaction. Then if they have drunk it and have had no symptoms they are safe and won't panic."

"Genius idea," agreed Stocky. "I was wondering how to approach it.

"I like that," agreed Dave. "I'm just the helpful friend trying to make sure nobody gets sick. That works for me."

With the details sorted and the pizza long gone the group broke up for the evening. Shutting the front door, Reggie paused for a moment to gather her thoughts. What followed was going to be the most difficult part of the evening to navigate. Taking one last calming breath Reggie reluctantly moved away from the front door and headed into the lounge. She knew her parents were patiently waiting, for yet another explanation and apology from their eldest daughter.

CHAPTER 16

Things were going well, almost too well. Reggie ticked off yet another task on her to do list and sat back in her chair. Sitting clustered around various tables, the decorating committee were busily adding sparkle to the fire helmet templates. Other tables were industriously working on the flame and water ideas that Stocky and Dave had come up with the night before. Reggie cast her eyes down the list, satisfied with the thick forest of ticks. Prizes, food, glow sticks, DJ and even tickets were sorted. She had even managed to contact all the parent helpers and give them their assigned roles for the evening. She still had to complete the decorations, but looking around the room she could tell that the committee had that under control. They would be dry in plenty of time to put up after school tomorrow.

One thing she still needed to organise for herself was a costume. She planned to dash into town this afternoon on her way home and hopefully find something cheap. Reggie needed to get home as quickly as possible. If she was going to be helping Stocky once the disco was out of the way, she needed to take full advantage of the time she had left. This evening was going to be a book marking and paperwork extravaganza.

The thought of going home was not exactly a pleasant one. Reggie winced as she recalled the painful conversation with her parents last night. The mood of the room, which had been frosty to begin with, had quickly chilled to sub zero temperatures. Some very harsh words had been spoken, quite a few of them by her usually laid back father.

Reggie was relieved when the ping of her phone pulled her attention back to the present. She reached into her bag and checked the message.

This is Jake. Got your number from Stella. Need to see you today.

Reggie's stomach lurched as her eyes read and re-read the message, searching for hidden meanings.

"He has my number," she murmured. "He wants to see me." She allowed her mind to drift back to the way his liquid brown eyes had warmed her to the point of melting when they last met. As she read the message again she noticed that it didn't mention wanting to see her but instead said 'need'. Either he was madly in love and couldn't wait to see her again (which was highly unlikely), or this wasn't about her at all. The butterflies continued to flutter hopefully in her stomach as she crafted her reply.

Have to go to the costume shop in town at 3.30pm. I'm free after that. We could get coffee?

She pressed send and waited anxiously for his reply, which arrived quickly.

No. Meet in churchyard. Won't take long.

Shit! - Definitely not a declaration of love. The butterflies settled into an apprehensive churn. Reggie feared she was heading for yet another uncomfortable conversation. The churchyard Jake was referring to was very different to the overgrown shambles she had walked through with Stocky at the weekend. This was a busy crossroads for foot traffic in the centre of the town. All the gravestones had been moved and laid flat around the edges, leaving a wide expanse of manicured lawn. Paved pathways crossed at the centre leading to different areas of the town. Benches were artfully positioned and on sunny days students gathered there between lectures and people with young children ate picnics on the grass. It was actually a lovely place to meet.

Reggie pushed Jake and the imminent encounter from her mind. She spent the remainder of the day focused on her disco responsibilities and her wonderful class. She couldn't afford for anything or anyone – no matter how heart-stoppingly gorgeous, to mess up her one chance at redemption. But as she dashed out to the car park at the end of the day, Reggie couldn't help the feeling of foreboding, which settled over her. Luckily the costume shop was just to one side of the churchyard so she wouldn't have too long to wait before she would be put out of her misery.

Reggie paused outside the old-fashioned shop. The large window display was filled with mannequins wearing a bizarre range of costumes. Cleopatra stood next to a clown - who had his hand on the shoulder of an army officer, who seemed to be dancing with Cat Woman. Ignoring the strange tableau, Reggie studied her reflection in the glass. Her skirt, fitted blue top and jacket combo made her look like any other young professional. Reggie was thankful she had opted to wear heels today, and even more thankful that the stars had aligned to give her a good hair day. If she was heading into a tricky situation then at least she knew she was looking good.

"Costume first," she muttered.

The wooden-framed door opened easily as she pushed it and a bell jangled overhead as she stepped inside. On previous visits, Reggie had seen wall-to-wall racks bulging with plastic covered costumes on wire hangers. Today the racks were mostly bare, with groups two or three forlorn costumes clustered together. Puzzled, Reggie wandered along the worn carpet towards the wooden counter at the rear of the shop. A short man with unruly grey curls and small round glasses beamed at her as she approached.

"Ummm, are you closing down?" Reggie asked, gesturing to the lack of costumes.

"Oh no love, anything but," the man replied. The man continued to beam, revealing a perfect set of false teeth.
"I'm having the best week I've ever had. The university is having a huge costume party to welcome the new first year students. That's pretty much wiped me out. Then to top it off some

primary school is having a costume disco tomorrow night so nearly all my kids costumes are gone too. So… what kind of costume are you after, young lady?"

"Do have anything from the emergency services; like, police, fire fighter, doctor, surgeon or nurse?" Reggie asked hopefully.

"Oh no love," he shook his head. "Let me think for a moment."

He pushed his spectacles further up the bridge of his nose and stared around the room thoughtfully. Reggie noticed that the denim jacket draped over his chair matched exactly the shade of his denim shirt. After a moment spent scanning the room he gave Reggie a quick assessing look.

"In your size I've got two Cat Women costumes and a Britney Spears." He pointed to a nearby hanger, which seemed to have three strips of cloth hanging off it." Seeing Reggie shudder, he glanced at the racks again. "If you want to cover up more, I do have this Darth Vader left. The gentleman was supposed to pick it up this morning, you can have it if you like." Reggie shook her head sighing.

"Thanks but it has to be emergency services." Reggie turned and headed towards the door.

"Oh no love," he called after her. "I hate to let you down. Let me have one more look."

He strode out from behind the counter and walked along the racks, checking costumes as he went. Reggie turned and paused, allowing herself a tiny smile as she noticed that he was wearing jeans to match the shirt and jacket –a triple threat.

"Aha!" he announced triumphantly and pulled an outfit off the rack. "This is the naughty nurse." Reggie's face fell. "Now don't be put off love, we need to be creative. Yes, it's very short and shows a lot up top."

Reggie studied the skimpy costume as he pointed out the obvious.

"But," he continued, "this costume is probably a size too big for you." He glanced meaningfully at Reggie, who shook her head, unable to follow his logic. "It means," he spoke slowly, "that you can wear clothes under it." Seeing understanding dawn on Reggie's face he beamed his toothy grin. "All you need is a T-shirt and leggings underneath and you're a nurse who's definitely not naughty."

A few minutes later, with a final wave of thanks and a promise to return the costume on Thursday, Reggie was back on the street. She headed around the corner and into the alleyway leading through to the churchyard. As the alley opened up to meet the lawn, Reggie scanned the pathways. There were a few people busily making their way towards the different exits and a group of students sat chatting on a bench. Reggie's chest jolted as she recognised the solitary figure sitting on a bench in the centre of the lawn, not far from where all the paths converged. Reggie, shifted the costume bag to her left hand, straightened and strode purposefully forward. She could feel him watching her approach. Nervously she bit her lip, concentrating on the suddenly difficult task of walking in a straight line. She stopped a couple of metres in front of the bench and chanced a glance upwards. His eyes, brimming with emotion sent a shockwave through her. Even in misery he was gorgeous. Needing a distraction, she spoke.

"I'm so sorry about your cousin," she said.

He nodded, continuing to stare at her. The silence stretched out between them. Eventually she had to look away. Why didn't he speak? Trying to hide her nerves she moved and sat on the bench placing her bags between them. Finally, he straightened up and turned towards her.

"Are you trying to hurt me?" There was anger in his tone and a new hardness to his stare.

"O..of course not," Reggie stammered, shocked by the hostility in his voice. "Why would you think that?" Jake made no attempt to hide his fury.

"Dave, murdered my cousin," he spat out. "And what do you do? You stop investigating him and start working for him… Are you crazy?" he yelled.

Reggie felt the anguish in his voice cut into her like a knife. She struggled to find the right words.

"Look!" she spoke quietly. "You're hurting. Something awful happened to Caroline and you should be angry. But the police… they think it was either suicide or Dave. They aren't looking any further. I spoke to Dave and I believe him when he says he didn't do it."

"Bullshit!" Jake launched himself off the bench. Before he could speak Reggie quickly continued.

"I just want the truth. I was the last person to see Caroline alive. I feel I owe her. I want to find out the truth for her. Don't you want that?"

She looked up, refusing to flinch as her questioning gaze met his molten stare. Unable to remain still Jake began to pace.

"Just who are you?" he ground out. "You think you're a better judge of character than the police? Dave turns on the charm, gives you a sob story and you fall at his feet. You're just a little girl playing grown up. First you play teacher then detective. What next? Then when it all turns to crap, people like me have to come rescue you…"

As his tirade continued Reggie began to fade it out; her thoughts focused inward and her own anger began to grow. Time after time over the past few weeks she had been forced to listen politely while her boss, colleagues, parents and even her friends berated her choices and questioned her actions. She thought about the many apologies she'd had to make and the countless hours she had put in to make amends for her actions, not to forget the hours spent trying to help Stocky with his career crisis. As the fury rose inside her it formed an icy cold reservoir of calm, pooling in her lungs and spreading out through her veins. Slowly she rose.

"Stop!" Her voice rang out, ice cold and her unexpectedly arctic stare cut him off mid-sentence. Her frigid, clipped tones speared the distance between them. "You do not know me," she spoke slowly, her voice cold. "We are not friends, so you do not get to criticise or judge me. If you need to yell at someone, choose someone else. We are done here!"

Calmly Reggie gathered her bags and walked away along the path, her high heels performing a model strut that even Bitch Face Fossington would have been proud of. All Jake could do was stare. In fact, he continued to stare long after Reggie had disappeared into the alleyway.

By the time Reggie reached her car her heart was galloping at an alarming rate and she could feel the heat from her rushing blood staining her face. She hadn't felt this good in ages. Finally, she'd been back in control of a situation and even got the have the last word. She remembered the stupefied look on Jake's face as she'd turned and walked away. Men are such dumbasses she thought - especially the good-looking ones. Ignoring the dirt she leaned against the car door for a moment, gathering her thoughts. It was time to take back her life, and to do that she needed to do three things. First she needed to make tomorrow's disco the event of the year. Secondly she had to earn some extra money so she could regain at least a sliver of her independence. Thirdly and finally, it was becoming more and more important to her to find out the truth of how Caroline Thomas died.

CHAPTER 17

Reggie stood motionless in the centre of the school hall. The curtains were drawn and the lights turned off. On the stage in front of her, the DJ's equipment was set up ready to go. Lights of various colours were flashing on and off in a random sequence. The DJ himself, Reggie suspected, had slipped out for a quick pre disco smoke in the staff car park. Slowly, Reggie began to move around the room making a final check. The decorations looked amazing. Her wonderful decorating committee had really given it their all. The fluorescent flames were glowing brightly and the helmets and water droplets sparkled beautifully in the disco lights. Reggie had even found time to create a fluorescent fire hose to go with the droplets. She smiled. It was so satisfying to finally accomplish something she could be proud of. The highlight of the day so far had been working with two of the other teachers to decorate the hall. The three of them had laughed and joked as they worked together. It was probably the first time all term that she hadn't felt like the hated outsider. It felt really good to finally be part of a team, even if only for a couple of hours. She just needed the rest of the evening to go off without a hitch. Reggie checked her watch; just enough time to go and change into her costume before people started to arrive.

Pleased with her achievements, she headed into the toilets, opened her bag and froze. Unbelievable! Mind racing, Reggie ransacked her bag. Shit! With disbelief she checked her bag again and stared helplessly at her reflection in the mirror.

Un-freaking-believable! The leggings and t-shirt were missing. Both were essential items in creating the non-naughty nurse costume. How had this happened? She had been so organised. This morning she had even placed the items on the kitchen bench next to her lunch so that she wouldn't forget them.

She leaned heavily on the edge of the sink, groaning as she remembered her quick lunchtime dash to spend precious money on a sandwich from the bakery. Forgetting her lunch had been an inconvenience earlier on. Now it was a major disaster.

A bass beat began to boom through the walls. The DJ was literally getting the party started. She forced a calming breath. "Think, think!" Reggie faced the mirror and took stock. The top she was wearing wouldn't look too bad under the nurse outfit. That would solve the cleavage issue. Reggie took several more steadying breaths. The short dress was going to be a challenge. She looked down in frustration at the skirt she had chosen to wear to work. Useless! In desperation Reggie scanned the room and her eyes came to rest on the tangled jumble of clothes sitting in a cardboard box in the corner. This scruffy pile was affectionately nicknamed the dump. It was where teachers deposited the unclaimed items of uniform and sometimes underwear that children left lying around on the classroom floor. Every now and then, when the smell of sweat (and Reggie suspected, urine) became a bit too much to bear, Ms Darwin would choose a volunteer to take the pile home and wash it.

Reggie leaned in close and gently inhaled. Her nose wrinkled and her stomach recoiled at the odour. It wasn't a fullblown stench but was definitely on its way. She sat back on her knees and studied the pile. All she needed was a pair of large PE shorts. Then at least if she had to bend over, nobody would see her G string undies. She tutted. Avoiding visible panty line had seemed important this morning. Holding her breath, she leaned into the pile and began to rummage. After a quick pause and a frantic dash to wash a nameless sticky substance off her fingers, she took another huge breath and dived back in. This time she emerged victorious, holding a pair of clean-ish blue shorts.

Looking in the mirror Reggie had to admit that the finished result wasn't bad. The shorts were snug under the dress, acting a little like bike shorts. At least her dignity would be more or less intact. Reggie's long legs (one of her best features) did look good in the short nurse's dress and white pumps. Buoyed by her problem-solving success, Reggie headed back towards the hall.

"You can do this," she whispered. "Make it fun for the kids and don't bend over." Self-consciously she reached for the hem of the very short dress, pulling it downwards.

Reggie moved quickly along the corridor; the pulsating beat of the music lifting her spirits. Rounding the corner at speed she collided heavily with a large solid body heading in the other direction. Knocked off balance by the impact Reggie braced to hit the floor. Strong arms reached quickly out to steady her and she found herself enveloped in a tight bear hug. Words of embarrassed thanks froze on her lips as she glanced up at her rescuer. Jake's highly amused face looked down at her.

"This is the third time in a week you've been in my arms," he grinned. "Anyone would think you had a thing for me."

Reggie's initial jolt of attraction was quickly overtaken by anger. Realising he was still holding her, she shrugged free. Thinking quickly, she grabbed his arm and propelled them both through the nearest doorway into the small photocopying room. She moved as far away from him as the space would allow and let her anger boil over.

"What the hell are you doing here?" she ground out. "If you've come to tell me more about how pathetic my life is I can assure you I got the message yesterday… Also, you've also picked a really bad time," she admitted. She paused for breath, confused by his smile.

"I volunteered," he replied, continuing to smile.

"Volunteered for what?" she snapped. His obvious enjoyment of her confusion sent her temper soaring.

"I offered to be one of the firemen to run the game at your disco… so I could see you… and apologise." He was now openly grinning. Reggie's eyes flashed.

"Then why are you laughing at me?" She accused. Jake shook his head, trying to force some order into his thoughts. "Well?" Reggie's tone was arctic.

"Ok, ok!" Jake raised his hands in defeat. "I came here to apologise. I planned out exactly what I would say... but then you are standing there like that." Seeing Reggie's confusion, he sighed and continued. "You are wearing that short, short dress with your long, sexy legs... you are so angry and beautiful at the same time." Reggie's stunned eyes met his.

"Oh" was all she could manage in response. Their eyes remained locked as he moved slowly to close the gap between them. Reggie bit her lip nervously. "You're here to apologise?" She whispered.

"Yes." He lowered his mouth gently to brush against her lips. Then moved away slightly to study her face.

"And you think I'm beautiful?" she murmured.

"Definitely!" His smile dazzled and mesmerised. Her lips parted slightly as he leaned in towards her. At that moment the DJ decided to amp up the volume. The thumping bass brought Reggie crashing back to reality.

"Oh my God, the disco!"

She pushed past Jake and out into the hallway. She pulled back the locks on the entrance doors and threw them open. Hoards of excited little firemen, police officers, nurses and the odd super hero surged in. Reggie began the job of collecting tickets from tiny sticky fingers and ushering them towards the darkened hall. She listened to the excited giggles and shouts of the smaller children as they discovered the transformation from school hall to disco wonderland. The older children exchanged jokes and complements; their excitement thinly covered by a veil of assumed worldliness - befitting their status as seniors.

Reggie stood in the corner of the school hall and found she was grinning. The night was a success. The hall was full of happy children. The food and glow sticks were selling like hot cakes, and Jake had kissed her. Flushing, she decided to think more about that later. As if her thoughts conjured him up he appeared next to her. He leaned in to shout over the music. She shivered as his arm brushed hers.

"It's going really well," he shouted. "Did you organise everything… like the decorations?"

"Yes, I'm really pleased with them. I've had lots of compliments from teachers and parent helpers. Especially the fluorescent hose pipe. It really seems to make everyone smile."

"I'm not surprised," Jake grinned. "Were you thinking of anyone particular when you made it… maybe me?"

"What?" Reggie's confusion was reaching epic proportions. "I don't get it. What is it about my decorations that is so damn funny?" Jake turned her around to face the largest wall in the hall, where Reggie's hosepipe centrepiece took pride of place.

"Take a really good look," he laughed.

For a moment all Reggie could focus on was the feeling of his hand on her arm, setting her nerves on fire and turning her insides to molten lava. She made the effort to block out everything but the scene in front of her. Jake felt the moment when realisation hit. Her body stiffened and then sagged slightly. It took another few seconds for Reggie to fully appreciate the horrific truth of what she had created on the school wall.

"It's a p…penis," she stammered. "I've put a giant glow in the dark penis on the wall, and it's ejaculating shiny sperm!" Reggie tried to take a few calming breaths but it wasn't working. "I'm going to get fired," she mumbled to herself… this is bad… so bad… Can't breathe… need air."

Reggie dashed through the side door of the hall and out into the welcoming darkness of the playground. She sank on to the nearest wooden bench, her shallow breaths coming quickly.

"Lean forward, put your head between your legs. Take a big slow breath in… then out again."

Jake's voice was an oasis of calm. Reggie's breathing slowed. She began to take in her surroundings, the cool breeze on her skin, Jake next to her on the bench - his hand gently rubbing circles on her back. Jake broke the silence.

"It might not be as bad as you think... The headmistress might think it's funny."

Reggie stared thoughtfully into the inky blackness of the playground.

"No," she replied. "I don't think Ms Darwin even has a sense of humour." Reluctantly she stood, straightened her dress and pulled the hemline down as low as it would go. "Time to face the music."

The pounding beat and steamy heat of one hundred excited, dancing children slammed into her as she walked slowly back into the school hall. With one notable exception, the evening really had been a huge success. Reggie made her way through to the school entrance hall where food and glow-sticks were selling out fast.

"Ah there you are Miss Quinn." Ms Darwin's ever-pristine form seemed to materialise from nowhere.

Dressed more for the boardroom than a school disco, her mere proximity was intimidating enough to induce fight or flight mode in Reggie.

"M..Ms Darwin... I can explain." Reggie managed to force out.

"What a marvellous evening." Ms Darwin's voice boomed. "The children are having a wonderful time. Dancing and games with educational fire safety tips thrown in. What could be more delightful?" She smiled blandly at Reggie as if daring her to disagree.

"Um... yes," Reggie cautiously agreed. "You're not angry?"

"Miss Quinn, I believe it is important for all of us to celebrate our successes, while also being mindful of the opportunities we are given to improve as we move forwards." Ignoring Reggie's blank stare Ms Darwin swept on. "Let us ruminate on this evening for example. The PTA and I are delighted with the huge amount of funds raised and the efficiency with which the evening was organised. We are overjoyed to be able to utilise your skills and hand over the running of all future school discos to you." She widened her smile and seemed to be waiting for a response.

"Thank you," Reggie replied dubiously. She wasn't sure what she was expected to say but this seemed to please Ms Darwin.

"Of course," Ms Darwin responded as if a huge honour had just been conferred. "Now there are two key areas where I see the opportunity for improvement as we move forward," she continued. "Dress code." Ms Darwin briefly scanned Reggie's outfit, causing Reggie to fidget uncomfortably with her hemline. "I will be updating the school dress code policy to include a minimum skirt length requirement." Reggie squirmed. "Secondly, I will in future be personally checking all decorating committee artwork before it is displayed, to avoid any" (she paused raising her eyebrows), "accidental misinterpretation of the images."

Reggie's face burned red. Ms Darwin nodded and then swept off towards the group of eagerly smiling PTA mums. Reggie stood for a moment in bemused shock. She wasn't fired. She still had a job. She may even have just been complimented.

"Welcome to the world of teaching," a voice next to her laughed. Reggie turned to see Kate, one of the teachers who'd helped decorate the hall earlier. She was grinning at Reggie. "You do well at something and they pile on more work and responsibility. Welcome to the club." Kate patted her arm before heading off towards a group of girls gathered outside the toilets.

An hour and a half later all the children had been collected and the hall, with the help of the PTA and Jake had been returned to its normal state. Reggie and Jake walked out into the car park towards Reggie's car.

"Thanks for staying to help clear up," said Reggie

"You're welcome," Jake returned her smile and checked his watch. "I have to head over to the station in a few minutes. I'm on call tonight. But I wanted to talk to you first... about Caroline."

"Oh!" Reggie's face fell slightly.

"No, don't worry," he rushed to reassure her. "I'm not going to shout." He raked his hands through his hair trying to find the right words. "I did come here to apologise. I had no right to take my anger and frustration out on you yesterday. It was wrong and I'm sorry."

"Thanks, I appreciate that," she replied, smiling shyly.

"To be fair," his eyes twinkled, "you put me in my place pretty spectacularly." She answered his smile with one of her own.

"Yep, It felt pretty good having the last word." Jake's smile faded and he took a moment to arrange his thoughts.

"I've been thinking a lot about what you said about getting the truth for Caroline. The more distance I get from it, the harder I find it to believe that Dave would have killed her."

"You should talk to him. He's taking it really hard. He can't stand to go home and it hurts him that friends and family just assume he's guilty."

Jake nodded, his face a confusion of conflicting emotions.

"I think it would be easier," he said with difficulty, "if there was someone else to blame. It's just so hard to imagine anyone wanting to hurt her. She was such a lovely, caring person."

Reggie watched as his thoughts turned inwards and he struggled with his grief. She knew that nothing she could say would be able to ease his pain. So, she simply reached out to hold his hand in a small gesture of comfort and waited. Eventually he broke the silence.

"If what you say about the police not looking for other suspects is true then maybe it is a good idea for someone else to be investigating... I would like to get the truth for Caroline too."

"I'm meeting with Stocky and Dave tomorrow, said Reggie. "I'll let you know what we decide to do."

"Ok, thanks," Jake replied, opening Reggie's car door. She climbed in and reached for the door handle, pausing when he quietly spoke.

"Reggie, you'll be careful?" Her eyes met his troubled gaze.

"Of course!" He reached down gently pressing his lips to her forehead.

"We'll talk soon," he murmured. As he straightened, he ran a finger gently over the healing scar above Reggie's eye. A small smile twitched at the corners of his mouth. He closed the door and watched as she drove out of the car park. He stood lost in thought, long after the sound of the engine had faded away into the distance. Eventually, he shook his head, walked over to his own car and headed to work.

CHAPTER 18

Reggie was still riding the high of her disco success the next day, as she drove across town towards Dave's pub. There had been a decided thaw in the attitude of some (not all) of her colleagues. Kate had even chosen to sit next to her in the staffroom at lunchtime, much to Reggie's surprise.

"You did a great job with the disco," said Kate. "Everyone's talking about it."

"Really?" Reggie smiled, remembering the Ms Darwin's praise the previous night.

"Yes, it's the most money we've made in years." Kate unwrapped her ham roll and looked across at Reggie. "I think… no, I know I owe you an apology. I've been pretty cold to you since you started here. I'm ashamed to say that I listened to the rumours about you and I shouldn't have."

"There were rumours about me? Asked Reggie. "Was it Veronica?"

Kate sighed. "I think so, although she's very clever about the way she does it. I should have known better because she did a similar thing to me last year when I was newly qualified.

"What were people saying about me?" Reggie asked.

"Erm…" Kate's face reddened but she continued, "that you didn't like the school or how it was run, and that you thought you were the only decent teacher here."

"Wow!" Things were beginning to fall rapidly into place. Reggie recalled all the strange glances in her direction and whispered conversations of her colleagues at the beginning of the school year. Reggie realised that she been doomed before she'd even had the chance to make her first mistake. Although, she had to admit that there was a seed of truth in the rumours. She had been ridiculously overly confident during her first few days but that had well and truly been stamped out of her now – to the point where she was second-guessing everything. Reggie glanced across at Kate who was hungrily devouring her lunch.

"What do I do, should I go to Ms Darwin?" Kate held up a finger while she finished chewing her mouthful.

"Definitely not. There are a few things you need to know about Veronica and Ms Darwin. They go way back – to teacher's college. They were like best friends or something. Apparently until a few years ago Veronica was a lot of fun. Then her husband left her and she became more and more bitter.

"But Ms Darwin must have noticed?" asked Reggie.

"Veronica puts on quite the act for Ms Darwin. "You saw what she was like comforting Mr Banks when you destroyed his classroom." Reggie shifted uncomfortably at the memory and shrugged. "When Ms Darwin is around, Veronica comes across as fierce but passionately devoted to the job." Kate paused and shook her head. "The problem is that I never went to Ms Darwin so she's even less likely to believe you now. Your best bet is to just keep working hard. The disco was a great start and people were impressed. People will stop listening to rumours once they see the real you."

Reggie smiled at Kate and finally felt less alone. Kate was her fist ally and Reggie was determined that she would be the first of many.

Reggie pulled in to the pub car park and chose a space close to Dave's office door. She knocked and Stocky opened the door to a much bigger room than she'd anticipated. Dave was certainly not a tidy man. The room seemed to double as an office and storage area. Boxes of napkins and glasses were stacked off to the far side, next to boxes of crisp packets in a range of flavours.

This area had some order to it (probably the duty manager's organisation). The remainder of the space acted as Dave's office. There were a number of shelving units on the walls all filled with papers and boxes containing who knew what? Dave's large desk boasted a computer that was hemmed in by more paper work, with some even overflowing into piles on the floor next to a large filing cabinet. Stocky's laptop was set up on a small desk pushed up to the side of the larger desk. It was conspicuously empty of papers. Stocky probably had to clear the debris off to make some space thought Reggie.

"Hi Reggie, grab a seat." Dave looked up from his comfy chair behind the desk. Reggie scanned the room and finally noticed an old wheelie desk chair almost hidden under boxes of condiments. She stacked the boxes in the corner and wheeled the chair so she could sit across from Dave. Stocky had returned to his smaller desk so the three of them made up the three points of a triangle all facing inwards.

"How was the disco?" asked Stocky. "Were the decorations a big hit?"

"They were actually very popular," replied Reggie, cringing slightly as the image of the massive fluorescent penis flashed into her mind. "It went well. I think my job is safe for now."

"Fantastic news, now you can focus on keeping me out of prison," quipped Dave.

"Ok then, you'd better get me up to speed on what you have been doing."

"Well," said Stocky. "We've actually accomplished a lot. As you know we decided to start with the wine as that was our best clue." Reggie decided not to point out that the wine was their only clue. "Once he got thinking," continued Stocky, "Dave actually came up with a pretty detailed list of people who he had given wine bottles to."

"It becomes quite easy to focus when the alternative is prison," Dave admitted. "The main thing I can't remember is who I gave multiple bottles to and also exactly how many extras people took at the end of Caroline's birthday party."

"But," said Stocky, trying to remain positive, we have managed to track down a lot of them by using your faulty batch idea."

Reggie cast her mind back to their discussion at her house before the school disco.

"So you told people that you were recalling them because they could cause an allergic reaction?"

"Yes, once I told them that, people were really keen to help. Quite a few people had already drunk the wine but suffered no ill effects."

"Well, they wouldn't be ill would they?" Reggie countered. "We made the story up."

"I had this theory," said Stocky, pausing.

"Go on," urged Reggie.

"No matter how hard we tried Dave and I couldn't come up with anyone who would want Caroline dead. Everyone liked her and nobody except Dave would benefit from her death. So, I thought, what if the whole thing was a mistake? What if the wine actually was faulty and it was just a horrible accident that Caroline drank it?"

Reggie mulled over this new information. "How would you explain the wine being left on the doorstep?" she asked.

"I thought about that," replied Stocky. "It could be someone from the party who felt guilty for taking too many bottles, so decided to give one back. Anyway, it doesn't matter anymore because since then, several of the people I've spoken to have already drunk their wine and they are all fine. I've still got a few more people to ring but I doubt anything will come of that."

"It was a good theory," Reggie agreed. "We need to keep an open mind."

"And it made a damn sight more sense than murder," added Dave. "I know it's selfish of me but I think I could deal with all of this more easily if it was just a tragic accident."

"Let's not forget," said Reggie, "that until the autopsy is completed, we won't know for certain that it is the wine that's poisoned!"

"That wouldn't help me anyway," Dave added miserably. "Caroline hadn't left the house that day so if it was something she ate rather than the wine, the police can still point the finger at me." Reggie turned to face Stocky.

"What's the situation with the police, Stocky? Did you manage to get any information from Teresa when you took the surveillance photos to the station?"

Stocky grinned and leaned forward, closing his laptop lid. "I found out lots from Teresa. She is totally onboard with keeping us in the loop. We were right! Dave is definitely the only suspect at the moment. There is a backlog with the autopsy and the lab results - apparently there always is after the summer holidays; it takes them a while to catch up. They aren't worried about Dave because they have his passport so he can't get far. Teresa reckons they should have the results from the wine bottle and Caroline's stomach contents in a couple of days." He saw Dave's grimace at the mention of Caroline's autopsy. "Sorry Dave," he apologised.

"It's alright, Reggie needs to know everything we know," Dave reassured.

"So," Stocky continued. "As soon as the results are back they will execute search warrants on Dave's home and the bar and will most likely re-arrest him. They already have people following Dave to make sure he doesn't try to get rid of any evidence."

"Have you noticed anyone following you?" asked Reggie.

"No," Dave gave a small smile. "I think they are slightly more skilled than Stocky is at surveillance."

"Hey!" Stocky protested, his feathers well and truly ruffled. "You didn't spot me that last time at the hotel."

"So what's next," said Reggie quickly, in an attempt to change the subject.

Stocky scowled, opened up his laptop screen and counted his list of names.

"I've got six more people to call about the wine. A couple of people had passed the wine onto friends, so I need to check them out. Then I'm going to drive around and collect all the unused bottles. After that, I thought I'd start looking into Caroline's recent clients and contractors she worked with – like painters and builders," he explained.

"What about your girlfriend Dave?" Reggie asked. "Did you give her any bottles of wine?" Dave had the grace to look uncomfortable at the mention of his lady friend.

"Yes," he answered. "I quite often grab one or two bottles to give to her when I see her." He thought for a moment. "But she prefers white wine and I can't remember giving her any of the bottles with a bow."

"Are you sure?" asked Reggie. "Because jealousy would give her an excellent motive."

"Nah," Dave shook his head. "It's not like that with Sabrina. She's all about fun with no strings attached."

"What if she couldn't resist?" Reggie smirked. "You're the whole package Dave. What if being with you changed her? What if she couldn't stand the thought of such a prize with someone else and just had to have you all to herself?"

"No!" Dave ignored the heavy sarcasm in Reggie's tone. "I don't even think she knows my last name. We met at the bar one night. In fact, she hasn't even been back to the bar since."

"I have to admit," agreed Stocky, "she doesn't exactly sound like crazy stalker material."

"Shit!" Dave began rummaging amongst the papers on his desk with urgency.

"What's up?" asked Stocky.

"It's Sabrina. I forgot, I'm supposed to meet her on Saturday." He finally located his phone amongst the desk debris and began typing a message. *I need to cancel… wouldn't feel right after Caroline-*

"Wait!" Reggie was thoughtful for a moment. Dave stopped typing and watched her pensively. "I know you think it couldn't be Sabrina," she said. "But, I think that Stocky and I should at least meet her and check her out."

"I suppose it couldn't hurt," Dave admitted, placing his phone down on the desk.

"We can go in your place to the meeting," said Reggie. "We'll explain your situation and why you can't be there. Then we can judge her response."

"We can also give her the spiel about the contaminated wine and see if she has any," added Stocky.

"Yes, that would work," agreed Reggie. "Between now and then you will have time to finish your wine phone calls and start looking into Caroline's work contacts and clients."

Reggie was thoughtful for a moment, a new idea occurring to her. "I've just realised we also have a whole different angle to investigate," she announced. "You both said that you couldn't think of anyone who would want Caroline dead. What if Caroline wasn't the target? What if you were the target all along?" Reggie gestured towards Dave. There was a moment of silence while the enormity of what Reggie suggested sank in.
"I mean," she continued, "no offence Dave, but I bet you piss people off all the time. All those lovely blond ladies you love so much. I bet some of them have boyfriends or husbands who'd be keen to get some revenge."

"I'm not that bad," Dave protested. Seeing Reggie roll her eyes, his body sagged slightly. "Maybe I am that bad," he admitted quietly.

"Maybe it's time to write a new list of names for us," said Reggie.

"I remember..." Stocky interrupted the silence, "that I watched an episode of Poirot once." The others stared blankly. "You know... Hercule Poirot the great Belgian detective! There are films and a TV series, like; *Death on the Nile* and *Murder on the Orient Express*."

"Now I know who you mean," said Dave. "I think I saw that Nile one at Christmas one year."

"The books are by Agatha Christie," Stocky confirmed.

"Aaah, I know who you mean, she did Miss Marple," said Reggie.

"Yes Miss Marple was a detective in a different series of books," said Stocky. Anyway, in this one episode Hercule Poirot was investigating a poisoning."

"So," Reggie interrupted, "We are now taking detective advice from a fictional character?"

"If we can pick up tips from Magnum P.I. there's a lot we can learn from Hercule Poirot," stated Stocky.

"Fine," Reggie sighed. "Carry on."

"Right, so, Poirot is narrowing down who the murderer could be and he says that the murderer has to be a woman because men choose more violent ways of killing people; men don't choose poison."

"That's fantastic news, it means I'm off the hook," said Dave. Reggie thought for a moment.

"I suppose it makes sense," she agreed. If any husband or boyfriend wanted to get revenge for Dave sleeping with their women, they would probably just beat him up or hit him with something large."

"Which means," said Stocky, "that we need to focus on any of Dave's lady friends who might not be happy with the way things ended."

Reggie watched Dave fidget uncomfortably in his chair and nibble on his thumbnail.

"What's the matter?" she asked.

"Umm… it's just that I'm a bit of a love 'em and leave 'em kind of a guy. So… there may be quite a long list," he admitted.

"Can you at least remember their names," Reggie asked sarcastically.

"Of Course I can," Dave reddened, "and I never delete phone numbers so I have them all here." He picked up his phone and waved it in Reggie's direction.

"Well at least that's something." Reggie's voice took on a slightly less judgemental tone. "If you can make a list of names, phone numbers, addresses - if you have them, anything else you know about them and maybe approximate dates when you were seeing these women; I bet Stocky could use his IT wizardry to get us more information, right?"

"Sure, no problem. What's the plan?" Stocky asked."

"I think you should finish off your wine investigation then start on friends and colleagues and find the addresses for these women. On Saturday you and I can go and meet Sabrina. Then if we don't have anything concrete by then we can visit some of these women on Sunday."

"That works for me," said Stocky.

"Great," Reggie felt better now that they had an organised plan of action. "I really need a coffee." She said.

Dave had been sitting back in his seat listening carefully to their planning.

"Me too," he added. "If you head through that door to the bar and ask Alex she'll sort you out with drinks. Stocky, you want anything?

"No thanks." He was already furiously typing and didn't look up from his screen.

"You get the coffees and I'll start writing the list," said Dave. He frowned and began to scroll through his phone contacts list.

Reggie walked through the door and emerged behind the bar on the left-hand side. This was the area she and Stocky had been watching during their failed surveillance operation the previous week. The bar was very quiet at this time of day. It was too late for lunchtime patrons and still too early for the after work crowd. Alex was busily cleaning the glass window on a beer fridge. She looked up when she heard the door open. When Reggie asked for the coffees she smiled and headed over to the coffee machine.

"Sure hon. You're Stella's sister, aren't you?" Reggie nodded. "I work weekend shifts with her, and we've been out drinking afterwards," Alex continued. "She's crazy fun," she grinned, "and she drinks like a fish."

"Yep," Reggie replied with a rueful smile. "Work hard, play hard, that's Stella."

She thanked Alex for the coffees and headed back through

the office door. Stocky was still engrossed in whatever online search he was doing. She moved across to the large desk and could see that Dave was adding names to what was already looking like a lengthy list. She placed a cup next to him and quietly took her seat opposite. For a couple of minutes she sipped her coffee, enjoying the busy silence. Her thoughts turned to Jake and she wondered where he was today. She hoped he'd taken her advice and spoken to Dave. Once the thought had taken root in her mind she just had to know the answer.

"Um… Dave?" she asked.

"Yes." He continued looking down at his list.

"Have you spoken to Jake yet?" Dave paused and looked across the table at Reggie.

"He sent me a message yesterday," he was thoughtful for a moment. "I think we're going to be ok. He wants me to let him know how your investigation is going. I'll ring him when I finish this list." He chewed on the end of his pen frowning down at the paper.

"How many names do you have?" Reggie asked, trying to keep her tone neutral. He stared at the paper for a while, not answering.

"Twenty so far but I feel like I've missed someone." Dave picked up his phone and started to search through the contacts list again. Eventually he shrugged and sat back. He pushed the list across the desk to Reggie.

"You've certainly given us a lot of suspects to look into," she remarked.

"I just want you to know," Dave said, "that seeing it written here in black and white does not make me proud. It sounds ridiculous but I didn't realise I was this bad." Reggie glanced down the list. "Maybe this time was different," Dave continued. "Maybe she really was going to get a divorce," he added sadly. Seeing the pained expression on his face, Reggie's heart softened slightly.

"You know Dave, it's never too late to make a change."

CHAPTER 19

Reggie was well aware that she had a large amount of ground to make up with her parents. Hard work, determination (and a little bit of luck) had saved her teaching career - for now. It was time to put the same skills to work on Project Parents. Reggie reminded herself of this, when her alarm sounded at the crack of dawn on Saturday morning. If she wanted to complete an impressive amount of cleaning chores before Stocky arrived at 11am, it was time to dig deep and find some early morning energy. She dusted, polished; unstacked the dishwasher, cleaned bathrooms and toilets and finally when she knew everyone was awake, Reggie vacuumed the house from top to bottom. She was sitting enjoying a celebratory coffee at the sparkling kitchen table when Stella emerged, grumpy and tired. She hugged her robe around her and dropped into the seat opposite Reggie.

"The whole house stinks of bleach," she complained, "and you woke me up with the vacuum."

"You went to the toilet, you were definitely awake... I checked," Reggie replied. Stella placed her arms in front of her on the table and slowly lowered her head onto them. Layers of hair, pyjama and robe muffled her petulant reply.

"I was going back to sleep but you ruined everything."

Reggie knew the signs. Stella was hung over. Reggie rose and poured her sister a coffee. She then rummaged in the pantry, emerging with a packet of cheese puff crisps, which she opened and placed carefully next to the coffee by her sister's elbow.

"Thanks Reg." Stella groaned as she lifted her head and

delicately placed a crisp into her mouth. Four more crisps and a couple of sips of coffee and she was already well on the way to feeling human again. Reggie saw the signs of improvement from across the table.

"Tough night?" she asked. Stella yawed and moved her head around experimentally.

"Not really," she replied, rubbing her eyes as she cast her mind back to the previous evening. "After my shift a few of us went to the new club on Gate Street. We had a few drinks and danced for hours. The music was great. You should have come. What did you do last night?"

"I marked two sets of school books and did most of my planning for next week's lessons," Reggie replied.

"Reg, it was Friday night," Stella was horrified. "What is wrong with you? You used to know how to have fun." Reggie's temper snapped.

"Now I have to hold on to my job, whilst keeping Dave out of prison; at the same time as trying to convince Mum and Dad that I'm not a lost cause," she replied bitterly. "And let's not forget…" Reggie's tone verged on hysterical, "that I'm doing all this without a penny to my name."

"Ok, ok. I'm sorry," Stella soothed. "I can see you've got a lot on your plate, but that's why you really need to take a break. I'm having my 'all I can drink while Dave pays' night, at the bar tonight." She grinned. "Why don't you come along and relax for a while? You can have a few of my free drinks. It might help put things into perspective."

Reggie felt very tempted. It would be great to forget all her worries for one evening.

"Thanks, but no," she said firmly. "It sounds like Dave will be re-arrested at any moment and we don't even have one bit of evidence to help him. It's so frustrating."

"Can I help?" Stella asked. "I know Dave really well. What are you working on?"

"Tracking down the wine hasn't helped at all so now we have a list of all of Dave's ex-girlfriends. Stocky and I are going to try and visit them to see how they felt about Dave."

"Do you have a copy of the list I can look at?" Stella asked.

"Sure," Reggie stood and headed upstairs to retrieve the copy from her bag. When she returned to the kitchen Stella was sitting up thoughtfully, looking far more alert.

"You know, quite a few of Dave's exes still drink at the pub," said Stella.

"Really? Dave seemed to think that he had broken a lot of hearts."

"Typical male ego," laughed Stella. "He thinks that women are little planets orbiting around him, basking in the warmth of his sunshine."

"And women don't... bask in his sunshine?" asked Reggie.

"Of course they do," Stella replied impatiently. "But what he doesn't realise is that the vast majority of women who get involved with him know exactly what he is." Seeing that Reggie still had no idea, she tutted and continued. "Dave is fun for a short while. He's generous, he's giving but he's shallow. Women enjoy being the centre of his attention while it lasts, but it soon wears thin and so everyone moves on. Generally, there are no hard feelings and it is easy to stay friends with Dave afterwards."

Reggie looked quizzically at Stella. "Should we be seeing your name on this list then?" She asked. Opening up the paper she passed it to Stella.

"Hell no! I don't mix business with pleasure." Stella smoothed out the paper and ran her finger down the list. "I know quite a few of these. Look," she pointed at a name, "Hayley was out with me last night. And these four," she jabbed her finger at various places on the list. "They usually turn up at the bar at some point during the weekend. They weren't there last night, so chances are they might make an appearance tonight." She smirked as an idea formed in her mind. "Now you have a legitimate reason to come out with me tonight. I can introduce you to some of Dave's exes and you can drink some free drinks and just maybe have some fun for a change." She sat back triumphantly and waited for Reggie's inevitable agreement.

"You might actually be onto something Stel. I've been wondering how best to talk to these women." She nodded her head thoughtfully. "It's actually perfect. I'll talk to Stocky and he can come too."

"The more, the merrier," grinned Stella. She was feeling re-energised and looking forward to a busy night, drinking away Dave's profits.

Reggie refocused her thoughts on the list. "You said that most of the women were fine after they broke up with Dave. Can you take another look and see if you can see anyone who took the breakup badly. It might narrow down our suspect pool."

Stella grabbed a pencil off the bench and studied the list. She put a dot by four names.

"I don't know who they are… but maybe I'd recognise them if I saw a picture," she mused. "These two," she circled the names. "Neither of these have been to the bar since Dave stopped seeing them." She tapped one of the two names. "Mandy, as I remember was one of those beautiful but crazy insecure people. I think Dave quickly regretted getting involved with her. I remember she was really demanding and high maintenance. She was definitely not happy when Dave ended it. You should ask Dave about her."

"Thanks," said Reggie. "I will. You've actually been a big help Stel. Thank you."

"All part of the service," Stella grinned. She stood up. "I'm going to go and relax in the bath with a face mask before Mum and Dad get back. I'm assuming they went Saturday morning grocery shopping?" she asked.

"Yes they did. Just try not to make a mess in the bathroom. I really want them to be impressed when they see how clean the house is," Reggie pleaded.

"Don't worry Cinderella," Stella winked. I'll put in a good word for you."

She swept out of the kitchen and headed up the stairs. Reggie busied herself putting the cups in the dishwasher and re-wiping the kitchen table. Then she filled the kettle. If Stocky arrived in the next few minutes he would have time for a cup of tea before they had to leave. She heard Stocky open the door just as she placed the steaming mugs of tea and coffee on the table.

"Perfect timing," she called out as he walked into the kitchen.

He shrugged out of his jacket and sat gratefully down in front of his tea. Reggie sat opposite and recapped her conversation with Stella.

"That could totally work, you know," agreed Stocky. "People would be more likely to chat to us at the bar than if we knock on their front doors. I'll ring Dave now and ask him."

Reggie sipped her coffee and tried to follow the phone conversation. After Stocky's initial explanation of the idea most of the talking was coming from the other end.

"Aha," said Stocky... "Yes, I understand" ... "mmm ok" ... "Yes I'll tell her" ... "See you tonight." Stocky put down his phone, replaying the plan in his head. Reggie's impatience got the better of her.

"Well?" she asked.

"Dave is definitely on board with the idea. He will be working on the bar so he says he can point out people we should talk to. He agrees that Stella will know most of the women. He even says he'll give us a couple of free drinks so we blend in. He went to great pains to remind me that he is paying us for this so getting drunk is not an option."

"Ok, so what is it that he wanted you to tell me?" Reggie asked.

"He wants me to remind you not to take any crazy pain medication," Stocky smirked. "He doesn't want a repeat of last time."

"It was an accident." Reggie bit back. It's not like I set out to make myself look completely ridiculous." She scowled at the painful memory of her humiliating encounter with Bridgett Fossington.

"Don't worry," said Stocky. He leaned across the table to pat her hand. "Bitch Face will get what's coming to her one day."

Reggie drained her coffee cup, placed it on the table and forced her thoughts in a different direction.

"So, what's the plan for this morning?"

"I spoke to Dave about it yesterday. His plan was basically the same as the day Kelvin and I followed him. He was going to pick her up at her office in Waverly and then take her to the same hotel. He says she won't wait around so we will need to be on time."

"What does she do?" asked Reggie.

"She is a lawyer at the firm of Spratt, Caulder & Associates," replied Stocky. "Dave thinks she is one of the managing partners."

"But her last name is Warrington, not Spratt or Caulder. If she's the boss shouldn't her name be up there in the heading?"

"Apparently, changing the name when the partners change is what they do in America." Replied Stocky. "In the UK firms tend to keep the original name, as it is usually well known and respected in the community."

"Makes sense." Reggie checked the clock on the kitchen wall. "We should get going if we are going to be on time for Miss Sabrina Warrington." Stocky quickly tidied away their mugs while Reggie ran upstairs for her bag.

Stocky started his car and headed in the direction of the small village of Waverly. Reggie cast her eyes over the tidy interior, much tidier than her own car. A blue folder on the back seat slid from side to side as they took turns on the winding road.

"What's in the folder?" she asked.

"I printed out a copy of all the surveillance pictures I gave to the police. I thought it would be a good idea to keep them for my records at work," Stocky replied.

Reggie reached through to the back seat for the folder. She flicked through the pictures, unable to hold back a chuckle at the one of Dave waving at Stocky. She continued through the stack, pausing at a picture of Dave signing for a package.

"This is the third picture where Dave is receiving a

package," she said.

"I think there are actually a couple more further on in the pile," said Stocky. I assumed it must be stock for the pub.

"No, deliveries from the brewery arrive in bulk and certainly not by a courier." Reggie was thoughtful for a moment. "Jake mentioned the packages to me last week. He was wondering if Dave was doing anything dodgy."

"That's another motive right there," replied Stocky. "If Dave has got himself mixed up in something illegal he could have annoyed somebody dangerous and they decided to get rid of him."

"If that is the case," said Reggie, "then he could still be a target. We need to talk to him about this."

"We'll go to his office after we meet Sabrina," agreed Stocky. "Dave wants to know what we think of her anyway."

They took the right turn and travelled over the bridge leading into picturesque Waverly. It was market day and roads were much busier than when Stocky had last been there. He saw a parking space on the side of the road and slipped in.

"I think this is as close as we are going to be able to get." He looked at the road ahead. The high street was closed to traffic today. Pretty market stalls with stripy awnings stretched as far as the eye could see. Traders selling a wide range of local produce were mixed in with stallholders selling artisan breads, cheeses, candles, arts and crafts and health products. Townsfolk mingled between the stalls, chatting and exchanging pleasantries.

"Waverly really comes alive at the weekend," exclaimed Reggie.

Stocky was too focused on the task ahead to enjoy the market scene. "We can get where we need to be if we head up the main street then cut through on the right between the chemist and the bakery. Come on, we need to be quick or we might miss her."

He locked the car and strode off towards the crowds. Reggie ran to catch up with him, pleased she had chosen to wear her converse shoes rather than boots with a heel. Reggie glanced longingly at a couple of the stalls as Stocky marched them quickly past. She made a mental note to come back when she had some money. She liked the look of some of the scented candles. They would look great in her lounge, if she ever managed to get her own place. Maybe she should start to buy a few things with her future in mind, she thought. Then living in her own home might not feel like such an impossible dream.

They took a sharp right at the chemist and walked into the quiet, cobbled alleyway. This led them to the side of the car park where Stocky and Kelvin had watched Dave meet Sabrina. Reggie recognised Sabrina instantly from the surveillance pictures. They didn't do her justice. She was insanely beautiful. Blond and gorgeous, thought Reggie wryly - Dave's kryptonite. Sabrina was standing beneath the Spratt, Caulder & Associates sign. The tiny white flower detailing around the neck of her knee length black dress complemented her outfit and matching heels perfectly. Simple and elegant thought Reggie a little jealously.

"Come on," urged Stocky. "She's checking her watch."

Sabrina saw them emerge from the alley. Her mild surprise at seeing them approach was quickly masked by a welcoming smile. Stocky extended his hand.

"Hi Sabrina, I'm Steven Stockwell and this is my associate, Reggie Quinn."

Sabrina shook his hand. "Nice to meet you both," She smiled and turned to shake hands with Reggie. "How can I help you both today? I'm afraid that my office is closed until Monday if you are looking for legal representation."

"No, no, we are actually here on behalf of Dave Thomas," said Stocky. Sabrina's face clouded with concern.

"Oh no, I hope he's ok. He's supposed to be meeting me here." Stocky rushed to reassure her.

"He's absolutely fine. Dave wanted us to come and explain to you why he can't be here today. I'm afraid there's been a death in his family."

I'm really sorry to hear that," replied Sabrina sympathetically. "Was it someone close to him?"

"Ummm... well... it's...like this..."

Stocky was struggling to find the right words. Having started off well, he was now paralysed by the extreme awkwardness of the situation. How were you supposed to talk to the girlfriend about the wife? He realised that he should have asked himself this question a lot earlier in the day. Reggie recognised the signs. Stocky was heading for a total system meltdown. She could watch it happen or she could step in and rescue him.

"I'm afraid his wife died." Reggie spoke loudly enough to cut through Stocky's stammering. Stunned, Sabrina locked eyes with Reggie. Time seemed to stop. Finally, Sabrina found her voice.

"Did you say wife?" She asked in amazement. Reggie nodded. Sabrina shook her head, dumbfounded. "That's... wow...I mean it's awful that his wife died but I would never have pictured Dave as the marrying type. He seems more of a 'love them and leave them' kind of a guy."

"So you had no idea he was married?" Asked Stocky, his game face back on.

"No. I actually thought we were very similar. Two single people looking for fun with no strings attached," Sabrina replied. She thought for a moment. "His poor wife must have had to put up with a lot."

"Yes," Reggie replied. "Staying married to Dave was quite a challenge." Sabrina nodded sympathetically,

"what happened to her?" Reggie grimaced.

"Actually she was poisoned."

"How did that happen?" Sabrina's faced paled. "Was it Dave?"

"The police think it's him," Stocky answered. "They are waiting on test results to come in before they can arrest him and issue search warrants."

"But we don't think it was him," Reggie jumped in. "We think it is more likely that the wine she drank was from a faulty batch." She reached out and touched Sabrina's arm. "That's another reason we wanted to see you. Dave gave out a lot of red wine bottles from the same batch to friends and business associates. We are trying to track them all down so we can see if the wine is faulty." Sabrina inclined her head thoughtfully.

"Dave has given me quite a few bottles of wine recently," she admitted. "But I don't really like red wine so he usually brings white. I don't think I can be of any help, sorry." She smiled in apology.

"That's ok." Stocky returned her smile. He was a little dazzled by her beauty. "We're sorry to have given you such bad news. Sabrina's smile deepened, becoming more intimate. Stocky began to feel like they were the only two people in the world. She reached out and took his hand, her eyes keeping Stocky transfixed.

"Don't be sorry." Her voice was soft, lyrical and almost hypnotic. "Thank you for taking the time to come and see me. I needed to know. I'll give Dave some space to deal with his grief."

Sabrina released Stocky's hand and he felt an uncomfortable sense of loss. She picked up her bag and walked gracefully over to a small black sports car and got in. Stocky remained transfixed, staring after her. Reggie's elbow in his ribs bought him back to reality.

"Hey!" he yelled. "What's that for?"

"She really did a number on you," laughed Reggie.

"I don't know what you mean," snapped Stocky. "She seemed wonderful."

Reggie spun around and grabbed his hand. She held it and stared meaningfully into his eyes. With her most seductive voice she imitated Sabrina.

"Thank you for taking the time to come and see me," she purred. Stocky snatched back his hand and stalked into the alleyway, Reggie's laughter echoing behind him.

Sabrina watched their progress through her rear-view mirror. She continued to stare until they had both disappeared from view. Her perfect mouth settled into a hard line. Decision made, she raised a delicate finger to remove a frown line from her brow. Then she reached into her bag to retrieve her phone. Polished nails danced quickly over the letters and she fired off a message.

There's a complication. Shut down location 1. Now!

CHAPTER 20

They were back in the car and had driven several miles out into the countryside before Stocky emerged from Sabrina's spell. He glanced across at Reggie, who had wisely remained silent.

"So, what do we think of Sabrina?"

"We know what you think," Reggie smirked.

"Come on," Stocky scowled, "take this seriously. We have to report back to Dave." Reggie took a moment to replay the conversation with Sabrina in her mind.

"One thing was very clear. Sabrina had no idea that Dave was married."

"I agree," said Stocky. "She was genuinely surprised when we told her."

"She didn't even get angry when she found out she'd been sleeping with a married man," said Reggie.

"Yeah, that's true." Stocky was surprised he hadn't spotted that detail himself. "I guess that means that we can take jealousy off the table as a motive."

"Then there was the wine," said Reggie. "Sabrina confirmed what Dave told us about her drinking white, not red; so, that ties in as well."

They drove in silence for a while, both weighing up possible avenues of investigation.

"Basically, we are back to looking at the exes," said Reggie. "I like the sound of Mandy. Stella seemed to think she was obsessed with Dave when they went out together. The only problem is that she never comes into the pub."

"Hmmm!" said Stocky thoughtfully. "We can go and talk to Dave about her now. If he doesn't have her address I can do a search for it. Then we can visit her tomorrow."

"We still get to go to the pub tonight though... right?" Reggie tried to keep the anxious tone from her voice. It had been weeks since she'd had a decent night out. Even a pretend night like tonight was better than nothing.

"Of course we do!" Stocky hadn't noticed her anxiety. "We need to talk to as many exes as possible. I think the relaxed setting (and the alcohol) will help them to be more honest."

The winding lane led them to a large roundabout where they re-joined civilisation. They drove along a busy street towards Stapwell town centre. The road was full of Saturday shoppers heading into the main shopping centre and the outlet stores beyond it. Reggie's stomach rumbled. She stared longingly as they crawled past a McDonalds.

"Can we stop and eat," she pleaded. "It's been ages since breakfast."

"No, this traffic is bad enough without adding a stop to our journey," Stocky replied. "Dave can order us something at the pub." He glanced across at Reggie's miserable face. "Reg, don't worry, they do really good nachos," he reassured her.

He could see that she was tempted.

"Ok," she said sharply. "But turn here and cut through the side streets."

Stocky took a quick right and wound his way through the rows of terraced houses in the residential part of the old town. He turned again and made his way past the severe brick walls of the local prison. The razor wire on top glinted brightly in the sun. Eventually he popped out at the bottom end of the main street and made his way around to the pub car park.

There was no answer at Dave's office door so they walked around to the main entrance. Saturday lunch was in full swing. Reggie's mouth watered as they walked past tables of people devouring nachos, wedges and fries. They made their way down to the busy bar area. The queue was fairly large so they moved

to stand at the side by the staff walkway. Dave was busy serving drinks but gave them a wave and motioned them to wait.
A few minutes later he came over to join them.

"Can you give me half an hour to help with the rush, then we can talk?" Stocky opened his mouth to agree but Reggie jumped in first.

"We need food," she growled. Dave smiled at her grumpy expression.

"Melissa will put an order in for you." He gestured for one of the staff to come over. "Get them whatever they want and put it on my tab," he told her.

Reggie's expression softened slightly at the thought of free food. It took them a few minutes to find an empty table and then a few more to wait for it to be cleared. Melissa bought over their drinks and assured them that the food wouldn't be far behind. Reggie sipped her Diet-Coke impatiently. She turned her chair to give her a better view of the kitchen doors.

"I forgot how grumpy you get when you haven't eaten," said Stocky. "You'd be a nightmare on one of those reality desert island shows."

Reggie wasn't listening; she'd spotted Melissa walking in their direction carrying three large bowls, brimming with food.

"Here's your carb' overload… enjoy." Melissa smiled and placed the three bowls in the centre of the table.

"Did we really need wedges, chips and nachos?" asked Stocky. Reggie already had a mouth full of hot cheesy wedges.

"Shut up and eat," she mumbled. Reaching across the table she dipped a chip into the aioli sauce. Five chips and four more wedges later, Reggie was beginning to feel human again. She swapped the bowls around and made a start on the nachos. The queue at the bar dwindled to one or two people, so Dave left his staff to serve customers and joined them at the table. He helped himself to a chip and looked enquiringly at Reggie.

"So, what's new?"

"You were right about Sabrina," Reggie answered. "She had no idea that you were married."

"Yeah, that would be right," said Dave. I don't usually mention that I'm married till later on when I'm trying to get rid of them."

"Classy," Reggie muttered in disgust. Stocky jumped in quickly to change the topic.

"She also backed up what you said about you giving her white wine not red wine."

"We can cross her off the list but unfortunately we have a large number of exes still to contact," said Reggie. "Stella thought we should talk to you about Mandy." Dave paled at the mention of her name.

"That chick was seriously unhinged. When she found out I was married she told me that if I didn't want to get divorced she could arrange for an accident to happen to Caroline. When I said no, she laughed and said that she was joking. She was a bit drunk. I thought it was the wine talking… You don't think she actually did it do you?"

"She's top of my suspect list at the moment," said Reggie.

"When did she last contact you?" asked Stocky.

"For a long time after we split she used to send me messages saying things like, 'you'll come back to me one day' or 'the universe will bring us together. That stopped about a year ago. I figured she'd found some other poor guy to harass."

"Do you have her address?" Stocky asked.

"I do actually, if she's still at the same place. I dropped her off a couple of times to a house on Telford Street." Dave paused for a moment. "I think number 22."

"Great! Reg and I will go and see her tomorrow," confirmed Stocky. Tonight, we'll try and meet up with as many of your exes as possible and see what we can find out." He gestured to Dave. "You and Stella will be able to point out and introduce us to them." Another thought occurred to Stocky. "Will Jake be working tonight? I bet he knows all your exes and he'd be in an excellent position to spot them as they arrive."

"No," said Dave. "Jake's rostered on at the fire station tonight. He wouldn't be any help anyway. I was always very careful when he was working. He probably had his suspicions but if he ever knew for sure that I was having an affair he would've gone straight to Caroline."

Reggie pushed back a wave of disappointment. Secretly she'd been hoping to wow Jake when she saw him, and hopefully erase the memory of the bedraggled mess she had been when they first met. She'd already planned an extensive hair and makeup session for later that afternoon. She also had her eye on one of Stella's newest dresses. It would take all of her negotiation and bargaining skills but it would be worth it. The stress of the last few weeks meant that Reggie had lost the few extra pounds she had been carrying around and she was keen to make the most of it. Reggie gave herself a mental shake. Jake or no Jake it was always good to get dressed up and feel fabulous. Thinking of Jake jogged her memory and brought the surveillance photos to the front of her mind.

"Hey Dave, what's with all the packages you sign for?" she asked "Are they for the pub?

"Packages?" asked Dave.

"Stocky has a stack of surveillance photos of you and in lots of them you are outside your office signing for packages."

"Oh those! They're nothing, they're Sabrina's. I just look after them for her till her office clerk comes to get them."

"Why on earth would Sabrina need you to look after packages for her?" asked Reggie.

"They have an asbestos problem at her firm's storage facility," said Dave. "She was actually really upset when she told me about it. She needed a temporary facility to store the company files in and she didn't know what to do. I did what I could to help her out."

Stocky made sympathetic noises while Reggie rolled her eyes. She could picture the scene; Sabrina reaching out for Dave's hand, her sorrowful eyes looking deep into his. He wouldn't have stood a chance. Wisely she kept her thoughts to herself. Instead, she asked,

"what exactly did you do to help?"

"I let her use the old World War Two air raid shelter to store her files."

"An air raid shelter," said Stocky, impressed. "That's totally cool. Can we see it?"

"No!" said Dave. "It used to join on to the beer cellars but that was bricked up years ago. There was a separate entrance by the side of the bar but I had it boarded over and plastered a couple of years ago. That's why it was a perfect secure storage area for Sabrina to use. She was really grateful when I suggested she use it."

"I bet," Reggie muttered under her breath. "There must be some way in. How does she get in there to store the files?"

"Sabrina never comes here." Dave shook his head. "It's always her clerk. He picks up any deliveries and then takes them to the shelter. There's a metal hatch in the ground at the back of the car park. That's the only way in or out now."

Reggie thought about the surveillance photos sitting in Stocky's car. "The packages in the pictures don't look big enough to be files."

"You're thinking about paper files," said Stocky. "Most companies store things electronically in the cloud these days. I'm assuming that the packages contain backup drives?" He looked at Dave, who nodded. "That's what I thought they were too," he agreed.

Reggie was still unconvinced. "If everything is in the cloud why would they need hard drives as well?"

"That's easy," replied Stocky confidently. It felt good to be talking about his area of expertise. "The new trend is for hackers to lock up all of a company's data and charge them a huge sum to get a code that will supposedly unlock the data."

"But the code doesn't always work!" Reggie guessed.

"Exactly!"

"So it's like kidnappers making a ransom demand then killing the hostage when they get the money?" Reggie asked. Stocky nodded. "Wow - brutal! I can see why Sabrina would need back up storage."

"We should probably check out the hatch anyway," Stocky suggested.

"Good idea," Reggie agreed. She pushed away the half empty nacho bowl, wiped her fingers on the napkin and downed the remainder of her drink.

Dave led them towards the bar. He paused at the end of the bar and tapped the wall. A hollow sound echoed back.
"This is the entrance I covered up. It's only a thin board. Easy to take down if I ever need to use it again."

He led them behind the bar and through to his office. Reggie carefully stepped over the piles of paper and around some carelessly stacked boxes. Once outside in the car park Dave walked around the building to a grassy area behind his office. An old but sturdy looking metal hatch sat amongst the weeds. A large, shiny padlock fastened it down to the ground. It reminded Stocky of the tornado shelters he had seen on TV.

"There's a set of steps going down from the hatch and then it opens out into two fairly large rooms," Dave explained.

Reggie stared down at the hatch. "I don't suppose you have a key for that massive padlock, do you?"

"Of course not," Dave was outraged. "I wouldn't betray Sabrina's trust. She's relying on me to help her." Reggie had to admit that she was impressed. Sabrina's power over the men she interacted with was strong and long lasting. Even Dave, the player, was well and truly under her spell.

"Dave I'm worried," she said. "We only have Sabrina's word that she's storing files. There could be something illegal down there." Dave raised an eyebrow clearly unconvinced. Stocky's imagination was piqued and he ran with it.

"They could be smuggling illegal animals. This could be where they hide them before they ship them off to the buyer," he laughed.

"And the packages I sign for aren't files," said Dave with a grin. "They are stacks of cash from the anonymous buyers."

"Hilarious," said Reggie dryly. "I still feel it's in your best interest Dave, if we get a look in there. You are the owner. You have every right to enter."

"Fine, but I want no part of it." Dave was serious again. "I don't want any way Sabrina can link it back to me. You can't go in there during the day as her clerk might turn up at any time. You'll have to do it at night."

"What does her clerk look like? Reggie asked.

"He's a big scary looking bald guy," replied Dave.

"That's the guy Kelvin and I saw pick Sabrina up at the hotel," said Stocky. "Looks more like he works for the mafia than for a lawyer."

Reggie cast her mind back over the surveillance photos. She looked over at Stocky. "I think he's on one of the photos you took at the hotel," she shuddered. "I wouldn't want to bump into him down in there." She gestured towards the air raid shelter.

"We can go in tonight," said Stocky, "after the bar closes. My uncle has some bolt cutters at his office. I'll bring them with me."

"Just don't get caught." Dave was beginning to have second thoughts. "I don't want to have to explain this to Sabrina or her clerk."

While Stocky drove back through the busy Saturday traffic, Reggie had time to reflect on their plans. It was great to be finally taking some action. She was feeling energised and looking forward to her evening out. Hopefully the exes would show up and would be feeling chatty. Then there was the issue of Sabrina. She was clearly using Dave but was it just for his storage space or was it something more? The idea of snooping through Sabrina's life was deliciously appealing. She couldn't be as perfect as she seemed... could she? Reggie squashed the twinge of guilt, she was following a legitimate lead. Searching the shelter was an obvious next step. The fact that she didn't like the way Sabrina managed to dazzle her friends and stir up their protective instincts was a completely separate issue. She was definitely not motivated by jealousy.

CHAPTER 21

Stella turned up the volume on the radio and danced her way back to join Reggie at the bathroom mirror. Both girls had mirrors in their own rooms, but where was the fun in that? As the oldest and tallest by one inch Reggie always went high and Stella low. Reggie added a swipe of mascara and stepped back to assess the finished look. It had taken an afternoon of work but she felt amazing. She ran fingers through her silky-smooth hair, enjoying the feel of it on her skin. She shook her head and it settled back into position perfectly. Reggie smiled at her reflection. Her make up always looked fantastic when Stella added her magic touch. She should do it professionally, Reggie thought. She moved her head slightly, admiring the way her eyes now seemed a brighter more vivid blue.

"You know you owe me big-time, right?" Stella stopped applying her own makeup to look over at Reggie. "That dress looks stunning on you?"

Reggie looked down and had to agree. The short blue dress skimmed her curves and showed just the right amount of cleavage. The length was perfect for her long, long legs, and would look even more flattering when she added heels.

The dress negotiation process had not gone well. In addition to the usual list of chores, Reggie now owed Stella a favour, to be decided on, as and when Stella needed it. Reggie figured she would worry about that when Stella called it in. For now, it was well and truly worth it to look this good. Stella smoothed her dress and stepped back to face Reggie. Her golden hair gleamed brightly against the black of the figure hugging dress.

"You look beautiful," said Reggie, truthfully.

"I know!" Stella laughed. "The men at the bar won't know what to do when the beautiful Quinn sisters arrive."

"Come on, Stocky will be here in a minute," said Reggie. "Let's wait downstairs."

The sun was setting as they drove the now much quieter roads into Stapwell. Stocky went over the final details of the plan. Dave had given him some money to buy drinks - just a couple for themselves, and as many as they wanted for the exes. It was agreed by all, that alcohol would help loosen tongues and maybe reveal any grievances the exes were hiding. Stella would introduce them to the exes in between her mission to drink Dave's bar dry.

"Try not to drink too much Stel," Reggie pleaded as they walked along the path to the main entrance. Stella flicked her hair and smirked.

"I can't promise that. Tonight, is going to be fun, I can tell."

Her mood was infectious. Grinning, Reggie linked arms with her and they walked in through the door. Stocky followed behind. He noticed the appreciative glances of the bouncers as the sisters walked past. He shook his head. This was definitely going to be an interesting evening.

It was still early and there was plenty of room as they made their way down to the bar. Small groups of early drinkers were sprinkled around, staking their claim on various tables.

"No exes yet," whispered Stella, "but we are certainly making an impression." Reggie glanced around the bar and met the interested eyes of several men. She surprised herself by smiling back at them. Stella's confidence must be rubbing off on me she thought. Over in the corner, Reggie noticed a band setting up. Stocky had warned them about this. If possible they needed to speak to as many people as they could before the band started to play at 9pm. After that it would be a lot more difficult to hold a decent conversation. Dave finished serving a customer and moved to meet them as they approached the bar.

"Whoa Reggie, you look hot," he said. "If brunettes were my thing you'd be top of the list."

"Thanks… I think," replied Reggie. "No, wait a minute, we are about to meet the women on your list and think one or all of them are capable of murder. So, I'll pass, on the compliment, thanks anyway." Dave shrugged and switched his attention to Stella.

"Drinks please Dave." She dazzled him with a smile. "I'll have a wine. Let's get his party started."

Dave smiled back. He would never admit it but he always found himself a little bit in awe of Stella.

"Princess Stella, I suppose you'll be drinking me out of business this evening," he joked.

"That's the plan." Stella took the glass of Chardonnay and nodded to the entrance where two blond girls were walking in. "That… and keeping you out of prison."

Dave gave Reggie and Stocky a few quick details about the two exes who were walking towards the bar. Freya, on the left was the manager of a clothes shop on the main street. She and Dave had had a lot of fun together over a year ago. It had lasted about a month and then they had both decided to move on. It was all very amicable. Amy had only gone out with Dave a few times, earlier this year. Then she called it off after meeting the man of her dreams at a conference. She was now engaged and Dave had met her fiancé a few times in the bar. He seemed like a good bloke.

Stella introduced everyone and Dave made sure they all had drinks. Conversation was easy as both girls were excited to finally meet Stella's illusive sister. It also seemed to Reggie, that they had both consumed a fair amount of alcohol before they had arrived.

The girls were happy to talk about their relationships with Dave. They both spoke of him affectionately and Reggie was relieved to find that Dave hadn't misled or mistreated either of the women. He may be a player but Freya and Amy had been very clear on the type of relationship they were having with Dave. It took skills to extricate yourself from a relationship and still remain friends. Reggie reluctantly admitted that Dave had some serious people skills. When Freya headed off to the toilet she tagged along.

Reggie washed her hands and watched Freya's reflection apply lipstick in the mirror next to her.

"Do you know many of Dave's exes?" she asked. Freya paused and smiled.

"Quite a few of Dave's ex-girlfriends are now good friends of mine. I guess we are almost a club." She put the lipstick away and began to powder her nose.

"Do all of the others get on with Dave as well as you do? Stella told me it was all very amicable but it has really surprised me how friendly you are with Dave," Reggie admitted.
Freya put the powder back in her bag and was thoughtful for a moment.

"I guess the thing is, that with Dave, what you see is what you get. He chooses women carefully and usually gets it right. We all know he's in it for a good time not long time, if you know what I mean." She turned to smile at Reggie. "And let's face it, the guy is a lot of fun."

"What did you mean when you said, usually gets it right?"

"Just before he went out with me he was seeing this girl called Mandy," said Freya.

"Stella told me about her. Apparently, she's a bit crazy."

Freya grimaced. "I'd say more like obsessed. She sent me a few nasty text messages – I've no idea how she got my number. Then she turned up at my house ranting about me stealing her man and that I should watch my back. In the end, I called the police and she stopped coming around."

"Sounds horrible," said Reggie. Were the text messages saying the same sort of thing?"

"They were usually short and to the point. It was like she considered Dave to be her property. I remember one said, 'Don't take what isn't yours,' another just said, 'give him back'. I never replied to her messages, and that was when she started to come to my house."

Alarm bells were beginning to ring in Reggie's mind. She definitely needed to talk to Stocky about this. It was vital that they tracked Mandy down tomorrow. "Can I ask you one more thing?" she asked.

"Sure," said Freya.

"Do you think Mandy would be capable of poisoning Dave's wife?" Freya wrinkled her brow and considered the question.

"I really hope that Mandy would have moved on by now. But, if she has managed to stay angry at Dave, and has been bearing a grudge for this length of time... then who knows?"

"Thanks," said Reggie. "I was thinking along the same lines. Let's get back out there."

They exited the toilets and moved back towards the others through the growing crowds. There was a queue at the bar and at some point, while they had been in the toilets the background music had been turned up. Reggie could see Stocky in deep conversation with a beautiful blond girl. Probably another ex-girlfriend she thought. As soon as he finished talking, Reggie would head over so they could compare notes.

Stella saw them approaching and waved them over. Reggie could see a full glass of wine in her hand and guessed she was on number two or even three. Stella was standing with a group of three attractive guys. When Reggie was close enough Stella threw her arm around her shoulders and pulled her close.

"Boys, meet the other beautiful Quinn sister. Reg this is Mike and his friends." Stella released Reggie and nudged her in the ribs. "Say hi," she stage whispered." The guys laughed and Reggie gave them an embarrassed smile.

"Hi," she said. The one Stella had pointed out as Mike leaned forward.

"Reg... is that short for Reggie?" he asked. Reggie nodded. "Are you the Reggie who tried to burn down the primary school?" Reggie sighed and nodded. Was there anyone in town who hadn't heard about it?

"It wasn't deliberate," she murmured. But Mike wasn't listening. He was too busy slapping his mates on the shoulder.

"You'll never guess who this is," he told them. "It's Jake's girl... the one who set fire to the school and dressed up as a hot nurse at the disco."

The boys were now whooping and jumping up and down patting each other on the back. Reggie shot Stella a confused look. Stella leaned in and shouted.

"They're Jake's friends, they're firemen."

Reggie nodded. The situation was becoming clearer. She was a bit miffed he'd told them about the nurse's outfit, although they had said it was hot. I suppose I should be grateful, she thought, that he didn't tell them about the penis artwork on the wall.

"We gotta send Jake a picture," yelled Mike over the music. "Jake'll freak when he sees who we are out with." Long arms reached over and grabbed Reggie around the waist. She felt her feet leave the floor and was manhandled in to the middle of the group.

"Stella take a pic," Mike shouted and lobbed his phone towards Stella.

Reggie watched Stella deftly catch the phone with her left hand without disturbing the glass of wine she was holding in the right. Stella gently placed her glass on the table and held up the phone to frame the shot. Reggie was helpless in the middle of the group. She forced a smile. Either side of her, burly fireman puckered up to kiss her on the cheek. Grinning at Reggie's discomfort, Stella snapped the picture. Three rather gropey hugs later and the firemen moved away in search of drinks from the bar. Reggie scowled at Stella.

"You enjoyed that far too much," she snapped. Stella sniggered.

"It was a little bit funny." She sipped her wine innocently. Over her shoulder Reggie caught sight of Stocky, still talking to the attractive blond girl.

"Who's that with Stocky, is she another ex?" Stella turned to follow her gaze.

"That's Chelsea. She went out with Dave towards the end of last year. She's really nice. I think she got a little bit clingy and that's why Dave got rid of her. She seemed to get over it quickly though. She's had a couple of boyfriends since then. Definitely not the murdering for revenge kind of girlfriend"

"It seems like all Dave's exes are lovely people – with the exception of Mandy," said Reggie. Stella raised her eyebrows.

"Mandy is interesting, that's for sure," she agreed.

Over in the far corner the band began to test out the sound levels on their instruments. Reggie leaned in towards Stella.

"It's going to get loud in here in a minute. I think I'll head to Dave's office so Stocky and I can compare notes."

The band struck up the opening chords and people began to cheer. Stella yelled back over the music.

"Good idea. When you've finished come and find me for a dance. My friend Hayley is coming in later. She's another ex you can cross of your list."

Stella grabbed Reggie for a quick hug. She drained her wine glass then thrust it into Reggie's hands. Reggie watched her sashay away into the crowd.

She looked over in Stocky's direction and found he was now alone. He was scanning the crowds looking for her. She waved and gestured towards the bar. They both fought their way through the boisterous crowd. Reggie arrived first, slipping behind the bar and through to Dave's office door. Across the far side of the room the band were now enthusiastically hammering out a popular cover version. Stella and Freya were part of a group dancing on a raised area. Reggie spotted Mike and his two friends among them. They were desperately trying to get the girls to notice them. Reggie allowed herself a smug smile of satisfaction. The boys had no idea what they were in for. Stella would lead them a merry dance before she nudged them gently into her reject pile.

Stocky finally extricated himself from the crowd and fell

in a heap on the floor of the bar.

"Too busy," he panted. "It's like swimming against the tide out there."

"Come on," Reggie bent to help him up. "There are bottles of water in Dave's office."

Stocky threw himself down into Dave's comfy office chair. He took the cap off a water bottle and murmured joyfully as he drank. It wasn't chilled but he really didn't care. The thick office door thankfully acted like earplugs, muting the noise from the bar. The peace and quiet settled gently over them. Loud music was wonderful when you were drinking and dancing but a nightmare when you were trying to track down a murderer.

Reggie moved a box onto the floor and sat opposite Stocky. It was time to share their findings.

"What did you find out from Chelsea," she asked. Stocky gulped down the dregs of the bottle. He placed it on the desk and wiped his mouth with the back of his hand.

"She's amazing. Did you know that she looked after her sick mother while putting herself through Hairdressing College?" His eyes glowed with admiration. "And she's been like a parent to her younger sister," he gushed.

"That is fascinating information," said Reggie dryly. "But do you think she could have poisoned Caroline?"

"Of course not," Stocky was indignant. "She told me that she went out with Dave a few times and realised she was looking for a more serious relationship. When she told Dave, he thanked her for her honesty - told her he was not the guy for her and they went their separate ways."

"That ties in with what Stella told me," Reggie agreed. "Did the future Mrs. Stockwell have anything else to say?" she teased.

Stocky reddened. "We chatted for a while, just to get background information for the case," he said defensively. "Anyway, what did you find out?" he asked, hoping to distract Reggie from any further comments. Reggie repeated her conversations with Freya and Amy. "Wow! Seems like Mandy is totally our next move, agreed Stocky."

"She sounds like a real piece of work, said Reggie. I'm a bit nervous about going around to her house," she admitted. "I'd rather not get beaten up by a crazy lady."

"Hmmmmm," Stocky was thoughtful. "Freya called the police because of Mandy, so there may be some information on file about her. I'll talk to Teresa in the morning and get her to check. If it turns out that she's the violent type, we can take reinforcements."

Reggie liked the sound of that, although she wasn't entirely sure who their reinforcements would be. An image of Stocky's computer geek friend Kelvin popped into her mind. He didn't strike her as the type to stand and fight. If things got really bad she could probably use him as a human shield. She hid her smirk behind her hand.

"So what next?" she asked. "I don't think we are going to find out anything more from the exes tonight. I really want to have a look in the bomb shelter and check out Sabrina's files."

"Dave says we can't do that till the place is empty," said Stocky. "He doesn't want to take the chance of anyone seeing us. He doesn't want to let Sabrina down."

"Oh please," Reggie snapped. "She's up to something and he just can't see it because he's too far gone under her spell to think straight."

"You may be right," said Stocky quietly. "But I think you need to give Dave a break. He's doing the best he can to cope with the guilt of Caroline's death. He doesn't want to be responsible directly or indirectly for causing anyone else pain."

Reggie wouldn't admit it but Stocky's explanation made a lot of sense. It was easy to believe that Dave's laughing and joking exterior was the sum total of his emotional range. Reggie knew that wasn't true. She pictured the heartbroken man who had sat at her dining table pleading for her help.

"Fine, I can wait," she said. "What are we going to do for the next couple of hours?"

"I thought I'd use the time to do some internet searches on Mandy. The more we can find out, the better prepared we will be when we meet her." Stocky left Dave's office chair and moved over to his laptop. He sat down and lifted the laptop lid. "What will you do?" he asked. Reggie stood and smoothed her dress. Grinning, she reached up to check her hair.

"It would be a shame to waste all this," she winked. "I think I'll go and mingle for a while."

Reggie walked through the doorway into a wall of sound and bodies. She stood for a moment at the end of the bar enjoying the party atmosphere. Dave and his bar staff were frantically serving drinks to the mass of people pressing at the bar. Anyone not queuing seemed to be dancing or at least nodding their heads to the music while they drank. The dance floor was a writhing mass of happy, arm-waving bodies. The band finished one song and moved straight into another. This received a cheer from the dance floor, the dancers instantly recognising the beat of another popular song. Reggie grinned. She loved it when there was this kind of energy between a band and their audience. Unable to resist, she began to slowly weave her way through the crowds towards the dance floor. She joined the group dancing with Stella. After some high-fives and a couple of enthusiastic hugs (from the firemen) Reggie relaxed with the rhythm and gave herself over to the joy of dancing. She felt amazing. It was so good to put all her worries about work and Dave to one side and focus on enjoying the here and now. Reggie loved the fact that the right dress, matched with killer heels, and of course - great hair and make-up, could boost your confidence a mile high.

She literally felt like anything was possible right now. Reggie smiled across at Stella who pointed at the girl next to her. Judging by her stunning looks and blond hair Reggie guessed that this must be Hayley, another ex. Dave really did have excellent taste in women. Reggie knew instantly that there was nothing new that she would be able to add. Mandy was going to be the new focus, as soon as Reggie had fulfilled her urge to snoop through Sabrina's files. She checked her watch - one hour forty minutes until the bar closed. Another ten or fifteen minutes after that for everyone to clear out of the car park, and then she could open the bomb shelter. Until then, she had nothing to do but enjoy herself and dance.

CHAPTER 22

Dirty glasses rattled in protest as Reggie heaved another full tray onto the bar. She tutted and pulled down her dress which had ridden up again. Her outfit was not designed for heavy lifting. Across the room the band were wheeling out the last pieces of their equipment. Thank goodness they'd soon be gone. Frustrated, Reggie leaned on the bar looking out into the open space. Two of the bar staff were quickly wiping down tables, while a third gathered the remaining glasses. Behind the bar a barman stacked clean glasses onto the shelves, clinking them musically together. The scent of hot cleaning fluid in the open glass washer almost blocked out the sour smell of spilled beer, not yet cleaned off the bar. The duty manager finally finished checking the last till and took it to the office, where Stocky was still working industriously on his laptop. Surely there couldn't be much more to do before everyone left for the night?

Now that the lure of the music had gone Reggie was impatient to move onto their search. Forty minutes had passed since Stella, along with a couple of the exes and their drunken fire-fighter escorts had departed in search of more music and dancing. Stella had hugged Reggie tightly and loudly proclaimed how much she loved her. Her words only slurred very slightly. It was an amazing feat Reggie thought, considering how much wine she had managed to consume. Dave had already left for the night, keen to maintain plausible deniability.

A final glance around the room confirmed that close up

would be imminent. Reggie made her way through to the office. A dull ache in her feet reminded her she was still wearing heels. She wished she'd had the foresight to bring a change of footwear and clothes. She glanced down at her dress. Stella would kill her if she got dust or dirt on it.

"They're going to close up soon," she said. "We should get going." Stocky nodded and closed his laptop.

The duty manager was organising coins into moneybags on Dave's desk. He paused and smiled up at Reggie.

"Thanks so much for all your help clearing up tonight. Let me know if you want to pick up a few shifts. We are always looking for hard workers."

"Thanks, I'll think about it." Reggie returned his smile. She wondered how keen he would be to hire her if he knew where her motivation to help came from. She just wanted them all to leave so there would be no witnesses when she broke into the bomb shelter. Stocky led the way out into the dark chill of the car park. Reggie shivered hugging her arms around her.

"I've got a hoodie in my boot you can borrow, said Stocky.

Reggie shrugged into the warmth of the jumper and counted the cars remaining in the car park.

"Ten cars, that's a lot more left than I thought."

"Some will have been left by drinkers who don't want to drive," Stocky replied. "They'll come back to collect them in the morning." He opened the car door. "Get in!"

Stocky started the car and cranked up the heating. He drove out of the car park and into a nearby side street. Reggie was grateful that he left the engine on and the heat running.

"How long do we wait?" she asked.

"Dave gets an alert on his phone when the alarm is set. He's going to send me a message. Then I guess we wait another five or ten minutes for everyone to leave."

When Reggie didn't respond he glanced across at her. She was slumped down in her chair, arms crossed tightly over her chest, staring stonily off into the distance – a statue except for the tiny movement of her jaw as she clenched her teeth together.

Stocky sighed inwardly. He knew that look. Reggie had reached the end of her patience. She was also probably hungry, which always soured her mood. If he didn't act fast he would soon be bearing the brunt of her angry frustration. He thanked his lucky stars that he had left extra food in the boot, just in case. He hopped out of the car and was soon wafting a packet of Doritos and a Diet-Coke under Reggie's nose. She took the food and opened the packet hungrily. She began to munch and the tension quickly left her body. A hint of a smile touched her lips. She took a sip of the Diet-Coke.

"Thanks Stocky, I needed that," she eventually spoke.

"Remind me to go on holiday if you ever decide to go on a diet," Stocky replied dryly.

Stocky's phone beeped an incoming message and he reached to pull it out of his pocket.

"Dave says the alarm has been set. We'll wait here for ten minutes then leave the car and walk back to the pub."

"OK." Reggie took another sip of her drink. "While we are waiting you can tell me everything you found out about Mandy."

"There's not a great deal to tell," said Stocky. "She doesn't have much of a social media presence. She certainly isn't someone who narrates her life online.

"So, no pictures of her dinner, or exciting posts where she checks in at the supermarket?" Reggie joked.

"No, it's a shame," Stocky replied. "If that were the case then we'd be able to track her movements and have a fair idea where she was around the time the wine was left at Caroline's house."

"Anything else?" asked Reggie.

"Well, she has an excellent credit rating and the house she lives in she used to rent, but bought off her landlord last year. She has a flatmate living with her to help pay off her mortgage."

Reggie ignored the twinge of jealousy and refused to even think about the number of years it would take for her to afford her own home. Instead she summed up Stocky's findings.

"Essentially you're saying she's bat shit crazy but financially sound!"

"She certainly keeps the crazy part hidden on line," said Stocky.

"I was really hoping you'd find incriminating comments or at least something to show her malicious nature," said Reggie.

"Maybe she's just too clever to leave a trail like that for anyone to follow. Which means we need to be even more careful when we meet up with her. With that in mind I sent a message to Teresa. She's working a shift tomorrow morning and said she would see what she could find out about the police complaint."

"Good idea," said Reggie. "I'd also like you to find out more about her life before we meet her."

"Like what?"

"Like …is she a black belt in Karate? Or did she study knife throwing at circus school?"

"I think we can safely rule both of those out," laughed Stocky. "Anyway it doesn't really matter. She wouldn't need to be a black belt to kick our asses."

"True," Reggie returned his smile. We aren't exactly Ninja warriors, are we?"

Stocky checked his watch. "I think we've waited long enough." He grabbed the bolt cutters off the back seat and jumped out of the car, quietly making his way along the deserted street. Reggie followed along behind. No matter how softly she tried to walk, her heels rang out loudly on the footpath. Frustrated, she bent and removed them. The blissful chill of the floor soothed her aching toes. She stood still for a moment, eyes closed, luxuriating in the numbing relief.

"Hey, come on," Stocky hissed from the street corner. Reluctantly, Reggie opened her eyes and padded towards him; the shoes swinging in her right hand as she walked.

At the entrance to the car park they paused to listen for activity. When Stocky was sure that they were alone, he led them into the main body of the car park. Up ahead the pub stood silently in a pool of darkness. Reggie was relieved to see no lights in any of the windows. She counted the remaining cars, just six left now and no sign of their owners. They cautiously moved towards the rear of the car park where the side of the building hid the bomb shelter hatch from view. At least if anyone did happen to come into the car park they wouldn't be able to see what we are up to, thought Reggie. The floor became rough gravel at this point. Reggie carefully picked her way across using grassy weed patches as stepping-stones to protect her bare feet as much as she could.

Reggie's eyes were focused on where she was putting her feat so she failed to see Stocky as she rounded the corner. The impact forced a whoosh of air out of Reggie's chest and a startled cry from Stocky.

"What are you doing?" he hissed angrily, reaching down to retrieve the fallen bolt cutters.

"Sorry, I was watching the ground." Reggie winced and shook a sharp stone from between her toes. "Why did you stop?" Stocky straightened up and stared along the path.

"We've got a problem that's why. Look!" Reggie followed his gaze. She was surprised to see that someone had parked a car along the side of the building. She strained her eyes to more clearly identify the outline of the car. It looked like a very old and battered Vauxhall Astra. Reggie opened her mouth to say they could work around the car but stopped. Something wasn't right. She realised that she couldn't see the entrance hatch for the bomb shelter. She squinted and scanned the area hopefully. Eventually her eyes came back to rest on the car and the enormity of the problem sank in. Someone had carefully parked the car to cover over the entrance hatch to the bomb shelter.

"It's going to take a lot more than bolt cutters to get us in now," muttered Stocky.

Reggie brushed the stones off her feet and put on the heels. Ignoring the protest from her toes she tiptoed over to the car for a closer look.

"Maybe we can push it out of the way?" she asked. She leaned hopefully on the boot of the car. Stocky joined her and they both pushed. The car rocked slightly but remained firmly over the hatch. Stocky used the torch on his phone to peer into the driver's window.

"The hand brake is on, we've got no chance," he scowled. Reggie moved around to a small patch of rough grass next to the car. She sank down to her hands and knees and peered underneath. She pulled her phone out of the hoodie pocket and focused its torch beam onto the padlock on the hatch. Stocky joined her and shone his light in the same direction.

"Even if one of us shuffled under to break the lock we'd never be able to open the hatch wide enough to get in," Reggie said crossly. Stocky scrambled to his feet.

"Oh well, we tried." He brushed the dirt and stones off his jeans. We'll come back when the car isn't here. There's nothing else we can do." Reggie remained on the floor, sitting awkwardly on the grass - her legs bent to one side of her body.

"No!" She looked up at him and Stocky recognised the stubborn set of her jaw. "Don't you see," she continued. "This car being here, it's important. A padlock is more than enough security for dusty old files that no one cares about." Putting a car on top - that means I'm right. There's a lot more in there than legal files, and they're obviously worried someone might try to get in. We need to get in there quickly, before they get a chance to move things out."

Reggie began the tricky and unflattering procedure of getting up off the floor in a short dress and heels. Stocky reached down to help pull her up.

"You are probably right," he admitted. He carefully avoided looking at Reggie, who was fighting to bring her errant dress down from where it seemed to be tangled with the hoodie around her waist. "The problem is that we have no other way in. Even if we got into the pub, Dave blocked the other entrance with a wall." Stocky chanced a glance and was relieved to see that Reggie had won the battle and was now fully covered and smoothing the wrinkles out of her dress.

"The wall… that's our way in," she said.

"You want to smash down a wall in Stella's dress?" he

asked, unconvinced.

"Well, yes I do." Reggie glanced down guiltily at the dress. "But maybe not tonight. Don't you remember? Dave said the wall is thin and flimsy so he can easily take it down if he wants to. All I need to do tonight is make a hole big enough to get a decent look. Then if the car is still blocking the bomb hatch tomorrow maybe I can convince Dave to take the wall down."

"Fine," said Stocky, admitting defeat. "Let's ring Dave and see what he says." Hopefully Dave would veto the idea, he thought. Then he could finally go home to bed.

Reggie reached for her phone. After a surprisingly quick conversation, she disconnected and was all smiles.

"He went for it," she announced.

"What!" Stocky was incredulous.

"Apparently he's been worrying on the drive home. He's managed to convince himself that the lab results will definitely come in tomorrow and he'll be arrested for Caroline's murder. Right now, he's open to anything that might help his case."

"What about the wall? Stocky asked.

"I have to make sure the hole is small enough to cover with a beer poster until we decide on our next move.

"And what about keys?"

"That's the easy part," she beamed. "Dave keeps a spare set in a lock box on the drainpipe around the corner - next to the bomb hatch. Apparently, Sabrina's clerk uses them to collect parcels from Dave's office if the pub is closed." Reggie's phone vibrated and she pulled it out of her pocket.
"That'll be Dave," she said. "He's going to text the lock box combination and the alarm code for the pub."

"So we're really doing this," said Stocky. The plan seemed straight forward enough. They weren't even breaking and entering, now that they had the alarm code. Yet Stocky couldn't shake the unease he'd felt ever since he had seen the car sitting over the hatch. Maybe it was because, until that moment he'd been 100 percent sure that they were on a wild goose chase, based solely on Reggie's visceral and unreasonable dislike of

Sabrina. Now he wasn't so sure.

Reggie tiptoed awkwardly across the gravel to the drainpipe. Using the light of her phone she set the combination of the lockbox. It opened with a satisfying click. Reggie crunched triumphantly across the stones to Stocky, waving the precious key.

"Are you sure we should do this?" Stocky asked uneasily. "We could leave it till tomorrow morning and wait till daylight."

"No, the car changes everything." Reggie was adamant. "Putting the car over the entrance was a temporary fix for them. They can't leave it there for long. Sabrina knows that if Dave sees it he will have to ask questions. Whatever is down there is important and I think they will be coming back for it soon."

"You think they might come tonight?" Stocky shivered.

"It is a definite possibility." Said Reggie. "It's what I would do. Wait till the pub is closed there's no one around then come back to move whatever is down there."

"I don't like this." Stocky was beginning to panic. "We are dealing with people we know nothing about. Neither of us is equipped for situations like this." Reggie placed a comforting arm around him.

"That's why we will be clever about it. We won't put any lights on and draw attention to ourselves. I'll slip inside for a quick look while you hide out here and keep watch. I'll only be in there for ten minutes max and then we can go home. If anyone arrives, text me and we'll both stay hidden until they are gone."

"You promise, just ten minutes?" Stocky was slightly reassured.

"Yes, maybe less if I can't see anything." Reggie pointed to a small patch of ground between two parked cars. "If you sit down there you will be able to keep watch on the road without anyone seeing you and you'll be able to see me when I come back out."

Stocky looked around warily, his thoughts conjuring up hidden foes.

"Swap," said Reggie. She held out her shoes and reached

for the bolt cutters. Reluctantly Stocky relinquished his only protection and ruefully looked down at its replacement. He supposed that some damage could be done with the heels, but didn't feel any safer. Reggie retrieved the key from the hoodie pocket and crept towards the office door.

"Make sure you close the door behind you, just in case," Stocky hissed after her.

She nodded and continued towards her destination. Stocky used the time to crawl into the relative safety of the space between the two cars. He sank into the welcoming darkness. Reggie had been right. He was hidden but still had an excellent view of the road at the car park entrance. Reggie reached the door and turned. She stared into the inky black, unable to see Stocky's position. She tensed, suddenly feeling very alone. When waving didn't work, Stocky shone light in his face and gave her the thumbs up. Reggie flexed her shoulders as they relaxed, smiled and waved. She threw a quick glance over her shoulder before slipping the key into the lock and disappearing into the building.

The click of the door shutting echoed loudly through the quiet night. Stocky shifted position slightly so that he could keep an eye on both the road and the office door. His heart galloped loudly in his chest. He slowed his breathing to try and compensate. Clutching one of Reggie's heeled shoes tightly in his left hand, he checked the time on his phone and reluctantly began to wait.

CHAPTER 23

Reggie was relieved to see the alarm keypad illuminated on the wall next to her. She quickly pressed the code. The alarm deactivated and she let out a long breath she hadn't realised she was holding. With the exception of the glowing keypad and the standby light on Dave's computer, the room was immersed in total darkness. Reggie switched on her phone's torch function and swept its narrow beam around the room. The room seemed much smaller and its jumbled contents more of a challenge. She hesitated before stepping into the minefield of boxes. When you removed the human element from the building it became colder – quite unfriendly and alienating. Holding her torch ahead of her she resisted the urge to check over her shoulder. Purposefully she stepped around a stack of boxes and over a pile of paperwork. The torch wobbled in her hand as her bare feet hopped from one uncluttered area to another.

Reaching the door at the far end she spun around, placing her back to it. Her torch swung around wildly as she checked around the room for… she didn't know what.

"This is ridiculous," she whispered. "You were here an hour ago, it's just the same."

Her voice wavered, holding less conviction than she'd hoped for. Now that she had reached the door her feet were reluctant to move on. She remembered how massive and intimidating the open, unfilled space had seemed on the morning she had come to collect her purse. For a moment she considered going back to get Stocky. At least if he were there she would be forced to put on a brave face. He was terrible in situations like these. She would have to be the strong one.

"I am strong," she murmured. Ignoring the instinct to run, she hugged the bolt cutters tightly to her chest and reached for the door handle. Decisively she strode into the area behind the bar, torchlight and eyes deliberately fixed on the familiar shapes of glasses, shelves and beer taps. The gentle hum of the drinks fridges was an unexpected comfort.

The air was much colder in here. The absence of body heat had allowed the cathedral like space to quickly take on the chill of night. She turned towards the main body of the pub and forced her torch to swing a wide arc. Its delicate beam reached tentatively out, much too quickly overpowered by the cavernous black hole. Reggie strained but her eyes could only make out a couple of tables before the light fell away to nothing.

"Shit!" She held the bolt cutters in a death grip. I should have brought a proper bloody torch, she thought to herself. She needed action. Wondering about who or what could be out there was a rabbit hole she did not want to spiral down into. Reggie forced her feet to continue their journey along the somewhat sticky floor. She paused at the far end. The wall she needed to work on was captured in the shaky torchlight. It was only two or three metres past the end of the bar. It might as well be miles away. To reach it she would need to leave the solid tangible structure of the bar. She would need to step out into the unknown.

Reggie realised she needed to dig deep and find some courage. She moved her light around behind the back of the bar. It bounced off the mirrored wall behind racks of spirit bottles. The reflected light managed to brighten up the area a fraction. The light fell on a row of expensive vodka bottles. Reggie scanned along the row and selected the most expensive looking one.

"Aha, found my courage," she managed a cheerful smile.
A couple of shots of this and she'd be ready to leave the safety of the bar and tackle the wall.

Outside, Stocky checked his watch. Only six minutes since she'd gone in. It felt like an eternity. He shifted his position again, brushing at the sharp stones underneath him in a futile attempt to be more comfortable. The prized anonymity of this dark hidey-hole came with a variety of unpleasant downsides. The coldness of the night seemed to intensify in this spot. Add to that the damp, seeping up through the loose stone chippings and Stocky was chilled to the bone. The adrenaline of the first tense minutes of waiting had abated. The only remainder - a cold trickle of sweat running uncomfortably down his back. There had been no sign of anybody, dodgy or otherwise. He had abandoned his death grip on Reggie's shoes in favour of blowing warm air on his numb fingers. This also helped block the very pungent odour, which seemed to hover, like a cloud in the air all around him. Four more minutes... He would give her four more minutes and then he'd ring her.

This night had gone downhill rapidly after they had seen the car sitting over the entrance to the bomb shelter. The instant he'd seen Reggie's face he had known that there was no point talking her out of it. She was on a ridiculous crusade to vilify Sabrina. At least he could bring it to a speedy conclusion. He checked his watch...seven minutes. Three more minutes till he could ring her and get the hell out of here.

A thunderous blast ripped through the silence, echoing percussively in the air. The shockwave erupted through the floor propelling Stocky onto his feet, all his instincts screaming to flee. He sprinted blindly, throwing glances behind him searching for the danger. He found smoke. Billowing smoke churned inexplicably out from under a car. He stared, his brain struggling to catch up with real time events. Then he realised. The car was over the bomb shelter hatch.

"Reggie!" he screamed, sprinting back towards the office door. It was locked. He threw himself repeatedly at the sturdy wood, pumping the handle and slamming his body against it.

When it wouldn't budge, he grabbed for his phone, fingers fumbling as he dialled. His breathing erratic, he listened in despair as Reggie's voicemail message kicked in.

The wind had changed direction and black acrid smoke engulfed him. Coughing and spluttering he stumbled to a safer spot and fell to his knees. His lungs were on fire. He dialled 999 and choked out his plea for help.

All he could do now was wait. He fell back, exhausted, his breath rasping raggedly – clean, cool air soothing burning lungs. Across the car park, smoke still billowed skyward. He noticed the windows where he had stood with Reggie… was it only last week? Finding proof that Dave was cheating had felt like everything. Now one of the windows had cracks in the pane. A wisp of smoke plumed out, engaged in a carefree dance to freedom. Stocky choked back a sob. The enormous effort brought on a new round of painful coughing.

"She has to be ok," he rasped. In the distance, finally there was some hope. Multiple sirens split the night air. Stocky staggered to his feet to meet the trucks as they arrived.

CHAPTER 24

Reggie decided that three was probably the magic number when it came to drinking shots of courage. The first two warmed their way down to her stomach leaving reassurance and relaxation in their wake.

"One more should do it!" She smiled sheepishly at her wavering reflection in the mirror. Even in this terrible lighting she could see the flush of alcohol on her cheeks. Fumbling to open the bottle while holding on to the light and shot glass, her hand slipped. The glass dropped and rolled around on the floor. Swearing under her breath, she bent to the floor to retrieve it.

The blast reverberated through the entire building, shaking it to its foundations. Reggie was thrown forward onto the ground, her head and the concrete floor connecting with a sickening thud. Above her, mirror glass and spirit bottles exploded off the wall. Through the fog of pain Reggie fought to move her arm up to protect her head. Glass rained down on her, a monsoon of razor droplets. Somewhere in the distance a phone was ringing. She fought to keep her eyes open. A white sail billowed out overhead as it ran up the mast… That wasn't right. She battled for control. As the darkness filled her mind she realised her mistake. She wasn't on a ship. The old cinema screen was falling towards her. Mystery solved she gave into the welcome darkness.

Stocky was frantic. He ran at the first vehicle to make it into the car park. The police car swerved and screeched to a halt, narrowly missing him. Stocky barely noticed.

"She's in there," he screamed, his fist banging on the bonnet. "You've got to get her out." Multiple sirens drowned out his next words. Two fire engines followed by an ambulance and two more police cars erupted through the entrance, fanning out to take up positions at various distances from the building. Stocky was choking again. Hacking coughs left him doubled over against the police car.

"Sir, you need to calm down." A comforting hand was placed on his shoulder. "You need to tell us everything you can, so that we can get to your friend." The police officer's voice was soothing. "Then we can get you checked out at the ambulance over there."

Stocky nodded and took a shaky breath. He glanced up at the Ambulance. The driver had opened up the back doors and his partner was already carrying a medical bag towards them. Closer to the building, fire fighters were pouring out of their trucks and setting up for action. One figure broke away from the others and sprinted towards him. Stocky strained his smoke-filled eyes until the familiar face came into focus.

"Jake," he yelled. "Thank god you are here... you've got to get her... the door was locked... smoke everywhere." Panic tightened its grip. "I..I..I couldn't get in," he stammered... She... she won't answer her phone.

Stocky began to shiver, his body once again shaken by a coughing attack. Someone wrapped a blanket around his shoulders. It didn't seem to help.

"He needs oxygen," said the ambulance driver. "We have to take him to the ambulance."

"Wait a minute!" Jake's tone allowed no argument. "He can help us." The ambulance driver paused and Jake stood in front of Stocky. He put his hands on his shoulders forcing Stocky to focus on his face. "Who's in there?" he asked quietly.

"Reggie... she went to investigate the bomb shelter." Stocky's breathing was coming in short gasps, but he continued to look at Jake. Jake swallowed. His expression hardened. He pushed all emotion aside to focus on his job.

"What was she doing in there and where do you think she might be?"

Stocky responded to the quiet urgency in his tone. He answered carefully.

"She went in through the office. She was heading to the wall at the end of the bar. She was going to make a hole in it with bolt cutters to try and see what was in the bomb shelter."

"Do you think she made it that far before the blast?" asked Jake ungently.

"Y…yes." Stocky began to shiver again. "Sh…sh…she had plenty of time."

"I really need to take him now," the ambulance driver stepped in.

"Yeah, thanks. I've got what I need." Jake was already turning to sprint back to the group of fire fighters.

The ambulance driver led Stocky slowly over to the ambulance. The plume of smoke from under the car had lessened. Stocky watched trance like as a group of fire fighters in full breathing apparatus attached a hook to the car. They were preparing to tow it off the bomb shelter hatch. He allowed himself to be gently settled onto a gurney inside the ambulance. An oxygen mask was placed over his face and he took his first steady breaths.

Outside, matters were moving forward with organised precision, born of lengthy experience. The Fire Crew Manager briefed his team.

"External assessment shows no substantial damage but there will probably be damage inside. The building could still be unstable with high risk of falling debris." It was decided that Jake (because of his knowledge of the bar) along with fire fighter Travis Dixon would make the first entry into the building, to perform a safety analysis and initial search for Reggie. They heaved the weighty tanks of air onto their backs and connected the air supply to their headgear. Meanwhile a group of fire fighters prepared to force open the door with a battering ram. Two quick punches had the wood around the lock splintering and the door gave way. No smoke came out through the opening. A positive sign.

Jake switched on his helmet light and stepped through the doorway. The fire fighters took stock of their surroundings. The bright beams of their lights pierced through the murky darkness of the office.

"The explosion really shook up this place," said Travis. He scanned the jumble of boxes and paperwork.

"No, this is actually pretty standard for in here," Jake replied wryly. "This is Dave's office. Just like his life, it's a mess." He paused at the far door. "The main bar is through here. Because it was an old cinema the ceilings are very high, so we could be seeing some fallen debris and potentially hazardous areas."

Jake swung the door and held it open. Their lights illuminated a scene of chaos. The blast had distributed broken glass over a wide area. The bar itself was inaccessible. The huge cinema screen had come down. Its heavy support beam was wedged between the front and back of the bar. The screen itself was draped over the length of the bar like a parachute. The air was still partially clouded by the remnants of smoke from the explosion but he worst of it had thankfully dissipated.

"Reggie should be just past the far end of the bar. We'll have to go around through the main area," said Jake. "Let's check the ceiling." They swept their light beams upwards and followed the contour of the roof. The ceiling was intact except for an area over the main floor, where a giant chandelier had previously hung. Jake illuminated a path down to the floor and found it scattered in several pieces among chunks of fallen plaster. "We'll avoid the area near the chandelier. Stay close to the bar and we'll only have broken glass and a couple of fallen tables to deal with."

Travis agreed and radioed their findings to the crew manager. The pair crunched through the carpet of glass. They negotiated the fallen furniture and made their way to the wall.

Their torches scanned the floor.

"No sign of Reggie." Jake kept the panic out of his voice.

"We should check the area behind the bar, under that lot." Travis gestured to the folds of fallen screen.

He lifted the nearest folds while Jake got down to floor level. Jake crawled through the space and into the bar area. He was grateful he had gloves to protect him from the myriad of broken bottles and mirror shards. Relief shot threw him as he saw a figure on the ground ahead. He shone light on her and saw her fingers twitch.

"She's here and she's alive," Jake shouted. He crawled back out of the space. "We need to move this screen back to get better access."

Between them they heaved at the giant folds hanging over the end of the bar, forcing the heavy material to fold back on itself. Travis used two bar stools to weigh the folds down so they would stay in place.

"Wow," Travis exclaimed. That's not something you see every day. They both paused for a moment, staring down at the unusual tableau in front of them. The folds of the screen had formed a cocoon around Reggie. The white material glowed softly around her in the torchlight. If it weren't for the head wound Reggie would have looked like a napping princess in an Arabian Nights tent.

"Is that a shot glass she's cuddling?" Travis asked.

"Yes, it is," Jake sighed. "I'm going to do a medical assessment before we move her."

He gently ran his hands over Reggie, searching for broken bones and wounds.

"She has a head wound but the rest is surface cuts and bruises from all the broken glass. She probably inhaled some smoke too. Have the ambulance ready. I'm going to bring her out."

Jake bent down next to Reggie and gently lifted her hand off her face. He held it in his own and gently stroked her cheek.

"Reggie can you hear me?" he asked. Her response was a

tiny murmur so he continued. "You're safe now. I've got you and I'm going to look after you."

He slipped an arm under her and held her gently for a moment, brushing the glass off her clothing. Then he carefully lifted her off the floor and settled her as comfortably as possible against him. He began to retrace his steps through the pub. Stirred by the movement Reggie opened her eyes for a moment. She smiled up at him.

"I knew you'd come," she murmured, her voice a husky whisper. Her eyelids drooped and she settled against his chest. Jake allowed himself a small moment of relief. His hold tightened possessively and he followed Travis outside to the waiting Ambulance.

CHAPTER 25

Reggie opened her eyes and stared up at an unfamiliar ceiling. She spent a moment pondering her surroundings, trying to remember how she had ended up there. Had she drunk too much? Her head certainly hurt enough for several hangovers. She lifted her hand to rub at the pain but her mother's concerned voice stopped her.

"Stay still darling. There's a bandage on your head and a drip in your arm. We are so glad you are awake. We have been so worried."

Elisabeth patted Reggie's arm soothingly. Her father's tired face appeared over her mother's shoulder.

"Hi Reggie," he smiled down at her. He ran a hand through his dishevelled hair. "Great to have you back in the land of the living. We missed you."

Reggie tried to return their smiles but pain shot through her head at the effort. Elizabeth noticed her wince.

"The nurses said to tell them when you wake and they'll bring some pain medication for you," she said.

"I'll go." Michael headed for the door.

Elizabeth patted Reggie's arm again and watched her husband's retreating back.

"It was hard for him seeing you lie here and not be able to do anything to help."

"How long have I been here?" asked Reggie. "In fact, why am I here… what happened?" Elizabeth's face clouded with new concern.

"What do you remember?" she asked gently. Reggie thought for a moment, trying to clear the fog from her brain.

"Stocky and I were in the pub car park," she began slowly. "We couldn't get into the bomb shelter, so Dave gave us the code to go in through the pub." She concentrated, ignoring the pain as she screwed up her face. "I was in the pub," she said triumphantly. "I remember. It was really dark and I dropped a glass…" Her face fell… "But, I don't know what happened after that."

"Don't worry," her mum's voice was cheerful. Reggie's memory seemed to be intact. "I can tell you what happened. There was an explosion at the pub last night. You hit your head and have some cuts from all the glass - mostly on your legs. Stocky's jumper protected your arms and you managed to cover your face."

"What about Stocky?"

"He's fine." Her mum reassured her, before Reggie could panic. "He was treated for smoke inhalation. His mum took him home but he's determined to come back and see you after he's had a sleep. Jake was here most of the night too."

"Really?" Reggie was surprised and warmed by the thought.

"He was the one who rescued you. He was very worried and came here straight after his shift. He left a couple of hours ago to take Stella home," She shook her head at the memory.

"Is Stella ok? Reggie asked.

"Your sister has the beginnings of a very serious hangover." Elizabeth rolled her eyes. "She's gone home to sleep it off. She and I will be having a very long talk about the dangers of excessive drinking." Rant over-with, her eyes softened and she looked down at Reggie. "You were really lucky you know," Elizabeth said quietly. Seeing Reggie's confusion, she sighed and continued. "The police said that if you had been inside the bomb shelter you would have died."

Reggie stared, dumbstruck. She had been so determined to get into the bomb shelter. Stocky had tried to make her leave it until daylight but she hadn't wanted to listen. She'd been so caught up in her quest to discredit Sabrina.

At that moment the nurse appeared at her bedside and injected something into her IV tube. "This will help with the pain and let you get some rest," she soothed. Reggie nodded, the world already becoming foggy around the edges. She slipped away into a dreamless sleep.

When Reggie awoke the pain was still there but she felt more like herself, albeit a more fragile version than usual. She noticed with relief that her arm was no longer connected to a drip. Stocky was sitting in the seat next to the bed.

"Your mum and dad have gone to get some lunch," he explained. After effects of the smoke inhalation had left his voice croaky. "Are you ok? He asked.

"Yes, I think so," she replied. "Or at least… I will be".

"I was frantic when I couldn't get to you…" Stocky broke off, emotion overwhelming him.

"It's alright," Reggie reassured. "We are both okay and that's all that matters." Stocky nodded, thankful for the time to regain control.

"So, what the hell happened?" Reggie asked. Stocky glanced around uneasily.

"Reg, I'm really sorry. I'm not supposed to say anything until you feel better."

"Stocky," her eyes flashed angrily. "I was almost blown up. I think I have the right to know."

"Yes, I know you do." He paused for a moment, then after taking a steadying breath continued. "You've missed quite a lot. It seems that the bomb shelter was being used as a meth lab."

"Yes!" Reggie resisted the urge to fist pump the air and settled for a less painful bed pat instead. "I knew Sabrina was a criminal. Meth labs explode all the time - if you believe what you see on TV. Were they down there making it?"
Stocky shook his head.

"I spoke to Teresa this morning. She says that most of the chemicals and anything of value had been removed. There were only enough chemicals down there to destroy any forensic evidence left behind in the bomb shelter. Teresa says they found the remains of a timer."

Reggie let this news sink in. "You mean someone blew it up on purpose?" she asked.

"Yes!" he nodded. The police think someone was trying to get rid of incriminating evidence. They set the timer for when the place should have been empty. Then they placed the old car over the hatch to ensure nobody could get in."

"On the upside," said Reggie, "we know Sabrina didn't deliberately try and blow us up." She cast her mind back over the short conversation they had had with Sabrina. "We must have rattled her when we met her. Can you remember what we said?" Stocky was silent for a moment.

"Reg… it doesn't matter."

"Of course it matters," Reggie stared, incredulous. It's another piece in the jigsaw." Stocky rocked forward, rested his elbows on his legs and held his head in his hands. "What are you not telling me?" Reggie asked. Stocky's anguished eyes met hers.

"They think Dave did it," the words burst out. "They've arrested him for so many things."

"What … I don't understand?" Reggie bit back her growing frustration, forcing her voice to remain calm. "You're not telling me everything. Tell me properly. Start at the beginning. Don't miss anything out," she demanded.

Stocky ran his hands through his hair and sat up.

"I spoke to Dave's lawyer. As we expected, the results on the wine came through and it was poisoned. They arrested Dave first thing this morning. That's when things started to get even worse. The police then showed Dave all of my surveillance photos; do you remember I had to hand them in to Teresa?" Reggie nodded. "They showed Dave the pictures of him receiving packages. They contacted the courier firm and have reams of paperwork and signatures all in Dave's name. They say it proves that he was shipping in chemicals so he could manufacture the meth."

"What about Sabrina and the clerk?" asked Reggie.

"Dave told them about her and that she was a lawyer at Spratt, Caulder & Associates. The police spoke to Mr Spratt and Mr Caulder. Both gentlemen are in their mid-seventies and have never heard of anyone called Sabrina Warrington." Reggie frowned.

"Do you think they are covering for her?"

"No, I think she conned Dave. I think she arrived there just before Dave did and went inside with some excuse. When Kelvin and I were following Dave, they came out of the office almost immediately after Dave walked in."

"What about the clerk? Reggie asked.

"The only picture I have of him is by himself. There's no evidence to back up Dave's story that he was passing on the packages at all. All of the evidence points to Dave."

"But Dave wouldn't blow up his own pub." Reggie was adamant. "The police have to know that."

"The police say that by carefully limiting the size of the explosion, there was minimum structural damage," Stocky shrugged. "The majority of the damage in the pub is cosmetic. They say Dave was trying to kill two birds with one stone. He was removing evidence of his drug operation and could then use the insurance payout to refurbish the pub."

"The police must think Dave is very stupid," Reggie muttered.

"He is stupid! He's either a failed drug-manufacturing murderer, as the police think. Or, he fell hook line and sinker for a beautiful criminal, who has parcelled him up neatly and presented him to the police as her fall guy."

Reggie sank back against the pillows, staring up at the ceiling.

"So, it was all for nothing," she said quietly. "I got blown up and Dave is in an even more impossible situation than he was before." A tear slid down her cheek and she closed her eyes.

"Reggie I'm so sorry, don't cry," Stocky pleaded. He jumped to his feet and began pacing. "I'm not supposed to let you get upset. You need to focus on getting better."

He turned mid-pace as the door opened, fearful that Reggie's Mum would return and see her crying. Jake's head popped into view.

"Your mum said I could come in for few minutes." He took in the emotionally charged scene. "Is now a bad time?" He looked towards Stocky who grabbed his hand like a drowning man finding a life raft.

"No," Stocky gushed. Totally perfect timing. You can cheer her up." He squeezed Jake's hand. "Mrs Quinn can never know I made her cry." Stocky released Jake's hand and sprinted out through the doorway.

After a puzzled glance at Stocky's quickly retreating figure, Jake turned and focused his attention on Reggie.

"Hi!" Jake smiled his devastating smile. He moved the visitor's chair closer to the bed and sat down. Reggie was suddenly acutely aware of how awful she must look, and now he'd seen her crying.

As if reading her thoughts, he reached and gently brushed the tear off her cheek.

"Don't cry," he said. "I've seen you look way worse," he grinned. Reggie laughed, immediately feeling better. It was true. In most of their encounters Reggie had been suffering a major wardrobe malfunction.

"The nurse outfit was my favourite," he teased. "But after seeing the picture of you last night I may have a new favourite." Reggie was confused for a moment; then she remembered.

"Of course, the picture your friends took," she blushed. It seemed like a lifetime ago that Stella had taken the picture of her, squashed between the three firemen. Jake took her hand and gently held it between both of his.

"You rescued me," she said simply. "Thank you."

"I did - again!" He smiled, his eyes twinkling. "I've only known you for two weeks and I've already picked you up, unconscious, and carried you out of a building, not once but twice. If this was a fairy-tale you would be a very accident prone princess." Colour flooded her face. He squeezed her hand gently. "Reggie Quinn, you are a really complicated lady," he said.

"I never used to be," she whispered, her voice catching with emotion.

"What is it?" he asked quietly. "What's the problem between you and Stocky? Tell me, maybe I can help."

Jake listened thoughtfully while Reggie went over their whole investigation. She talked through all of the dead ends and the theories that had led them to go back to the bar last night. As she talked, the burden began to lift. She realised that finding justice for Caroline, and worrying about Dave's future, weren't responsibilities she had to shoulder alone. It wasn't enough, but the fact that she was trying had to count for something. At the conclusion of her recount Reggie leaned back to rest her pounding head.

"Well, I can definitely help you with one thing," said Jake. Reggie opened her eyes hopefully.

"You can?" she asked.

"Yes. You said that you and Stocky were supposed to go and see Mandy today. I think you can definitely cross her of your suspect list. She's going out with the owner of the gym I go to. He chats to me sometimes when I go in. He told me that he and Mandy are both the jealous type and are both sick of feeling insecure in relationships. They decided to take all the doubt away by both getting that app that allows you to track where the other person is. He said it changed their relationship."

"So they basically stalk each other the whole time?" asked Reggie. "It doesn't sound healthy to me."

"Whatever works," Jake shrugged. "The point is that I don't think Mandy would be keen to sign up to something like that if she was trying to kill her ex. It will also be really easy to check on my friend's phone, to see if she was anywhere near Caroline's house the day she was poisoned."

"I've been thinking," Reggie frowned. "After everything that's happened I think that Caroline's murder has to be something to do with Sabrina," she said.

"You think Sabrina killed Caroline?" Jake asked.

"I think it's too big a coincidence otherwise. Besides, Sabrina is already involved in the illegal production of meth and was happy to potentially risk lives when she blew up the pub. Murder is a small step away from all that."

"But what's her motive?" asked Jake.

"That's the problem," Reggie replied. "I can't think of one. I was there when she found out Dave was married. She was definitely surprised and she really didn't care."

"So it wasn't Jealousy," said Jake.

"No, definitely not jealousy," Reggie confirmed. "In fact Sabrina seems to enjoy controlling and manipulating men. Finding out that Dave was cheating on his wife to be with her would be a bonus." She leaned her head back again and closed her eyes. "I know I'm missing something. There must be a connection. I just can't find it."

They sat in silence for a while, both trying to make sense of the situation. Eventually Jake spoke.

"The way I see it, right now, you have no way of connecting Sabrina to either the meth lab or the murder." Reggie winced.

"Yep we've got nothing."

"From what you've told me, quite a few people have helped you with different parts of the investigation."

"Yeah," Reggie agreed. "Teresa's been great with all the police stuff. Kelvin helped Stocky when he was following Dave. Stella was great with information and introductions to the exes and now of course you," she gestured towards him.

"Exactly! Everyone knows his or her own part of what has happened. Why don't you get everyone to meet up? You could go over the whole case and discuss all the evidence. Then between all of us maybe we can come up with a new angle or something else that will help prove Sabrina is involved."

The more Reggie thought about it, the more she liked the idea. Anything was better than continually churning the whole mess around in her head by herself and coming up with nothing.

There was definitely strength in numbers. And it was a real plus that Jake was counting himself as one of their team.

"It will need to be soon," she said. "I'll talk to Stocky and then as soon as I'm allowed out of here we can arrange something."

Reggie was relieved to see the nurse walk in holding pain medication in her hand. Reggie's parents followed closely behind.

"We have fantastic news," her mum announced brightly. "The doctor needs to check you over again and then if all is well we can take you home later on today," Reggie managed an exhausted smile. It would be great to get out of the hospital room and be able to relax at home.

"Now don't you worry about anything," her mum beamed. "I spoke to the lovely head teacher at your school; she was very understanding."

"She was?" Reggie was astounded.

"She asked if there was anything you needed and said she would find someone to cover your class tomorrow. She said she hoped you would be better for the Roman trip later in the week. She told me that the whole thing was your idea. Very impressive darling." She lent down and kissed Reggie on the cheek. "I don't always show it, but I am proud of you, you know. I need to give you more credit for the wonderful woman you have grown up to be."

Reggie smiled weakly, amazed and a little overwhelmed by her mum's emotional outpouring. Reggie had almost become used to being the family disappointment. Hiding her emotions, she swallowed the painkillers and passed the empty cup back to the nurse.

I'm feeling much better already," Reggie assured her mum. "I could probably do with a short nap now though. Jake, do you think you could talk to Stocky and arrange the meeting for me please?" She settled back onto the comfy pillows.

"Of course, I'll go and ring him now." Jake jumped up, said his goodbyes and headed out of the room. Reggie was able to fully relax for the first time in a long while. She drifted off into a blissfully untroubled sleep. Her parents settled themselves into their chairs to watch over her and wait.

CHAPTER 26

It was decided that the meeting should take place in Cairn so that Reggie wouldn't have far to travel. Stocky suggested they meet at one of the pubs in the town, as Monday night would be quiet and pubs were unlikely to be busy. Jake came up with the Narrowboat Inn next to the canal. The old pub had a small taproom bar at the back. If they could take over that room they would be unlikely to be overheard. The decision made, Stocky set about contacting everyone to arrange the meeting. He was hopeful that Dave's bail hearing would be on Monday morning. His lawyer was confident that bail would be granted and he would be released by Monday afternoon. Stocky mentally checked off the names: Reggie, Stella, Teresa, Kelvin, Dave, Jake and himself. That made seven. Surely between them they could come up with something new!

Reggie spent most of Monday attached to the comfortable couch in her lounge. She wore her favourite flannelette pyjamas and alternated between watching movies on TV and snoozing. Reggie's mum had taken the day off work to fuss over her and Reggie wasn't allowed to lift a finger. This arrangement initially worked well. Reggie was still feeling delicate and her head tender. Being wrapped up in a cocoon of blankets and plied with warm drinks and tasty treats was a welcome display of motherly concern. By the afternoon however, Reggie's pain levels had lessened and she began to focus more on the upcoming meeting. Her efforts to leave the couch were met with strenuous resistance by Elizabeth. Tempers began to flare as the frustrated patient clashed with the under-appreciated nurse.

By the time Reggie's Dad arrived home, an uneasy truce had been established. Elizabeth was calming her nerves with a pot of tea in the kitchen. Reggie, meanwhile, had retreated upstairs to her bed. She was busily making notes for the meeting later on. It was important to make sure that all aspects of the investigation were discussed. She couldn't shake the feeling that the clue they needed was hidden somewhere in the details.

Shortly before 7pm Reggie made the effort to look a little more presentable. Before she'd left the hospital, nurses had changed the bandage covering her stitches. Thankfully they'd replaced it with a much smaller dressing. She still had to wait another day before washing her hair but at least she was now able to tie it back in a tidy ponytail. She gently pulled a pair of comfortable jeans over the cuts on her legs and chose a fitted shirt with buttons, so she wouldn't need to pull it over her head. Reggie rejected the idea of make up; you were supposed to look bad after surviving an explosion. At least she had survived, and all in one piece. Reggie refused to think about what could have happened. Instead she went downstairs in search of Stella and some painkillers.

"Come on, let's go," urged Stella. She grabbed her bag and keys and headed out through the door. Reggie rushed to catch up, ignoring the twinge in her head.

"Why are you so keen all of a sudden?" she shouted at Stella's back. "You thought the idea of Stocky and I investigating was a joke." Stella froze, then turned back to face Reggie. Her fierce expression stopped Reggie in her tracks.

"That was before some evil bitch almost killed my sister. I'm going to find her and make her pay." Reggie could see the rage simmering under the surface. She reached out and placed her hand on Stella's arm.

"It's over, I'm ok," she said gently.

"Just make sure you stay that way," Stella fumed.

Yanking her arm away Stella strode off towards her car. Reggie couldn't resist a tiny smile. Sisterly love ran deep. It was reassuring to know that despite all the bickering, Stella always had her back.

The Narrowboat Inn was a short journey from Reggie's house. Stella and Reggie had both, on more than one occasion made the walk home from there after closing time. Stella turned into the car park, her headlights illuminating the lime-washed building. Reggie loved the old pub. It had existed in various forms since the fifteen-hundreds. Dave had pulled in just ahead of them, so Stella chose the spot next to him. Reggie waved and was grabbed in a fierce bear hug as soon as she was within reach of him.

"Careful," Stella snapped. "She's injured." Dave gently released Reggie and stepped away.

"I'm so glad you are ok. I don't want anyone else to get hurt because of me." Reggie realised Stocky must have shared their new theory about Sabrina with him. She smiled reassuringly and linked arms with him.

"Come on Dave, I'm fine and it's definitely not your fault."

She led him decisively towards the entrance. It was odd she thought, that she was the one injured in the explosion, but it seemed she was going to be cast in the role of providing comfort and reassurance to her friends.

They were the first to arrive. Luckily the cosy taproom bar was empty. They pulled two of the round wooden tables together and arranged the heavy stools around them. Dave and Stella ordered drinks at the bar, leaving Reggie to gaze around the familiar room. The bar was a simply furnished practical space. The decoration consisted of a few rows of brasses hanging on leather straps next to the bar and a small collection of historical photos and drawings of the pub and canal through the ages, around the walls. Reggie's eyes were drawn to a photograph of an old narrowboat being pulled along the canal by a horse. Things moved at much slower pace back then. Life must have been so much simpler she thought wistfully.

Dave and Stella returned with the drinks and the others began to arrive. Jake was first. She responded to his wave with a grin and watched as Jake and Dave shook hands and hugged. Teresa arrived next. Out of uniform she looked younger and definitely more relaxed. Her long blond hair was down and shone in the bar lights as she ordered her drink. Stocky and Kelvin arrived together. Kelvin as usual looked like he had grabbed random black items of clothing off the floor of his bedroom. Today's T-shirt of choice sported a faded Guns N Roses logo and a mysterious food stain, possibly ketchup.

Reggie was pleased to see that Stocky had bought a folder and notebook. She reached down into her bag and placed her own notebook on the table. When everyone had settled themselves and their drinks at the tables, Stocky took care of the introductions.

Reggie noticed with dismay, the moment that Kelvin set eyes on Stella. His jaw dropped and he stared across the table with puppy like adoration. She nudged Stocky, who shrugged and sighed inwardly. He had seen this look on Kelvin before and knew there was nothing he could do to avoid the inevitable train wreck. If Stella had seen Kelvin staring she was doing an excellent job of ignoring it... for now.

Between them, Stocky and Reggie ran the meeting. They talked through the entire investigation, answering questions and listening to suggestions as they arose. Stocky jotted down notes of new ideas and insights as they occurred to people.

"So Mandy is definitely in the clear then?" asked Teresa.

Jake explained what he knew about Mandy's current relationship. Then Reggie explained the new theory about Sabrina.

"The problem is," she said, "that we have two separate crimes – the meth lab explosion and the murder, but nothing to link either one to Sabrina. In fact, we can't even link the two crimes together because we have absolutely no motive for why Sabrina would want to kill Caroline."

"She could easily have got the wine from me," said Dave. "I gave Sabrina a box with a few leftover bottles from Caroline's surprise party. I thought they were all white but when I think back, I was in a rush and grabbed a few bottles without checking."

"We know Sabrina doesn't drink red wine," said Stocky. "So that would be the obvious bottle to choose if you were going to send poisoned wine to someone."

"But we still don't know why!" Reggie was becoming frustrated. Jake reached across and squeezed her hand gently under the table.

"Look, why don't we take a break and get another drink," he said. He looked across at Stocky. "What have you got in the folder?" Stocky glanced down at the folder in front of him.

"That's just a copy of all the surveillance photos we took, he said dismissively."

"That's great," said Jake. "We'll get a drink, then pass around the pictures. It can't hurt." There were murmurs of general agreement and people began to move towards the bar. Kelvin leaned across to Reggie.

"Your sister is a goddess," he whispered loudly. "I feel like this is fate; I think I'm in love. I'm going to ask her out." He began to stand up but stopped when Reggie grabbed his wrist.

"I really wish you wouldn't do that," she urged. Kelvin sat down again thoughtfully.

"Why… are you worried about Stella? Do you think I'll break her heart?" he asked. Reggie was sure that Stella would likely break his face if he tried to make a move on her. Before she could reply he grabbed her hand. His expression was so sorrowful that she froze. "Do you think it will compromise the investigation?" he asked. "That's it isn't it. I'm being really selfish. If Stella and I are together we will only be able to think of ourselves and our love."

Reggie was stunned into silence. Jake nudged her and she managed a small nod. Kelvin smiled compassionately and patted Reggie's hand.

"I can wait if that's the case," he offered magnanimously. He stood up releasing Reggie's hand. "It will be just like Shakespeare," he said. "I'm so awesome at unrequited love."

"Do you think we should warn Stella," Jake whispered, when Kelvin was a safe enough distance away. Reggie's smile was sly.

"Definitely not. Where would the fun be in that? Besides," she added, "she'll eat him alive. At least let's give him the element of surprise."

The others returned to the table with fresh drinks and bags of crisps. Stella passed a Diet-Coke across the table to Reggie. Stocky opened up his folder and removed the pictures.

"These were taken when I was carrying out surveillance on Dave. I'm not sure how much use they will be," he apologised.
He split the photos into two piles and placed one in the centre of each table. People began to delve into the piles and look through them. Stella reached for one picture. She held it up, laughing.

"This one is still my favourite," she grinned. It was the picture of Dave waving at Stocky.

"Hey it was a steep learning curve," said Stocky defensively. "Dave never saw us the last time we followed him."

"That was because you had me and my awesome disguises," Kelvin said. Stocky rolled his eyes and was about to reply when Kelvin cut him off. "Let me see that!" He snatched a photo out of Teresa's hand. "I know that guy." He stared at the photo for a moment, trying to place the man. He nodded his head. "I definitely know this dude. He comes into Starbucks."
Dave looked over his shoulder at the picture.

"That's Paul, Sabrina's clerk," he confirmed. "He's the one who collected all the packages from me." Kelvin frowned, biting his lip thoughtfully.

"No," he eventually said, "that's not the name he uses." Kelvin continued to think… "Davis," he looked up triumphantly. "Davis is the name he gets me to write on his coffee."

"That could be his surname," Reggie joined in excitedly. "His name could be Paul Davis." She looked across at Teresa. "Now we have his name you could look him up on the police system, couldn't you?"

"Yes, I could do that tomorrow morning. That's no

problem," Teresa answered, her eyes lighting up at the prospect of a lead.

"No need my friend." Smiling smugly, Kelvin punched Teresa playfully in the arm. All eyes turned expectantly in his direction. "I knew I was good at this detective stuff." He smirked mysteriously at the group. Reggie's patience was at an end.

"Stop messing around!" She banged the table with her fist. "Tell us what you know," she demanded. "Do you know where he is?"

"No!" Kelvin saw Reggie's eyes narrow. "But, I know where he will be," he continued hurriedly. "The guy – Davis, comes into Starbucks every morning during the week, at around 8.30am for coffee. That's where he'll be tomorrow morning."

Kelvin sat back, satisfied that his news had awed the others into silence. Teresa recovered first and switched into professional mode.

"We can definitely use this information," she said. "Paul Davis is a person of interest in the meth lab inquiry. The police need to talk to him." She stood up. "I'm going to ring Sarge and see if he can contact Detective Inspector Andrews." She looked across the table at Stocky and Reggie. "Do you remember - he was the detective who interviewed you?" They nodded.

"He seemed like a pretty decent guy," said Stocky. Teresa moved towards the doorway, mobile phone in hand. "This is the break we have been looking for," Stocky was energised.

"If the police can find Paul Davis, we should be able to convince them that Dave was duped into passing on the packages." Dave cleared his throat- his cheeks tinged red.

"It still doesn't clear me of murder."

"But once the police have the Clerk he can lead them to Sabrina," said Reggie.

"You see it all the time on TV," Stocky agreed. "The first person arrested makes a deal and gives up the main guy."

"This is real life not TV," said Stella dismissively. I think we should wait and see what Teresa has to say when she comes back." There were murmurs of agreement from the group. The euphoric mood of a few moments ago deflated suddenly. Reggie wondered how Stella could always manage to do that with just a few words. While they waited, the group quietly passed around the remainder of the surveillance photos, hoping for another unexpected clue. Finally, Teresa returned and there was a definite bounce in her step.

"I have good news," she announced. "Sarge spoke to Detective Inspector Andrews. He's very keen to talk to Paul Davis. They ran his name and he's wanted in connection with other crimes."

"I knew it," Stocky slapped the table, rattling the glasses. "It is just like on TV." He cast a meaningful glance in Stella's direction.

"Shush," said Reggie impatiently. "Let her finish!"

"Because of his record," Teresa continued, "they are also interested in anyone associated with him, especially anyone further up the chain – like Sabrina." Stocky opened his mouth to comment, closing it quickly when Reggie's elbow connected sharply with his ribs. "They have come up with a plan," announced Teresa, her eyes sparkling brightly. "They are going to wait for him to show up at Starbucks and then follow him for a while to see if he leads them to Sabrina. If nothing comes of that they'll pick him up and take him in for interview. And the best bit of all…" Teresa was now quivering with anticipation. "Because I brought the information to them I get to ride along." She sat back on her stool, feet tapping with nervous energy. "This is going to be so good for my career."

Dave stared numbly at Teresa. It took a while for the ramifications of the police plan to sink in.

"You mean… I could be ok? This could all be over?" he asked quietly. Relief coursed through him releasing the knot of tied emotions that had been slowly squeezing ever tighter. Light headed, he rested his arms on the table and placed his forehead on the cool wooden surface. Embarrassed, Teresa gently patted his back. A moment ago she had been so selfishly overjoyed at the prospect of advancing her career that she'd forgotten about

Dave and his pain and loss.

"So what now?" asked Stocky. Teresa was once again the trained professional. She took her hand off Dave's back and sat up, straightening her shoulders.

"I have to report to Stapwell branch at 7am. As soon as I find out anything I will let you know. I'm really hoping for a positive outcome." She looked around the group. "We wouldn't be able to do any of this tomorrow if you hadn't all played your part."

Dave sat up and ran a hand through his hair. His emotions were safely under control.

"I can't thank you all enough," he said. It means so much to me that you have all stuck by me." Stella squeezed his shoulder.

"Hopefully tomorrow will be the end of it all and you can begin to try and move forward," she said. "Then you can fix up the bar and we can get back to work."

"Meeting up like this has helped far more than I could have imagined," said Stocky. "I'll make sure that all of you are kept in the loop. As soon as Teresa gives me any information I'll send a group message to all of you."

The meeting broke up after that; people finished drinks and began to drift off to their cars.

Stocky reflected on the evening as he drove home. He had to admit that he was amazed. He'd gone along with the idea of a big group meeting because it seemed to make Reggie feel better. He'd secretly thought that it was a waste of everyone's time. Who would have thought that his terrible surveillance pictures would have been useful, or that Kelvin of all people would come up with the name and location of the clerk? It was actually looking like he might close his first case and bring some money into his uncle's business. Stocky smiled as he visualised the scene. His uncle would have to eat his words and his mum would be forced to stop talking about jobs at McDonalds. Stocky checked his watch 9.30pm. In just over twelve hours he should have some news. Teresa seemed confident. Stocky really hoped she was right.

CHAPTER 27

Reggie could, and probably should have taken another day off school. But today was the day before her Roman school trip and she wanted to make sure her darlings were ready. They greeted her with the excitement of a long lost relative. Then proceeded to bombard her with questions about her injuries and the explosion. When all the questions had been exhausted, they moved on to petulant moaning about the injustice of being left with a supply teacher the previous day. Reggie soothed ruffled feathers and apologised again and again. She'd been warned at teaching college that classes were very loyal to their teacher and could feel abandoned when a teacher was away sick or on a course.

Reggie hid a smile as one child outlined how outrageously the supply teacher had treated him. Reggie knew the retired teacher was a grandmotherly lady who planned really fun activities, and the children adored spending time her. Reggie made sympathetic noises and patted backs until everyone seemed satisfied that their complaints had been heard.

It took a lot longer than usual to settle the class and they had only just begun their morning spelling games and activities when Stocky's message came through.

The police followed Paul Davis but no sign of Sabrina. They picked him up. Going to interview him.

That seemed fairly positive thought Reggie. If Stocky was right, he would cut a deal and then the police could forget about Dave and focus on tracking down Sabrina.

Reggie turned her focus back to her Roman trip. The education centre had sent some pre-visit activities. There were Roman soldiers to cut out and colour in, and weapons to attach. The class embraced the activity with gusto. Reggie had known it would be a winner. The girls loved to colour in and the boys were in their element choosing and cutting out Roman spears, swords and shields. The morning flew by. The children ran off happily to enjoy play time and Reggie found herself humming as she wandered around the class collecting stray pencils and scissors.

"There you are. You're back then," barked a voice from the doorway.

Reggie turned to see her colleague and so called mentor standing with arms folded, aiming a frosty glare in her direction. Veronica was wearing her usual comfortable black trousers and sensible shoes. Today she had matched them with a knitted sweater. It's shapeless fit managed to make Veronica's bulky form look even larger and more intimidating. Reggie forced a polite smile.

"Good morning Veronica." Veronica ignored the pleasant greeting.

"I've come to see if you have completed all the necessary paperwork for our trip tomorrow."

Reggie knew that as her mentor Veronica should have gone over all of this with her and helped her complete the necessary forms. She also knew that Veronica was looking for any means necessary to discredit her with the Headmistress. This would be an excellent opportunity to make Reggie look bad. Luckily Reggie had sought out advice from Kate, and had double-checked her paperwork with the school secretary.

"Yes, I think I'm ready for the trip," Reggie smiled sweetly.

"What about the health and safety forms?" Veronica demanded.

"Done!" Reggie's smile widened.

"Risk assessment forms?" Veronica ground out between gritted teeth.

"Done!" Reggie was beginning to enjoy this.

"Permission slips collated and parent helpers confirmed?" Veronica spat out. Reggie could see Veronica was grasping at straws. This wasn't going the way she had intended.

"Done and done," Reggie beamed.

"Don't forget first aid kits and sick buckets," Veronica snorted. "No one wants to be covered in vomit!" Visibly annoyed, she spun on her heel and marched out.

"Thanks for all your help," Reggie called sweetly after her. Reggie took a moment to enjoy the victory. "Reggie 1 – Bitch-Witch 0," she laughed.

School was over for the day and Reggie still hadn't heard any more from Stocky. Hopefully no news is good news she mused. Perhaps there was a lot for Paul Davis to talk about. Teresa had mentioned that he was linked to other crimes. Reggie turned off the main road and followed the curves of her street around to her driveway. Stocky's car was parked outside her house and he was standing leaning against the passenger window. He didn't have the look of someone bringing happy news.

"Hi, is everything ok?" Reggie asked hopefully. Stocky pushed away from the car and walked slowly down the drive.

"No, it's terrible. Come on, I'll tell you inside."

Stocky waited until they were both sat at the kitchen table. He wasn't really sure where to start.

"Is Dave in the clear? What happened?" Reggie prompted.

"Davis didn't take the deal. In fact, he swears he's never heard of Sabrina."

"How can that be? We have photos," Reggie asked.

"Not of the two of them together," answered Stocky.

"But what about the packages?" Reggie asked. "Did he admit to collecting them from Dave?" Stocky sighed and spoke quietly.

"Yes he did." Reggie was confused.

"I don't get it. That's got to be good for us, right?"

"Paul Davis admitted to collecting the packages from Dave because he says he works for Dave. He says Dave is the big boss running the drug operation and that he is Dave's assistant."

Reggie stared open mouthed. Of all the outcomes she could have predicted this hadn't even crossed her mind.

"Reg, Dave is totally screwed. Paul Davis has made a deal with the police. He will get a reduced sentence if he testifies against Dave in court." Reggie boiled with anger.

"It's all Sabrina. He's doing it for her. He's another man she's got twisted up under her spell. It's disgusting. He's falling on his sword to protect her."

"Whatever his reason, he's taking Dave down with him," said Stocky

"There must be something we can do?" Reggie asked desperately.

"The only way out of this would be to find Sabrina and get her to confess," said Stocky miserably.

"And she's disappeared," said Reggie. Stocky nodded.

"Now that the police have Dave all tied up neatly in a bow for court they couldn't care less about Sabrina."

"Poor Dave," said Reggie. "How is he?"

"He's not doing well. He's spoken to his lawyer and he suggested Dave plead guilty to make a deal for less years in prison."

"But he's innocent!" Reggie felt hopeless. Stocky ran his hand agitatedly through his hair.

"With Paul Davis testifying against him, Dave will go to prison. If there is a way to reduce his sentence then maybe he should take it." It was a miserable thought. Reggie fetched them both a drink from the fridge and they sat in brooding silence, quietly sipping. Defeated, Reggie looked up.

"Everything we have done has made Dave's situation worse," she said bitterly. "We had the pictures and the police used that to link him to the meth lab. We found the clerk and now they are using him to put Dave in prison."

"Yeah. Dave would be better off if he had never met us," agreed Stocky, his face a grey mask of misery.

"I wish there was something we could do," Reggie

mumbled.

"Me too!" Stocky's troubled eyes looked across at Reggie, and then lowered to stare morosely into his drink. Without Sabrina, there was nothing anyone could do.

CHAPTER 28

"Seven, eight, nine, ten…" Reggie carefully counted the children onto the bus. It was a beautiful sunny morning, the perfect day to be marching around Roman walls. After a restless night's sleep Reggie had resolved to push her concerns about Dave to the back of her mind - for now. She needed to make today's trip a success. The disco had won her a reprieve with the head teacher and if today went well her job would be secure - for a while at least. Reggie had left nothing to chance. Everything had been checked and double-checked. She had even made sure that all children who had ever felt motion sickness were seated at the front of the bus, near the sick buckets. She checked the list on her clipboard one final time and allowed herself a small smile.

"We seem to be ready," growled Veronica begrudgingly, from behind her back. Reggie jumped and turned to face her.

"Yes. Looks like we are ready to go." Reggie smiled politely.

"I've looked over your arrangements." Veronica was using her sergeant major tone. "There are just a couple of changes. I will have Kate on my bus and you can have the extra parents."

"Oh, ok." Reggie tried to hide her disappointment. She had been looking forward to a chat with Kate on the way. It would also have been reassuring to have another teacher to back her up while she supervised a busload of excited children for the first time.

"And don't forget the snack on the way," Veronica added.

"But, I thought we don't let the children eat on the bus?" Reggie was sure that rule that was strictly adhered to.

"For goodness sake Regina." Veronica enunciated each syllable slowly, her tone heavy with malice. "We won't arrive until after the children's morning snack time. Do you want to have to deal with all the angry parents who say we have starved their children?"

Her finger poked accusingly at Reggie's chest. Reggie fought the urge to grab it and snap it off. She felt sorry for the children in Veronica's class. Being spoken to in this way, day in and day out would put a huge dent in your self-esteem, not to mention what it would do to your love of learning.

"If that's what you think we should do then of course I'll do it." Reggie replied, trying hard not to grit her teeth.

"I'm not saying they should eat everything in their lunch box." Veronica rolled her eyes. "A small snack should do it."

Message delivered, Veronica strode off towards the other bus. Reggie was sure she heard her mutter "imbecile" under her breath as she moved away. Reggie straightened her shoulders. She would not allow Bitch–Witch to ruin her perfectly planned day. Reggie forced a smile and climbed on to the bus. One final count and some quick messages and they were on their way.

Twenty minutes later, disaster struck. Up until this point, the noise level had been bearable. Lots of good-natured chatter and the occasional excited shriek. Only once had Reggie felt the need to stand up and tell the children to lower their voices. Now suddenly, half the bus seemed to be shrieking and the other half groaning. Reggie leapt out of her seat and launched along the aisle towards the back of the bus, the motion of the vehicle swinging her from seat to seat. News of the disaster had travelled fast. She had only moved a couple of rows back when a girl shouted across to her.

"Miss, Jonathan has been sick. It stinks." Reggie swore under her breath. She turned and lurched as quickly as she could to collect the stack of buckets and bags from the front. The stench hit her well before she reached ground zero. It was the unmistakable small of vomit with the distinctive tang of chocolate orange added in for good measure. Her stomach flipped in revulsion. Reggie quickly took in the scene. A very green Jonathan was holding his stomach and leaning over the side of the seat. Luckily the vomit had missed him and was sitting in an odorous pile on the floor. Next to him, his seat partner, was holding his hand over his mouth and dry retching. Oh my God thought Reggie. It's a vomit chain reaction. She thrust a bucket into the arms of each boy and turned to the people around them.

"Who else feels sick?" she shouted. A sea of hands shot up. Speedily she gave out the remaining buckets and extra bags.

"Hold your nose and breathe through your mouth," she ordered. "Then you won't smell it." She turned to Jonathan, who was still looking green. "What happened," she asked gently, hiding her anger as best as she could. "I thought people who get sick were going to sit at the front." She fought hard to keep her tone mild. Jonathan looked up miserably.

"I don't get sick usually. I ate my snack like you said I could and then I felt bad." Reggie's anger melted.

"I'm sorry you feel bad." She rubbed his back gently. "What on earth did you eat to make you feel so ill?" she asked.

"A chocolate orange snack bar." Well that explained the smell thought Reggie.

"I'm sorry Miss Quinn." Jonathan was near to tears.

"It's not your fault, Jonathan." She smiled down at him. "I'll get this cleaned up and then we will all feel better."

Reggie staggered back along the swaying aisle to collect the cleaning supplies. She had a very good idea who was to blame for the vomit and had the feeling she had been deliberately set up. Reggie would need to watch her back from now on. She shoved her hands into a pair of gloves and grabbed more bags and the cleaning supplies. As an afterthought she removed one of the laundry-pegs she'd attached to her clipboard and placed it on her nose. "Right, let's do this," she muttered and headed back into the disaster zone, a one-woman clean-up crew.

The coaches pulled in to the education centre car park and children gulped hungrily at the fresh air as they disembarked.

Reggie joined in, filling and refilling her lungs with relief. Kate pulled her to one side.

"What the hell happened?" she asked. Reggie quickly explained the eventful bus journey. Kate shook her head.

"Reggie, it's school trip rule number one." She said. "Nobody eats on the bus!"

"I know that, but Veronica said -" Reggie began desperately. Understanding dawned on Kate's face and she interrupted.

"That woman is a bitch and a bully," she said fiercely. "I told you that she made life miserable for me and the other new teacher last year. Maybe it's time for us all to team up and report her to Ms Darwin."

"What is her problem?" Reggie asked. Kate shrugged.

"Perhaps splitting up with her husband made her so miserable she thinks the rest of the world should suffer too. Or maybe she's just plain evil." They moved back towards the waiting lines of children. "Be careful," whispered Kate. "Once she's got her sights set on you, she won't give up."

They divided the children into their assigned groups and began the activities at the education centre. Reggie relaxed as she watched her children try on costumes, prepare Roman food and role-play a Roman feast. This was what teaching was supposed to be about. Her children were having an amazing time and learning a lot in the process. After a quick lunch and a look at some Roman innovations it was time for the highlight of the trip. The children cheered as the Roman Centurion marched into the room. He was dressed in full Roman army uniform, complete with sword and shield. The children listened spellbound, as he talked about his life in the Roman army. He passed his weapons around the group and a couple of lucky children were able to act out a play-fight. When it was time to begin marching, he taught the children the Latin words for left and right. Soon everyone was chanting "sinister, dexter," as they practised marching around the room.

Reggie couldn't fault the enthusiasm of the Centurion. He

was deeply immersed in his character.

"Halt," he commanded. The children obediently stood still. "We must do our duty for Caesar and for Rome. Today we march on the city walls of Deva Victrix to protect our town from its enemies. Are you with me?" The children let out a cheer. The Centurion held his sword in the air. "Advance!" he yelled. The children followed him out in two lines. He led them along a path and up a flight of ancient, worn steps until they all stood on top of the Roman town walls.

The walls provided an excellent view of the town beneath. Reggie could also see how over the centuries the town had expanded well past the original walled boundary. Reggie knew that for this final part of the day the Centurion would march them around the walls, stopping to explain key places of interest - like the Roman baths, along the way. Reggie looked back over her shoulder. Veronica and Kate's classes had finished the climb up on to the walls. The Centurion sensed their readiness and began the chant.

"Sinister, dexter, sinister, dexter," he bellowed. The children quickly joined in and the procession marched joyfully along. Reggie cast another look over her shoulder. Veronica was as sour-faced as ever but Kate was laughing and joining in the chant with her class. Her long brown corkscrew curls were bouncing up and down merrily as she marched. Reggie relaxed. Today had been a huge success. She was even looking forward to sharing her photos with Ms Darwin during the inevitable debriefing session back at school later.

As she marched, Reggie looked down into the busy shopping area. It was full of little boutique shops and restaurants. She resolved to come back and treat herself to a shopping day once her financial crisis was over. Across the square an attractive couple emerged from a tiny bistro. They kissed and then parted ways. The beautifully dressed woman turned as she crossed the square. Her hair glinted in the sunlight but it was her smile that captured Reggie's attention. Reggie stopped, nearly tripping several marchers. They skipped out of her way and Reggie stepped out of line, leaning over the edge of the wall for a better view.

It was her! It was definitely Sabrina. Sabrina was strolling towards the exit at the far corner of the square. Her lunch partner was still standing outside the bistro engrossed in his phone screen. Reggie had to act fast. Quickly she pushed through the marching line to the front. She sprinted past the Centurion towards the next set of exit steps.

"Don't worry she called back. I'll catch up with you. I've spotted someone I know."

Reggie dashed down the steps, pausing briefly at the bottom to check her target was still in sight. A quick glance along the marching line revealed Veronica's furious face.

"What are you doing?" bellowed Veronica. "You can't leave. Come back."

"Sorry, I won't be long. I'll catch up with you," Reggie replied, eyes never leaving Sabrina's back.

Thankful for her sensible boots Reggie set off at a jog towards the bistro. Almost past the bistro she changed her mind and paused for a moment. Sabrina was still twenty metres away from the corner of the square. Reggie had a few seconds to spare.

"Excuse me," she panted. The man looked up from his phone, curious at the breathless interruption.

"How do you know that lady you were with? It's really important," she urged. The man smiled.

"Felicity and I met at my café on the other side of the square." Reggie's eyes darted quickly in the direction he pointed. Café Zoe was nestled next to a pretty flowerbed. Small tables and chairs were arranged either side of the doorway, where hanging baskets continued the floral theme. "Do you know her?" he asked, still smiling.

"Yes I think so," Reggie answered. Her eyes were back on Sabrina's retreating figure. She only had a few more moments before Sabrina would reach the corner and make a turn. If Reggie didn't get after her she would lose her. "Look this is going to sound odd," she said, acting on a hunch. "But have you done anything to help her out recently?" she asked quickly.

"Why yes," he said, surprise in his tone. "Felicity has had some asbestos problems with her storage facility. I'm letting her use my empty warehouse until I sell it."

Reggie had no time to dwell on this new information. In the corner of the square Sabrina was turning left. She was going to lose her. She left the bewildered man and sprinted away. Reggie focused all her energy on reaching the point where Sabrina had last been visible. She arrived, breathless, but in time to see Sabrina make her next turn. She was heading into a more industrial area of town. Reggie followed carefully, keeping as much distance as she could. Internally her mind was racing. Dave wasn't the only one, she thought. Sabrina was pulling the same con on the café guy and perhaps lots of other men too. Café guy knew her as Felicity. She could be using any number of fake names.

The path Sabrina had taken opened out into a row of warehouses. Sabrina stopped to rummage in her handbag, so Reggie quickly ducked behind a skip. She watched Sabrina put on a pair of expensive looking leather driving gloves, and then watched her walk over to the first warehouse. Reggie was thankful she still had her phone in her pocket. She grabbed it, zoomed in and took pictures of Sabrina unlocking the padlock and opening the door.

Once Sabrina was inside, Reggie ran up for a closer look. She could see that there were windows around the side of the building but when she got there it was impossible to see anything. They had all been thoroughly covered from the inside. Frustrated, Reggie retreated back to the relative safety of the skip. She needed to do something but she also knew that if she wanted to keep her job she needed to quickly re-join the school trip. It was an impossible situation. Grabbing her phone, she dialled Teresa's number. She explained her predicament and gave a quick recap of her conversation with café guy.

"Wow Reggie, that's amazing luck finding Sabrina. Get out of there now and get back to your trip," Teresa instructed. "Leave the rest to me and send me the pictures as soon as you can."

Reggie could tell that Teresa was fired up and ready for action. Last time she had passed information on it had resulted in her having a ride along. With any luck, by the time Reggie got back to school Teresa would have Sabrina safely locked up in a cell at the police station.

Reggie calculated that the Roman visitor centre was a short walk from where she was. After a couple of turns she was pleased to see the buses and the children lined up in front of them. As she approached, Veronica broke away from the group and headed to meet her.

"You are finished," she hissed. "When we get back I'm going straight to Ms Darwin. You broke all the rules on adult to child ratios and put your class in danger."

"Look, I'm really sorry," said Reggie desperately. "I know I shouldn't have left the trip. It was an emergency. I really am sorry, and I know I need to make it up to you somehow." Veronica snorted.

"I don't want your apology, I want you gone! I knew sooner or later you'd mess up badly enough. I just needed to wait." Reggie felt the anger welling up inside.

"Just what is your problem with me? I have been nothing but nice to you. You never even gave me a chance!"

"You try teaching for thirty years and then watching all these flighty girls who think they know everything about teaching come breezing into school, with their laughing and joking and new ideas. Education is a serious business." Veronica folded her arms across her chest, a sneer fixed on her lips.

Reggie realised that apologising wasn't going to help. If she wanted her career to survive this trip then she needed to push back and go on the offensive. She stood up straight, matching Veronica's pose.

"I can't stop you from going to Ms Darwin," Reggie spoke quietly. "You need to know that if you decide to take this further then I will too."

"Ha, you have no credibility," Veronica laughed. "Nobody

would believe your word over mine." Reggie's insides were churning but she forced her expression into a benign smile.

"I've recently made some new friends on staff and they aren't happy with the way you treated them last year. After the 'snack time' stunt you pulled on the bus this morning-" Reggie noticed a tinge of colour around Veronica's cheekbones. She realised with relief that her words were having an effect, "-the teachers are about ready to go to Ms Darwin themselves," she finished.

Reggie watched Veronica's face as she took in this new turn of events. Her mouth gaped. Anger, frustration, surprise and even fear took its turn to paint over the canvas of her face. Reggie pressed on, hoping to force a compromise from her reluctant colleague.

"The way I see it, you've got two choices," she said. "You can accept my apology and know that I owe you, or we can all go to Ms Darwin and nobody will come out of this looking good – especially you." Reggie stood firmly in place watching hopefully for a positive sign. Veronica was motionless for a while. Her vivid red face the only outward sign of inner turmoil.

"OK," she said eventually. "You owe me and this is what I want. For the rest of this term you can do all of my playground duties every week." She glared at Reggie, who inwardly sighed but nodded. "And if anybody asks why you are doing it, you'll tell them you want to pay me back for all of my help and guidance so far this year."

"I can do that," Reggie replied carefully.

"That's not all," Veronica continued. "I want you to run two lunchtime fitness trainings each week for my netball team. It will help get them competition ready."

"I can do that too." Reggie held out her hand. Reluctantly Veronica shook it.

"Reggie, this does not mean we are friends." Veronica's cold stare met Reggie's quizzical glance. She turned abruptly and strode back towards the waiting children.

Reggie trailed along behind thanking her lucky stars. She

had hoped her first year of teaching would be a collection of successes and achievements. Instead it seemed to be following a pattern of career ending near misses. Her children were lined up patiently waiting for Reggie to count them onto the bus. One of the girls grabbed her arm and squeezed it. Reggie looked down.

"I had a great day, thanks Miss Quinn," she said shyly. "The marching was the best bit."

"Thanks Rachel," Reggie smiled down at her. "I'm glad you enjoyed it." The small hand grabbed at her arm again. "What is it Rachel?" Reggie asked. Rachel pointed across to where Kate was waving her arms, desperately trying to attract Reggie's attention.

"I think Miss Shepherd wants you," Amy giggled. Reggie mimed that she would message Kate on the bus. Kate gave the thumbs up and disappeared inside. Reggie turned back to her children.

"Right then, let's get you onto the bus. One, two three, four…"

CHAPTER 29

Reggie was desperate for news of Sabrina. She rang Teresa as soon as she arrived home. The news was disappointing.

"I can't tell you anything yet," Teresa insisted. "But I can say that your information has been very helpful and we are acting on it."

"That's it?" Reggie asked. "That's all I get?" After the action of earlier in the day Reggie had been hoping for results. Teresa took pity on her.

"Look Reg," she said sympathetically, "As soon as I can tell you something, I will. You need to go into the Stapwell branch tomorrow after school to make a statement about what you witnessed today. After that, Detective Inspector Andrews wants to talk to you."

Reggie felt a glimmer of hope that she hadn't been permanently shut out of the loop.

"Can I take Stocky?" she asked hopefully.

"Sure," said Teresa. "He can't be in the room when you make your statement but I'm pretty sure that Detective Inspector Andrews would like to talk to him too."

Time crawled by on Thursday. After the excitement of the school trip the previous day, the children were listless and hard to motivate. It turned out that both Veronica and Reggie had playground duty at playtime that morning. Reggie had to plead with a colleague to swap with her so that she could cover Veronica's duty in the morning and then do her own at lunchtime. Her old friend drizzle, made a return visit during the lunchtime duty slot. There was no way she was going to lose all the good will she had earned at the disco and Roman trip by calling wet playtime. By the end of the school day she was still slightly damp. She'd tied up her frizzy hair in a bun, using a florescent pink, tasselled hair tie – borrowed from Rachel Smith.

The only highlight in an otherwise dismal day had occurred before school even started. When Ms Darwin had called her into her office, Reggie had felt sure that Veronica had reneged on their agreement. With heavy steps she made her way to the seat in front of the imposing oak desk. It occurred to Reggie that however difficult this meeting would be, telling her parents she had been fired would be one hundred times worse. Reggie was surprised to find Ms Darwin full of praise for her efforts and organisation.

"I think we can add this to the list of outside school opportunities that we offer Year Three children every year," Ms Darwin smiled. "You are beginning to exhibit signs of the potential I saw in you at your interview," she said. "In fact, Mrs Barkwich went so far as to say that you didn't do a terrible job!" She saw Reggie's resigned expression. "Believe me," she continued, eyes twinkling with mirth, "that is high praise coming from Veronica."

Stocky was waiting for Reggie in the school car park at 3.30pm. It was easier to head into Stapwell together and Reggie was happy to sit back and let Stocky drive.

"How's Dave doing today?" she asked.

"He's been a lot more positive since he found out that you'd seen Sabrina." Stocky glanced across at Reggie. "I'm worried that we've given him new hope, when it may well come to nothing again."

"I know," she agreed. "It's so frustrating not knowing what's going on. Did you manage to get anything out of Teresa?"

"Nope," Stocky shook his head. "She clammed up tight as soon as I asked."

"Well at least Detective Inspector Andrews wants to see us. That's got to be a good sign, don't you think?" asked Reggie.

"I'm not so sure," said Stocky. "Maybe he wants to give us an official warning for meddling in police business."

Reggie sat back and brooded. A sombre mood settled over the car. She tried hard to remain positive but if recent experience was anything to go by, they were doomed. Every single time they had found evidence or thought they had made a breakthrough in the case, the outcome had been disastrous.

Stocky pulled into the police station car park. The Stapwell police station was a fairly new, purpose-built structure. It had the appearance of a sleek office building, built to suit the needs of the modern police force. The reception area was spacious, light and airy. They gave their names to the receptionist and they were shown through to a waiting room, complete with large fish tank and views of a courtyard garden. Reggie helped herself to a cup of coffee from the machine and chose a plush couch to sit on. It was a stark contrast to the broken plastic chairs Teresa had offered them. Stocky sat comfortably next to her and picked up a newspaper from the stylish coffee table.

"No wonder Teresa hates working at the Cairn police station. This place makes it look like a ruin," he said, echoing Reggie's thoughts. They didn't have long to wait before the familiar face of Detective Sergeant North appeared in the doorway.

"Hi," he smiled at both of them. "Reggie, I'm going to take your statement and then D.I. Andrews will talk to both of you. He ushered Reggie into a small interview room and Reggie reported the events of the previous day. It didn't take her long. She recapped seeing the couple at the bistro, her hurried conversation with the café owner and then what she had witnessed at the warehouse. She mentioned Sabrina wearing gloves, the photos she had taken of Sabrina unlocking the door and being unable to see in through the covered windows. When she had finished, Detective Sergeant North smiled.

"Thanks Reggie, that ties in with everything else we have." Before Reggie could ask any of the many questions whirling around in her head he stood up. "I'll take you to see D.I Andrews now. I bet you and Stocky have a lot of questions for him. Reggie smiled ruefully. Her poker face obviously needed work.

Detective Inspector Andrews's office was a large corner room with views of the river and the town. He rose from his desk as they entered, greeted them warmly, shaking both their hands before gesturing to the chairs in front of his desk. So far so good, thought Reggie. The Detective inspector's mood was jovial, not what you would expect if a reprimand was to follow. He took his seat and beamed across at them.

"It is not our usual practice to involve civilians in police matters," he said. "However, as this case moves forward we could really use your help Reggie. I'm getting ahead of myself." He paused for a moment to gather his thoughts. "I expect you are keen to find out if the information you gave to us yesterday has been useful in our ongoing enquiry?" he asked.

"Definitely," said Reggie eagerly. "Did you find anything in the warehouse?"

"I can tell you that police officers did enter the warehouse yesterday afternoon and it was found to be a working meth lab," answered D.I. Andrews.

"Were you able to arrest anyone?" Stocky asked.

"Unfortunately the premises were unoccupied." Reggie's face fell. "However," the Inspector continued. We did find some useful evidence, including fingerprints."

"Sabrina's?" Reggie asked hopefully.

"No, they belonged to her so called clerk – Paul Davis."

"That's good news because it links him to both of the meth labs." Stocky said excitedly.

"Exactly," D.I Andrews agreed. "We have had a very lengthy chat with Mr Davis today. When it became clear to him that the new fingerprint evidence would allow us to prosecute him as the ringleader, he began to crack. When he realised he would serve a minimum of fifteen years he finally admitted to working for Sabrina Warrington."

"Thank goodness!" Stocky sank back into his chair with

relief. Reggie grinned, speechless.

"I have to hand it to this Sabrina woman, she certainly had a large amount of influence over Paul Davis. He was very reluctant to give her name and when he eventually did, I am still not convinced he told us everything."

"Manipulating and controlling men is Sabrina's speciality," announced Reggie, finally finding her voice. "When I met the café guy he called her Francesca. Is Sabrina even her real name?" she asked.

"It is likely that both names are false," said D.I. Andrews "I have officers working on it at the moment. When I talked to the café owner he confirmed that he was lending the warehouse to Sabrina for storage. He had been receiving packages for her and Paul Davis had been collecting them."

"That's just like Dave," Stocky jumped in. The Detective Inspector nodded.

"And just like in your friend, Dave's situation, all of the paperwork led back to him. There is nothing to connect Sabrina to it at all. It would seem that Sabrina has a talent for making usually savvy businessmen act like love sick fools."

Reggie rolled her eyes and glanced across at Stocky.

"What was it you and Kelvin called her?" she asked. "A goddess?" Stocky ignored her and asked the logical next question?"

"So does this mean that Dave's off the hook?"

"Yes, all charges will be dropped," said the Inspector. "In fact it is our opinion that as we keep digging, more victims like Dave and the café owner will come to light."

"But what about Sabrina?" asked Reggie.

"At the moment we have no physical evidence of her at any of the meth lab sites." He looked across at Reggie. "You told us that you saw her put gloves on before she entered the warehouse. I imagine she is very careful not to leave DNA evidence behind."

"But what about the pictures I took?" Reggie asked. "They

proved that she went into the warehouse." D.I Andrews's cleared his throat uncomfortably.

"Unfortunately, when you took the photos you zoomed in too closely on Sabrina. There's nothing in the pictures to prove that it was that specific warehouse she was entering. Her defence team would easily have that evidence thrown out during a trial." Seeing her face fall he quickly continued. "But that is where you can help us Reggie." She looked up hopefully. "You are the only witness who can physically link Sabrina to the warehouse. The café owner never went there with her and says he passed on the keys to her clerk. When we find her - and I am hopeful that we will eventually track her down, we will need you to testify in court as a witness."

"Of course!" Reggie was elated. "I would love to help put her behind bars."

A chilling thought struck her. He hadn't mentioned Caroline's death.

"What about the murder?" she blurted out. "Is Dave still being charged with killing Caroline?" D.I Andrews smiled. He clasped his hands together, resting them on the desk in front of him.

"Our chat with Paul Davis revealed some interesting information. He was keen to emphasise how insignificant his role was in Sabrina's business. He freely admitted to fetching, carrying, collecting and delivering for her. When we asked him if he had delivered a bottle of red wine to Caroline's address he admitted that Sabrina had asked him to deliver it. He was shocked when we told him it was the murder weapon."

"Did he say why she killed Caroline?" Reggie asked.

"Davis strongly denies any knowledge of the murder," the Inspector answered. "When we questioned him further he couldn't think of any reason why Sabrina would have wanted Caroline dead. I don't think that any of us will know the reason for Caroline's murder unless Sabrina herself chooses to reveal it."

Stocky and Reggie jumped up and hugged tightly.

"We did it, Reg!" Stocky was incredulous. Reggie glanced

across at the Detective Inspector.

"Dave is definitely cleared?" she asked.

"Absolutely!" the Detective Inspector confirmed. D.S North was tasked with ringing Dave's solicitor after bringing you to my office. Dave has our apologies, commiseration for his terrible loss and good wishes for the future. Please impress on him that we will do everything in our power to track down Sabrina, or whatever her real name is, and bring her to justice… One more thing." The Detective Inspector stopped them as they turned to leave. "I have to admit that your help on this case has been invaluable… but I hope you aren't going to make a habit of involving yourself in police business?" he asked.

"No way," said Reggie forcefully. It's far too stressful. I just want to teach my class from now on."

"I totally agree," said Stocky. All this has made me realise that I need to try a lot harder to get myself a tech job and do something that I am actually trained for."

Reggie squeezed Stocky's arm as they left the police station.

"I can't believe we actually did it. Dave is cleared and can get on with his life."

"This calls for a celebration," announced Stocky. "I'll gather the troops. We can debrief back at The Narrowboat Inn tonight and drink to Dave's freedom.

CHAPTER 30

"I still don't believe it," said Stella. She took the dripping pan from Reggie and began to dry it.

"Stocky and I helped solve the case. Why is that so hard to believe?" Reggie scrubbed angrily at a stubborn baked on stain.

"I mean, that the two of you have no formal training but were still able to find evidence and put things together in a way the police couldn't. That's huge!" said Stella.

"Oh," Reggie was slightly mollified. "Well I guess it is. But a lot of it came down to luck." She placed the casserole bowl in the drying rack and began to scrub at the grill pan. "If I hadn't seen Sabrina on my Roman trip, Dave would still be charged with murder and drug manufacturing."

"Yes, but you didn't just see her, did you? You followed her and gathered evidence. Most people wouldn't have done that." Stella placed the dry pan on the bench and reached for another.

"Ok, I admit it," Reggie laughed. "I'm amazing." She turned to look at Stella. "Are you sure you won't come out tonight? I'm driving, and Dave will want to celebrate with you." Stella grimaced. "What's wrong?" asked Reggie. "You never turn down a free drink."

"That's apparently part of the problem, according to Mum," muttered Stella.

Understanding dawned. Reggie remembered her mum's threats to talk to Stella about her drinking.

"How bad was it?" Reggie asked cautiously.

"By the end of the conversation she had managed to blame

my drinking habits for everything, including you ending up in hospital."

"Don't worry Stel," Reggie soothed. You know Mum was just blowing off steam because she was worried about me. She's always waving you under my nose as an example for how I should get my life together. You're entitled to go out and have fun."

"Hmmmm!" Stella was unconvinced. "I think she may have a point. I could cut back a little. Anyway, if I don't go out tonight, you and I can definitely go out together for a huge celebration tomorrow night," she grinned. "There won't be any shifts at the pub for a few months, while Dave does repairs. So, I might as well make the most of it. What do you think?" she asked. "The beautiful Quinn sisters can dance the night away in Stapwell."

"Actually, it sounds amazing," agreed Reggie. "I finally get my first pay packet tomorrow and Dave owes me loads of money now that we've saved him from prison. I might be able to pay rent to Mum and Dad, go out with you and still have money left over for shopping." She smiled dreamily at the thought of finally being able to buy clothes instead of merely window-shopping.

Twenty minutes later Reggie was looking very presentable in jeans and a fitted shirt. She'd made extra effort with her makeup. After all it wasn't a good thing to look like you've been blown up every day. It would be good for Jake to see her looking like a normal human being. She grabbed her bag and walked past Stella in the hallway.

"Are you sure you won't come?" she asked. "Last chance!"

"No, I'll sit this one out," said Stella decisively. "But tomorrow is a different story, she smiled."

Reggie walked up the driveway into the glowing pool of lamplight that fell softly onto her car. She stepped towards the road, heading around to the driver's side. A slight rustling in the bushes stopped her. She stared into the darkness of her neighbour's driveway, expecting their angry ginger cat to fly out.

"You've finally decided to make an appearance." The voice

shot across the void between them. Reggie strained to see the hidden figure in the darkness. Sabrina stepped forward into the light. Its golden glow formed a saintly halo around her shimmering hair. As usual she was perfectly dressed. Reggie looked down, letting out a horrified gasp as she realised that Sabrina was holding a small gun.

"What do you want Sabrina?" Reggie forced her voice to remain calm. Her mind was racing, her brain screaming for help.

"A little bird tells me that you are an important witness against me. That little bird says that you are the key to putting me in prison." The angelic smile she wore for all the men in her life had been replaced by an ugly sneer. This is the real Sabrina thought Reggie. "You know what happens to key witnesses don't you?" Sabrina mocked. "They disappear!"

"What are you going to do?" Reggie asked, keeping her voice even.

"We are going for a little drive together in your ancient wreck of a car." Her brittle smile emphasised the hatred in her eyes.

"Sabrina, there's no point," Reggie reasoned. "It's over! Paul Davis gave you up to the police. He made a deal."

Sabrina snarled and Reggie saw a brief stab of fear pass through her eyes before the supreme confidence returned.

"Don't be ridiculous. Paul idolises me, he would never betray me, and certainly not for a runt like you." She pushed the gun further towards Reggie for emphasis, hands quivering slightly. "Men are weak," she smiled. "They look at me and see a beautiful, helpless damsel and they can't wait to be my knight in shining armour. I inspire their undying loyalty and devotion. No-one betrays me." The sneer returned and a hint of something beyond reason glittered in her eyes.

She's not completely sane, thought Reggie. Shit! Her panic became cold, petrifying fear. There would be no point in trying to appeal to her better nature.

"Throw down your bag," Sabrina ordered. "Take your keys and walk slowly around to the driver's side."

Reggie knew she needed to stall. Once she was in the driver's seat she was only a short drive away from becoming one of those unexplained missing people, whose car ends up at the bottom of a river or abandoned in a ditch.

"Wait a minute," Reggie searched her mind for something to say. "Caroline's murder," she blurted out. "I understand all the rest but why kill Caroline?"

"That stupid jealous bitch," Sabrina spat out the words. "She's caused me no end of trouble. That idiot Dave never told me he had a wife. Men are pathetic."

"I know you weren't jealous, so why did you need to kill her?" asked Reggie.

"Jealous!" Sabrina laughed. "Look at me. People like me don't get jealous. I'm every man's ultimate fantasy. That stupid woman left me a threatening message, saying she was coming after me and going to make me pay. I thought she was after my business. I've worked hard to build up my manufacturing sites and distribution lines. No one messes with my business! How was I supposed to know it was about her idiot child of a husband?"

"So you sent her the poisoned wine?" Reggie asked, determined to keep the conversation going.

"I dealt with the problem and got rid of her," said Sabrina coldly.

"But what if someone else had drunk the wine?" Sabrina shrugged.

"There's always collateral damage in business."

"She offered a drink to me," Reggie said indignantly.

"Ha, Sabrina laughed. "You win some you lose some. You should've said yes. It would've saved me the job of getting rid of you now." Her face settled back into its familiar sneer. She raised the gun, level with Reggie's chest.
"Enough talking. Walk around to the driver's side, now."

Realising she had run out of time, Reggie slowly followed the instructions. Sabrina tracked her progress with the gun as she moved.

"Now open the door and get in," Sabrina ordered. Reggie bent to pull open the door.

The heavy, metallic clang of scull meeting steel rang out, harshly echoing between the houses. Reggie flinched, expecting to feel pain. Feeling nothing she looked up in surprise.

"Ding dong, the bitch is dead," sang out Stella's beautiful voice from the other side of the car. Adrenaline still pumping, Reggie rushed around to the path. Sabrina lay in a heap on the floor and Stella stood fiercely over her brandishing a garden spade.

"Reg, get the gun," she urged. Tentatively Reggie moved towards Sabrina's lifeless form and pulled the gun from under her arm.

"Do you think she's dead?" whispered Reggie.

"Check for a pulse," Stella ordered. "If she moves I'll hit her again." Reggie took a deep breath and gently placed her fingers to the pulse point on Sabrina's neck.

"She's got a pulse," Reggie breathed out with relief.

"Right then," said Stella. "We need to tie up her hands and feet." Reggie was happy for Stella to take charge. The adrenaline of the last few minutes was seeping away, leaving her feeling weak and light headed.

"Do you want to go and look for rope in the garage or sit on her?" Stella asked.

"I'll sit on her," said Reggie, grasping at the offer to sit down.

Together they rolled Sabrina onto her front. Reggie stepped over her and sat on her back, legs astride. Stella passed the spade to her, just in case Sabrina regained consciousness. Reggie wasn't sure that she would be able to hit her now that the drama was over. Stella quickly returned with zip ties. She fastened them around Sabrina's wrists and ankles and helped Reggie up.

"Are you ok Reg?" Stella asked. Reggie nodded, the numbness beginning to subside.

"You should ring the police," she urged. Stella dialled and

together they sat on the kerb to wait.

Reggie threw her arms around Stella and gave her a fierce hug. "How did you know she was here?" she asked, incredulous.

"As soon as you left, I knew I was being ridiculous, missing out on celebrating with you and Dave, just to make Mum happy. I grabbed my shoes and bag and ran out after you. I heard talking and it sounded strange. Then you said her name and I knew I had to do something. So, I ran into the garage and grabbed the first thing I saw."

"Dad's gardening spade," smiled Reggie.

"I waited patiently until she turned and was busy watching you walk around the car, then I hit her as hard as I could."

"Thank goodness you came out after me. She was going to make me drive somewhere, shoot me and dump my body," Reggie shivered.

"At least one good thing came out of all this," said Stella, trying to lighten the mood.

"What?" asked Reggie.

"When Mum and Dad get home I'll be able to tell them that my love of socialising saved the day," she laughed. Stella's phone pinged with a message. "It's Stocky wondering where we are. I'll send a quick message back, letting him know what's happened."

While Stella typed, Reggie mentally replayed her conversation with Sabrina.

"Do you know," she said when Stella put down the phone, "Caroline's death was a mistake. She died because of a misunderstood voice message. Sabrina didn't even care, she called it collateral damage."

"That's awful," Stella agreed.

"I finally figured out the detail that I knew I was missing," said Reggie. "When Sabrina told us that she didn't know Dave had a wife, we focused on the fact that her surprise seemed real. We should have realised then that something was wrong about that. Caroline had already told us that she had left a message for Sabrina so Sabrina should have known that Dave was married.

The reason she didn't know was because Caroline's vague threats made Sabrina assume it was a challenge to her business, not a simple matter of jealousy."

"So if Caroline had been more specific in her voicemail, she'd probably still be alive today," said Stella sadly.

They sat in companionable silence for a while, until the welcome sound of sirens signalled help was on the way.

Everything happened quickly after that. The ambulance took Sabrina away. She was beginning to regain consciousness and groaned quietly as ambulance staff cut the zip-ties and placed her on a gurney. A police officer cuffed Sabrina's hands to the stretcher and followed her into the ambulance for the journey to hospital. More police officers gathered details from both sisters. Thankfully they were happy to wait until the next day for a full statement.

At some point Stocky and Jake appeared. Jake took Reggie's hand and stood next to her while she recounted the events of the evening. Reggie found his quiet presence calming, and drew strength from his warm hand gently holding hers.

Eventually, the last detail had been recorded and the remaining police car headed back towards the centre of town. Only the four of them remained. Stella and Stocky moved towards the driveway.

"Are you two coming in for a coffee?" asked Stella.

"Be there in a minute," Reggie shouted back. After all of the tension and stress of the last hour the cool silence of the night was a soothing antiseptic. Reggie realised she was still holding Jake's hand. When she started to move, he reached for her other hand, turning her to face him. She looked into his eyes. They were full of worry and concern.

"I thought I was going to die," she said simply. "I looked into Sabrina's eyes and I knew there was something broken inside her." Jake pulled her close. The hug was as much a comfort for him as for Reggie.

"It's over now," he reassured. "Because you kept her talking." He smiled wryly, "and because of Stella's deadly aim."

Reggie pulled back slightly to look in his eyes. She reached up to touch the worry lines on his forehead.

"That means you can stop worrying too," she replied. Jake dipped his head to kiss her softly on the lips.

"Worrying seems to have been my standard operating procedure since I met you," he whispered.

Reggie pulled him back down to her and deepened their kiss. All concerns drifted away on the evening breeze.

"Do you know that we haven't even been on a first date," laughed Reggie.

"That is easily rectified, said Jake, taking her hand again as they walked towards Reggie's front door. "If you don't mind, I'd like to have at least one evening with you where the action and drama are kept to a minimum."

"What do you have in mind?" she asked.

"How about a movie on Saturday night?" he suggested. "That way all the explosions and guns will be safely contained on screen."

"Perfect," she agreed. "Are you coming in?"

"Now that I know you are safe, I should really go and check up on Dave," said Jake. He was pretty cut up when he found out Sabrina had admitted to killing Caroline." Jake frowned. I know it was Caroline's message that set Sabrina's murderous plan in action, but Dave will have to live with the fact that if he hadn't had the affair with Sabrina, Caroline would still be alive..." Jakes voice faded away and he became quietly thoughtful. Reggie gently held Jake's hands, watching the wave of grief pass through him.

"You know," she eventually said, "blaming Dave won't help either of you. Dave made mistakes but Sabrina is the one who murdered Caroline and no-one could have predicted that." Jake nodded, his expression still sombre.

"I don't blame Dave. Sabrina is an evil woman. Thank God she didn't manage to kill you too."

Jake pulled Reggie possessively against him, wrapping his arms around her. Reggie relaxed inside the comfort of his arms, the soothing rhythm of his heartbeat slowing her breath. Reggie could have stood this way forever, and moved reluctantly when Jake eventually unwrapped his arms and held her away from him.

"I know Dave feels responsible for Sabrina trying to hurt you." Said Jake. "He's going to need personal assurance that you are okay."

Reggie could understand how badly this - on top of everything else, would've affected Dave; she had seen how concerned he had been about her after the explosion.

"Give Dave my love," she said. "Tell him it's not his fault. I'll go over to see him tomorrow, to prove I'm still in one piece."

"I consider myself a pretty brave guy," Jake smiled wickedly, "But I'd definitely rather not be here when you have to explain this evening's events to your mother."

"I imagine Stocky will make a run for it as soon as he hears their car pull up. He might have the right idea, said Reggie ruefully."

Smiling, Jake kissed her gently on the forehead. "Please avoid, explosions and crazy women holding weapons, at least until you see me on Saturday," he urged. Reggie watched Jake walk away into the darkness.

"I can't promise," she called after him, "but I'll try."

Reggie thought she saw him shake his head as he disappeared into the night. She reached for the door handle, a smile of bemusement on her face. Her first five weeks of teaching had served up occasional triumphs and more failures and disasters that she cared to count. She'd been reunited with Stocky and Teresa, made a raft of new friends and now she had Jake. It was early days but she had a good feeling about him. Whatever happened, she was determined to enjoy their time together. I can't wait to see what the next five weeks bring, she thought. I'm ready.